With a Twist

A BAD HABITS NOVEL

Hearts and Arrows
Deer in Headlights (Hearts and Arrows 1)
Snake in the Grass (Hearts and Arrows 2)
What the Heart Wants (Hearts and Arrows 2.5 Novella)
Doe Eyes (Hearts and Arrows 3)
Fool's Gold (Hearts and Arrows 3.5 Novella)

Hearts and Arrows Box Set

Hardcore (Erotic Suspense Serials)
Volume 1 - **FREE**
Volume 2
Volume 3

Bad Habits
With a Twist
Chaser - Fall 2015
Last Call - Winter 2016

Nailed - Erotic Shorts
FREE with newsletter subscription

Once
FREE short story on Amazon

Cover by Quirky Bird
Photography by Perrywinkle Photography

To Becca.
#TeamBashert

LIFE GOALS

Lily

OH, MY GOD. I CANNOT believe this is actually happening.

It was the only thought in my brain, and it echoed over and over again as I stared in the studio mirror, gripping the barre as Blane Motherfucking Baker nailed me from behind.

Maybe I should explain.

I feel like I should definitely explain.

See, this isn't the sort of thing I'd *ever* do under normal circumstances. I'd been busting my ass for years with the New York City Ballet — a job that left me with precious little social life or opportunity for dating — and even at that, I'd avoided hooking up with another dancer. Everybody else did it, but I'd seen the fallout. Not worth it.

But for *Blane Baker* I'd make an exception.

I still remember the first time I saw him. I was

fifteen, far away from home on a scholarship to attend
the School of American Ballet, sitting in the lunchroom
by myself. He walked in with a tray, laughing with a
friend, and my thoughts went something like this:

1) nvfjrugncpqdhhHNGGGGG.

2) Please, God, don't let him be gay.

3) HOLY SHIT, HE LOOKED RIGHT AT ME.

Which was the same moment I reached for my
phone to cover the fact that I was drooling. My fingers
bumped into the plastic cup, sending it flying, and
orange juice hit the ground with a slap. The cup
skittered across the floor to stop at his feet.

Attempt to look busy: backfire.

Blane laughed at me, that kind of unabashed laugh
that makes a teenage girl consider moving to Iceland.
He picked up the cup and brought it back to me,
smiling genuinely as he set it back on the table with a
wink. "Dropped something."

I melted into a steaming puddle of viscous glop on
the ground.

As if that wasn't bad enough, Nadia Anderson
walked in behind him, taking in the scene with a
horrible smile on her face. That smile said she wouldn't
forget, and when she hooked her arm in Blane's and
they walked away, the Lily-sized pile of goo turned into
acid, and I melted through the floor.

She sometimes still called me JuicyFruit, even seven

years later.

Whatever. I'm sure that kind of thing happened to him all the time. Blane looked like a freaking god — tall and blond, with blue eyes that I was absolutely certain could see through clothes, a smile so bright that girls literally tripped and fell when they saw it, and an ass that could probably crush a walnut, if it were positioned just so. And he just kept getting hotter with age.

I found out later that he and Nadia were in their last year at SAB, three years older than me, and had been dating since their first year.

Here are a few things you need to know about Nadia: she's a harpy, she's a remarkable dancer, and she owns Blane Baker. Nadia was the definitive reason why I would never have a chance with Blane — not during our one year together at SAB and not through our years working together in the company. He was always just a step ahead of me in the ranks, which kept us in each other's eyesight, but we'd never run in the same group of friends.

Until now.

The universe had given me three supreme gifts, and there was no way in hell I'd waste them.

I'd been promoted to principal dancer with the New York City Ballet.

I'd landed the role of my life as Odette/Odile in *Swan Lake*.

Nadia had broken up with Blane's sweet, sweet ass.

That same ass was currently flexing like a piston as he pounded me.

I glanced at my reflection, hoping I'd find myself looking sexy. In my head, I looked *so* sexy, all parted lips and long lashes, blond hair loose and wavy, like a bathing suit model in the Barbados. But no. I had the most awkward expression on my face, sort of a mix of surprise and confusion. I wiped it away and replaced it with something I hoped looked more appropriate. It was only marginally better, if not a little porny.

I gave up. He didn't seem to be paying attention anyway.

Blane's eyes were down, lush bottom lip between his teeth, hands on my hips as he moved faster, giving me a grand total of 6% of his attention, all of which was between my legs. He didn't bother with the rest of my body at all. And I couldn't find it in my heart to give one single shit.

Blane Baker, y'all. Blane Do-Whatever-You-Want-To-Me Baker. Making girls lose their minds since puberty, circa 1996.

Clearly, I was not immune.

He finally looked up, though not at me, making a face as he watched himself come with a sort of strangled grunt. I gasped and moaned, hoping I was giving him an appropriate amount of enthusiasm for his effort.

Blane slowed, trailing a hand down my back with a hum. "That was nice."

I pretended to be out of breath. "Right?" I sounded like an idiot. *Get your shit together, Lily. A-game.*

"I've been thinking about that for a long time, Lily." He smiled at me in the mirror as he pulled out and took off the condom, righting his pants when he turned for the trash.

My cheeks were on fire. "Me too." I adjusted my leotard and shook my head at my reflection, taking a deep breath and smoothing my chiffon skirt to fortify myself. My hair was a wreck, and I tied back the mess as the awkward silence stretched on. I wasn't sure what I was supposed to do. Ask him out for coffee? No, too desperate. Rehearse? I mean, it wasn't like that was actually what I expected to happen when he invited me to his 'private studio.' At least, I'd hoped that wasn't what he really wanted to do. I'd shaved and everything.

I realize how juvenile I sounded, but being around him kicked me straight back to high school. Normally, I was a fairly rational adult, a professional ballet dancer. Responsible. Not a complete idiot. I wondered briefly if proximity to him could actually affect my IQ.

He turned, and I flashed a smile. *Be charming, goddammit.* "Rehearsal's never been so exciting."

It might have been the lamest statement of my life.

Blane laughed, the sound deep and easy as he sauntered back over to me. "Most definitely. I'm happy to *rehearse* any time." He slipped a hand around my waist and kissed my hair.

My mental state deteriorated even further.

"Seriously," he said. "I'll give you tips anytime you want."

A laugh bubbled out of me at the joke. "Your tip. That's funny." But when I glanced up at him, he looked a little confused. I watched hopefully as it dawned on him.

"Oh, *tips*. I get it," he said with a chuckle.

At least he's pretty.

Just like that, I had a handle on myself again. I kissed him on the cheek and strutted over to my bag. My pointe shoes lay neglected next to my bag — Blane had jumped me before I'd even had a chance to put them on. So I traded my skirt for leggings, slipped on my flats and picked up my bag.

"See you tomorrow, Blane." I smiled and gave him the smolder eyes over my shoulder as I walked to the door. I hoped they smoldered, at least. After seeing what I looked like earlier, I couldn't be sure. When he smiled back, my stomach did a flipflop, and I twiddled my fingers at him before I left the studio.

And by leave, I mean skipped.

I had to tell Rose.

West

My wooden office chair squeaked as I leaned back, squinting at the paper in my hand, not realizing how dark it had gotten, my eyes on the words as I spun the chair around and clicked on the lamp switch. The words jumped into focus, and I scratched at my beard absently, willing my brain to pay attention to the essay I was grading.

Being a Literature TA for the illustrious Dr. Blackwell at Columbia wasn't without its merits. The experience would be résumé gold, and the connections I'd made would help me get into the doctoral program, I hoped. The application was in, the proposal made, and soon I'd know if I'd been accepted.

That didn't make my task of grading essays any more tolerable. Some were the kind of papers that only overeducated intellectuals can produce, sprinkled with regurgitations of things they'd heard professors — or worse, other intellectuals — say. Others were obviously a last minute noodle-toss of half-baked ideas. But then there were the gems: the inspired, collected thoughts of someone with original ideas and a brain between their ears.

Unfortunately, that wasn't the variety I was currently reading.

I sighed and laid the paper on my desk, glancing between the stack of graded versus ungraded essays, mourning the lack of progress and looking forward to the day when I'd have my own classroom and a TA to do this kind of thing for me.

I pulled the rubber band out of my hair, twisting it up into a fresh knot in the hopes it would somehow reset me, give me the kickstart I needed to keep slogging through these papers. So I picked up the essay and read the same paragraph I'd read three times. It didn't make any more sense to me.

My phone buzzed on my desk, and I thanked the universe for giving me a break. A picture of my sister that I'd taken when I went back home for Christmas popped up on my screen. She was standing in front of the tree in what had to be the ugliest sweater I'd ever seen: fire engine red with a lace collar and a gigantic felt Santa Clause on the front. She might have been twenty-three, but to me she'd always be three years old in overalls, her curly blond hair a mess.

Once, my buddy Cooper called her a knockout. I almost knocked him out.

I hit accept and pressed the phone to my ear. "Hey, Mags."

"Hey. Busy?" Her Mississippi drawl was so pronounced that I immediately slipped back into it myself, something that only happened when I went

to get settled in before I start teaching full time in the fall. I can sub here and there, use my little nest egg to lie around and take it easy. Start over."

My chest ached for her. "Everything's gonna be fine, Mags."

"Promise?" Her voice was full of hurt and hope.

"Promise."

She let out another breath. "If you could move to New York, then so can I. Though I honestly don't know how you did it alone. At least I've got you, Rose, and Lily."

I twiddled my pen in my hand and shook my head. "I lived on campus, and Cooper was my roommate, so I wasn't alone, not really. Coop's lived here his whole life and has got to be the best and worst guide to the city that anybody could have. He'd take me to a little-known art gallery and a members-only strip joint in the same afternoon."

She snorted. "Ugh."

I smirked. "I had help, and so will you."

"Thanks." I thought she might have been smiling on the other end of the line. "I've gotta get outta here, but it's terrifying, you know?"

"I know. New York's going to be good to you."

"Thanks. I was looking at this old room and all these suitcases and … I just needed a little reassurance, that's all. All better."

"Glad I could help, kiddo."

"All right. Well, this stuff isn't going to pack itself. Thanks again, West. Talk to you later."

"Good luck, Mags."

I set my phone back on the desk and sighed, worrying over Maggie, rubbing my beard. Getting her out of Jackson had been my idea. I just wanted her to find a way to move forward, leave her hurt where it belonged, and it hadn't taken much convincing on either side. Lily had offered to share a room with her without thinking twice, and Maggie jumped at the chance.

I sighed and looked back at the essay that mocked me from my desktop. The thought of picking it back up made me twitchy, so I stood and stretched, popping my back, ready for a proper break.

I pulled open my bedroom door and made my way through the living room looking for my roommate. The apartment I shared with Patrick Evans was a pretty typical bachelor pad — mismatched furniture, minimalist style, with books and art everywhere. I collected books like some guys collected phone numbers, and Patrick was always working on something. His room was basically an art studio with a bed in it. Mine was a library.

Patrick stood in the kitchen, pulling on his leather jacket. The light caught on his black hair, which was combed back, sides shaved short. His tattooed arms disappeared into his jacket one at at time, tattooed fingers appearing out of the ends of the sleeves, and he adjusted his collar to get it straight. More ink climbed out of the neck of his black-and-white striped T-shirt and up to his jaw, which had the line of a movie star. In fact, just about all of Patrick looked like a movie star.

He was an artist — primarily a tattoo artist, so good at what he did that people waited months for him to make his mark on their bodies. He'd done all of mine, including my sleeve, and had done pieces for Rose, too. Even Lily had one, though hers was on her ribs, where it could be easily hidden — a vine with a watercolor lily and rose. Rose had one to match.

"'Sup, man." Patrick jerked his chin at me with a half-smile. "Finish grading your papers?"

I shook my head. "Not even close, but I couldn't do it anymore. Where you headed?"

"Habits."

"Ah," I added knowingly. "Rosie workin'?"

He scowled. "How should I know?"

"So, yes?"

Patrick turned to pick up his keys, avoiding my eyes. "Pretty sure."

I glanced at the clock, but it didn't really matter what time it was because there was no way I was going back to those papers for at least an hour. "Want some company?"

He looked over and shot me a crafty smile. "Nobody likes to drink alone."

I grabbed my own jacket and shrugged it on. "Isn't that the God's honest truth?"

THIS GUY

Lily

I TROTTED UP THE SUBWAY steps at the 86th St. station with my bag bumping against my ass and my lips stretched into a smile. I had doodled Blane's name on my binder in high school. Named our imaginary children. Lay in bed, staring at the springs of the mattress in the bunk above me, imagining what it would be like to kiss him.

Now I knew what his dick looked like.

Crazy!

The guy walking in front of me gave me a look over his shoulder, and I realized I'd said it out loud. I blushed and tossed my hand in a wave. He just rolled his eyes and trucked on.

I caught sight of the black awning across Broadway with the word HABITS printed in slender white letters. To say I was a regular at the bar would be an understatement. My roommate, Rose, was a bartender there, and since Habits was on the same block as our apartment, our group of friends always seemed to end up there. The food was good, the drinks were cheap by New York standards, and the vibe seemed to be just right — chill when you wanted to chill, rowdy when you wanted to party.

Rose and I met when I responded to a Craigslist ad during my apprenticeship. Her roommate skipped on her, went back to Los Angeles where they were from without any notice, just a note and an empty apartment. She took everything with her, even the fridge magnets. Normally, I'm not the type to find a roommate on Craigslist, but I was armed with mace and adrenaline, and my mom was scheduled to call the cops if I didn't check in within an hour. Plus, her ad was hilarious. *Nocturnal lady bartender seeks clean, quiet roommate. Must love whiskey. Vaginas only. Penis denied on entry.* When I learned her name, I made a joke about lady parts and flower power, and the rest was history.

I pulled the brass handle of the heavy wooden door, catching sight of Rose through the inset window. She stood behind the bar, the wood so dark it was nearly black, with shelf after shelf of liquor bottles behind her. The planked floor was worn, and the walls were white subway tile all the way up to the exposed beams and pipes on the ceiling. Rose glanced over at me and waved, brown eyes twinkling, framed by shaggy bangs, long black hair braided over one shoulder.

I bounded over and leaned on the glossy wooden surface.

"Hey, Lil. You all right?" She smiled crooked as she looked me over.

I grinned. "Nope. Blane asked me to rehearse with him tonight."

Her eyebrow arched. "On your one day off for the week?"

"Mmhmm." I nodded. "And then I fucked him."

A shocked laugh ripped out of Rose, and I giggled until my cheeks hurt.

"Jesus, Lily," Rose said once she'd calmed down. "No wonder you look like you just found a million dollar bill. So how was it? Hot?"

My nose wrinkled up. "I'm sure next time will be better. The first time's always weird, you know?"

"No, I don't."

I threw a cocktail napkin at her smart mouth. "Shut up. You know what I mean."

"So, what are you guys? Like, are you just fuck buddies? Or are you guys going to see each other?" Rose poured me a glass of water.

"I don't know what it means, honestly. I'm trying not to read too much into it, but I won't pretend like there's not a part of me that wants this to be the beginning of something epic. He's my actual dream guy. It's like if Ryan Gosling showed up at your door dressed like Noah from *The Notebook*, bearing flowers and whiskey. You'd be stupid not to take that bike for a ride."

"Agree, because there is no one like Noah. He cannot be topped. I'd ride that bike to New Zealand." Rose handed me the water. "So tell me about this 'weird' first time."

If it were anyone else, I would have bullshitted, glorified it. But Rose would get all the sordid details. Okay, maybe not all, but I'd at least give her the gist. "He just wasn't very … attentive."

Her eyes narrowed. "Did you get off?"

I hesitated with her looking at me like that. "No."

"Ugh, Lily."

I huffed and rushed to explain. "Well, we were kind of in a hurry."

"Why?"

My mouth opened and closed again. "I don't know why, but I'm not questioning it. Plus, how can anyone perform full-on body worship on a studio dance floor?"

She was still judging me. "I feel like that's entirely possible."

I ignored her. No way was she bringing me down. "It was hot — for real. I was hanging onto the barre while he jackhammered me."

A laugh burst out of her. "Oh, my god."

"What?" I asked innocently. "That's pretty much what it was like. I was just so psyched that it was even happening that I couldn't concentrate."

"Do you usually have to concentrate when you have sex?"

"Rose, you're missing the point! It seriously doesn't matter if it was good or bad because *I banged Blane Baker!*" I squealed. I actually squealed, and Rose did too, party pooper or not.

A deep voice with what I knew to be a Mississippi accent boomed from behind me. "What are you two giggling about?"

My cheeks were instantly on fire as I turned to find West behind me, smiling crookedly from behind his dark beard, bright, blue eyes twinkling. I looked up at him with my mind tripping to change gears into a conversation with my other best friend. The one who I didn't generally enlighten on the literal ins and outs of my sex life.

Rose kept laughing, a loud, bawdy laugh at my discomfort. I leaned back on the bar, red-cheeked and stammering. "I … Ah, hey, West. What's happenin'?"

Rose laughed even harder.

But West just chuckled, shaking his head as he tucked an errant strand of dark hair behind his ear and took a seat next to me. "Nice try, Twinkle Toes."

I took the window to change the subject. "Whatever, Man-bun. Did you chop any trees down today, LumberWest?" I grabbed his messy, dark top knot and wiggled it.

He shrugged. "Couldn't. Left my flannel at home."

I chuckled. "Aw, well, there's always tomorrow." I slapped him on the shoulder and smiled at Patrick as he pulled off his jacket and sat next to West. "Hey, Tricky."

He rested his tattooed arms on the bar with the quiet smile he wore when he wasn't brooding. "Hey, Lil. Hey, Rose."

"Hey, Tricky." Rose smiled politely and leaned on the bar. "What are we drinking, fellas? Whiskey or beer?"

West shook his head. "Beer tonight. I have papers to grade and class first thing."

"Whiskey," Patrick answered with his eyes on her like laser beams. I didn't know how she could handle it, especially not since they used to date. Don't get me wrong — I was more than happy they got along. Rose did everything she could to pretend not to care about him, the number one tool in her arsenal being distance, and as much as possible. But Patrick had this ... *look* that made it seem like a lost cause. It was a look that said he'd fuck you up in the best way — the way that would have you begging for more. Legitimate fuck-me eyes. He wasn't even trying, either, just had a bad case of Resting Smolder Face.

Somehow it didn't affect Rose, just seemed to wash over her. I think he turned up the intensity just for her because the charge between them affected *me* just by proximity.

Rose poured drinks, and I took the seat next to West.

He eyed me, smiling before taking a sip of his beer as soon as Rose handed it over. "What's up with you today?" There was a little foam in his mustache.

"You got a little something right there." I grabbed a cocktail napkin and wiped the foam off before stuffing it in his mouth. "And nothing's up with me, Weston."

Rose snickered, and West spit out the napkin and stuck the wet part in my ear. I squealed, angling away from him, and bumped into the guy next to me. "Sorry," I smiled, but he just eyeballed me before turning back to his friends.

"Sure doesn't seem like nothin'," West smirked.

But Rose's smirk was even worse. "Lily had a date tonight."

I'd like everyone to meet Rose, the traitor.

I gave her a look that said I knew what scared her and where she slept. "It wasn't a *date.*"

West assessed me with his eyebrow jacked. "The lady doth protest too much."

"Ugh, West." I rolled my eyes. "Don't get all hoity-toity Shakespearean Lit on me now, buddy. It wasn't a date. We just rehearsed."

Rose leaned on the bar. "Alone."

"Sounds serious." West took another sip of his beer, laughing at me with his stupid eyes.

I swept a finger across them. "You guys are all assholes."

Patrick leaned forward with his brows up. "All of us?"

I forgave him, even though he was clearly mocking me on the inside. "Nah, you're all right, Tricky." I took another swig of my water and set it down. "I've got to be up at five, so you kids have fun."

"Night, Lily," Rose said sweetly.

I slid off my stool and grabbed my bag. "Nu-uh. Don't you 'Night, Lily' me. I might not be the only one getting up at five."

"I will cut you."

I leaned across the bar to kiss her on the cheek. "Sharpen that shiv, my friend. See you guys," I called over my shoulder as I left, swinging my hips like I could pretty much take over the world.

West

I watched Lily walk out the door of the bar, blond hair in the tight bun she always wore to rehearsal, hips swaying like a pendulum in leggings, bare shoulder peeking out of an oversized sweater. I'd never seen her giddy over a man before, all blushing and nervous. Her not-date had her worked up, that was for sure, and my curiosity was piqued.

I jerked a chin at Rose. "So who's the guy?"

Rose sighed and shook her head. "Blane Baker." She said his name as if I should know who he was.

I gave her a look and shrugged.

"She's had a crush on him since her second day of high school, and now he's been partnered with her. But the real trigger point is that he's recently single. And apparently into her."

My eyes narrowed. "She's never mentioned him before."

"Yeah, well," she scoffed, "most girls don't walk around talking about their high school crushes, do they?"

"Most girls don't, but I just figured Lily wasn't interested in anybody."

Rose raised an eyebrow. "Oh, so you tell her all about your conquests?"

My face screwed up at the suggestion. "No, but that's different."

She smiled a smile that told me she had my number. "Oh, is it?"

"It is. She knows I date. But Lily never dates, not

ever."

"That's not true, West. She's not a robot. She goes on dates. She just doesn't get serious with anyone."

"Well, that's what I mean," I blustered. "It's never been anyone worth her mentioning to us. She's always said she's focused on her career and all that. So what makes this guy special?"

"To be fair, she didn't mention him to us. *I* mentioned him to us."

My face went flat. "You know what I mean, Rose. She's never been like *that* over a guy before." I gestured toward the door.

Rose shrugged. "I don't know what it is about him, outside of the crush. You know how that can be — when you care about somebody, but they don't seem to know you exist. And then, one day, they see you."

I frowned.

"Anyway, he's apparently a brilliant dancer with loads of leads under his belt. She's partnered with him for three ballets this week alone, including his role as the prince in *Swan Lake*."

"Wow, that was almost fascinating enough to put me into a coma." Cooper took a seat and pulled off his jacket, resting his forearms on the bar with a flash of his Cartier watch. Even his smarmy bastard smile looked rich. "Who is this guy and why are we talking about him?"

I picked up my beer. "Lily's not-date tonight."

"Ah," he said with an understanding nod. "I just passed her on the street. Thought she looked a little extra chipper."

"Scotch?" Rose asked.

"Always." He turned back to me. "So Lily finally got laid? I'm not going to say she needed that, but man, did she ever need that."

Rose balked, retracting the scotch she'd been holding in Cooper's direction. "Hey, asshole. Watch your mouth."

His face went soft and amiable as he chuckled. "Aw, come on, Rosie. Don't be like that. I'm happy for her, really. Promise I'm not being a dick."

She gave him the glass, coupled with a hard stare.

I snorted. "You're kind of being a dick, but we wouldn't expect any less from you, Coop."

He just smiled. "I'm a dick with a heart of gold, Weston." He turned to the group. "So, do we like this guy or not?"

"We're not sure. None of us have met him," Patrick answered. "Lily seems stoked."

Cooper took a drink and set down the glass. "Well, she's a smart cookie. I'm sure he's not horrible."

"He'd better be not horrible," I grumbled and took a drink.

"Oh, yeah?" Cooper said with a laugh. "Or what?"

"Or I'll have an opinion about it."

Patrick snorted. "When do you *not* have an opinion?"

"I'm just sayin'. I think we can all agree that Lily deserves good things, so if this *Blane* guy doesn't treat her right, I'll have something to say about it."

Rose rolled her eyes and reached into the sink behind the bar to wash glasses. "Down boy. I'm sure we'll meet him soon enough, if it lasts."

Cooper smirked at me. "And *then* you can get out your shotgun."

I laughed. "My dad did that. Decided that the best time to clean it was when Maggie's prom date came to pick her up."

Rose shook her head. "So it's genetic? Or just a Southern thing?"

"Both." I drained my glass.

But Rose just kept shaking her head at me as she held out a hand for the glass. I handed it over, and she dumped it in the sink before turning to pour me a fresh beer.

Cooper jerked a chin at Patrick and me. "I don't suppose either of you are interested in going out tonight, are you?"

"Not me," I answered. "In fact, this'll be my last drink." Rose passed it across the bar to me.

Cooper leaned around me. "How about you,

Tricky?"

"Not this time."

"What, you're not trying to be *good*, are you, Trick?" Cooper needled him.

"Depends on your definition of good. I've got a six hour job in the morning."

"Well, I hope she's hot."

"It's for a dude."

Cooper sniffed. "This is exactly why I'll never take over my dad's company. Responsibility doesn't suit me."

Rose made a mock pouty face. "Aw, Coop. The playboy life is lonely, isn't it?"

He laughed, but I knew it was more true than he'd ever let on. "Don't hate. I've got plenty of people I can call."

"Ha. Like Astrid?" I asked.

He shrugged. "Lily's sister and I have an arrangement. We run in the same circles. It's convenient. Surprisingly, models and playboys get along very, very well."

Rose snorted.

Cooper turned to me. "Speaking of sisters, when does Maggie get here?"

"Thursday," I answered.

"Still need me to pick her up?"

"Yeah, but don't tell her. I'll be in class, and she wouldn't wait for me to come get her. Said she wanted to 'dive in' to New York."

Rose made a disapproving face. "You're a control freak."

My brow dropped. "Why, because I don't want my baby sister lugging nine suitcases through the subway? Alone? Not fair, Rosie."

"If she wants to, then let her."

Cooper shook his head. "I'm siding with West on this one. Pretty little thing like Maggie, alone in New York?"

I eyed him. "Keep talking like that, and I'm sending a chaperone."

"Don't worry. Your sister's virtue is safe with me."

The rest of us burst out laughing.

"What?" He asked innocently. "I *can* be good. I just choose not to be."

I chuckled. "Well, watch yourself, or I'll choose to break your face."

BITCHES AND BALLERS

Lily

THE AFTERNOON SUN SHONE THROUGH the high windows in the studio as the pianist began the Stravinsky piece again. We were rehearsing *Apollo* for the show that night, and our ballet master, Ward Stewart, stood with a stern look on his face and arms folded across his chest, salt and pepper hair neatly combed. He called instructions, counting and correcting as we went through the piece. He was one of the most insatiable masters in the company, and the one I worked with most often.

I wound around Blane with Jenni and Nadia in my wake, the three of us threading in and out of each other's arms in waves around him. Blane was Apollo, and we were muses — muse of poetry, muse of theater, and my part, muse of dance. It was the coveted spot, the muse that Apollo chooses in the end for the pas de deux.

The roles I'd landed since my promotion a few months ago still shocked me — as hard as I'd worked to get where I was, I'd never expected it. Or, I guess I should say that I expected it eventually, but I never felt entitled to it, or like I was good enough to actually have it for my own. I'd apprenticed under Isabell Lamont, and after she injured herself last season, she decided to retire. The day I walked up to the rehearsal schedule board and saw my name next to Firebird, I almost hit the floor. No one auditioned for a promotion. It was given based on merit and could happen to anyone, at any time. The day it happened for me was a flagstone in my life.

In any case, I was still a new principal, and Nadia had seniority over me, but here we were, dancing together, and I somehow had the bigger part.

It wasn't something she'd let me forget, either.

No one was surprised that Blane landed the part of Apollo with his golden hair and eyes like the sky. He was built like a Greek god, and with the grace of one, too. The pas de deux with him gave me life. But rehearsals were never easy with Nadia, and the part required absolute synchronicity between the three muses.

I dropped under Nadia's arm again, and she squeezed my hand, locking her wrist so I couldn't twist.

My ankle faltered, and I almost fell.

"Tighten up, Lily," Ward shot, eyes hard.

I glared at Nadia as I passed her, but she only smiled, and I pushed the rage away, focusing on the music and my body. I raised my leg in an arabesque, then Nadia, then Jenni. I bourréd away, then Nadia, then Jenni, and when I bent with my arms arched in fifth position over my head, they followed. We danced behind Blane around the studio before lining up next to him, and he leaned forward with the three of us against his back, our legs extended at intervals behind him.

The music ended, and Ward brought us around to give us closing direction. The tension hung between us — Nadia on one side of me and Blane on the other. We curtsied and bowed before making our way over to our bags as the pianist started up again. Blane and I would be staying with Ward, and Jenni and Nadia would leave for their next rehearsals. I grabbed my water and took a drink as Jenni sat and pulled on her warm-up booties.

I looked over my red-cheeked reflection in the mirrored wall. "God, I'm a sweaty mess." I shook my head. "I think I even have crotch sweat."

Jenni laughed. We'd always been friends — from being in the same class at SAB to dancing in the corps together. We'd even been promoted within a month of each other, both as soloists and now principals. She was my constant in the company, and in a world where the pressure and competitiveness of our jobs so often ripped friendships apart. She was a beautiful dancer and a gorgeous woman, with raven hair and creamy white skin that I'm almost positive didn't have a single freckle. She also had the longest, most graceful arms I'd ever seen.

She zipped up her bag. "Steamy crotches happen to the best of us."

I patted down my face and chest with a towel from my bag. "Reasons to wear a skirt, number one."

"The poor guys can't even avoid it."

"Nothing like some sweaty balls in tights to get the old libido going."

She chuckled, and I sat to untie one of my shoes.

"My shoe's dead. Look at the shank." I bent it, and the leather buckled in the arch. "Man, I just got these from the shoe room this morning."

"Ugh, I hate that. Will you have time to go before your next rehearsal?"

I sighed and pulled off my other shoe. "I'll have to make time."

She shook her head as she took a drink. "Only Ward would whip us so hard as to kill a pair of shoes in an afternoon."

I chuckled. "Sacrificing satin and leather, one concerto at a time."

She giggled and glanced behind me, jerking her

chin. Nadia was standing close to Blane at the far end of the room, a little too close for my comfort, and I felt my cheeks heat up when she touched his arm. Nadia and I actually looked a lot alike — same build, both with long, blond hair and blue eyes — but while I tended to fall a little closer to cute than foxy, Nadia had that stone-cold model sort of face. Harder, skeptical. A little pinched.

She said something to Blane I wasn't able to hear over the piano, and he pulled his arm from her grip. I couldn't read his expression before he turned to his bag, putting his back to Nadia, and she spun around scowling, her narrowed eyes connecting with mine. I met her glare with one of my own, hoping I looked like I couldn't be ruffled, even though my heart clanged against my ribs. She didn't even sit as she took off her shoes in a huff, stuffing them in her bag and leaving in a whirl.

"What's her problem?" Jenni asked.

Me. I shrugged. "Who knows. The diva rests for no one. Where are you headed next?"

Jenni zipped up her bag. "Rehearsal for *Four Temperaments* and then for my solo for tonight." She shook her head and glanced back at Blane. "You are *so* lucky to be partnered with Blane so often. And to dance *Swan Lake* with him, too? I'm so freaking jealous. I've wanted to dance Odette since I was seven."

My cheeks were still hot as I dug around in my bag for my flats and gave her the canned answer I kept on hand for when someone brought up the partnership. "We're only paired because of our height."

She shook her head. "No way. You are so in sync. Your lines are always perfect. It's sort of a remarkable thing to watch the two of you dance together."

I thought my heart might burst at the compliment. "Thanks, Jenni."

She smiled and raised an eyebrow. "Plus, you get to look at that ass every day."

I snickered. "I swear to God, when he wears tights, my uterus screams his name." I pulled on my booties and hopped up. "Ward, I need to grab another pair of shoes from downstairs."

He frowned. "You don't have a spare?"

"No, sir," I answered, wishing I'd grabbed more than one pair that morning. "These are brand new, and I blew out my backups yesterday."

He nodded, though he was clearly not pleased. "Quickly."

I curtsied. "Yes, sir." I gave Jenni a wave, and Blane caught my eye as I hurried to the door, giving me a smile that erased the unease from delaying rehearsal.

I hustled down the hallway lined with gigantic orange crates full of props, wigs, and costumes, the same that crowded almost every hallway of the building. NYCB had over four hundred ballets in our repertory, and that much *stuff* just takes up a ton of space. We had an entire crate just full of fake mustaches and beards. Seriously.

When I hit the end of the hall, I took the elevator down to one of my most revered spots in the entire theater.

The shoe room was a place of worship — a quiet space packed with shelves that housed thousands of handmade shoes for the dancers in the company. On average, we went through a pair of shoes per day of rehearsals, and many of us wore brand new shoes for performances. Each pair was special, because each would play a part in our success.

That room was full of possibilities. Full of dreams waiting to be made.

I made my way through the aisles until I came to my stall, marked with my name. I looked up like I always did, taking a moment to appreciate the stack of shoes — *my* shoes — handmade by Freed of London to my specifications. I'd tried a dozen makers' shoes when I apprenticed until I found the right fit, the perfect balance and cut. The moment I found my maker, whose stamp was branded into the shank of every pair of my shoes, it was like the moment when Cinderella put on that lost glass slipper.

I grabbed two bags of shoes and turned to leave,

stopping dead when I looked up.

Nadia stood at the end of the aisle with her hands on her hips and a smile I could only equate to a Disney villain. "Hey, *Lily*." My name from her lips was venom.

"What's up," I said in lieu of a greeting, picking up my feet.

She shifted to block my path as I neared her. "What's going on with you and Blane?"

I met her hard gaze with one of my own. "I don't know what you're talking about."

"Don't bullshit me, JuicyFruit. Everybody knows you've got a thing for him." She snickered. "God, you watch him with those big puppy-dog eyes of yours. Do you really think he could ever be interested in you?"

I kept on glaring at her, imagining that I could light her bun on fire by sheer will of mind. "Well, you set the bar pretty low."

But she was unshaken, just stretched her slimy smile even wider as she looked down her nose at me. "You know, he's always made fun of you, ever since the first time he saw you. It was so pathetic in high school, watching you trip all over yourself when he was around."

Humiliation and anger slipped over me, but I'd never let her know. "Too bad he's not interested in you anymore."

Her eyes narrowed, even though her smile stayed in

place. "Just don't get comfortable, Thomas."

A burst of adrenaline shot through me. "Maybe you should just let him go. Seems like he doesn't want you anymore."

Nadia edged closer. "Fuck you, skank."

She'd boxed me in — I'd either have to slink away and go the long way around or get physical. I chose the latter, plowing through by way of slamming my shoulder into hers. "Grow up, bitch."

She didn't respond as I hurried out, and I think we were both a little surprised by my reaction. I wasn't one to pick a fight, but you come at me, and I'll bite. My nerves hummed as I blew down the hall and to the elevator, thankful that she didn't follow me. I was already in trouble with Ward — pretty sure murdering Nadia in the shoe room wouldn't help my case.

By the time I got back to the studio, Ward was already working with Blane. He gave me a nod as I opened a bag of shoes and dropped them on the floor to step on the toe boxes, then sank to the ground next to my duffle bag. I picked up each shoe to break the shank before digging out my sewing kit and pink darning thread.

First was the elastic across the top, then the satin tendon ribbon with a small strip of elastic that would lay against my ankle for give. Every stitch was sure and quick — something I'd done thousands of times. Once

I'd scored the bottom and covered the toe and shank with resin, I was ready to go. Seven minutes was all the process took. Jenni and I raced once.

Ward stopped the pianist and instructed us to set up for the beginning of the pas de deux. Blane's eyes were on me as I approached, and he smiled as we got into position, slipping his hands around my waist, pressing his chest against my back. Ward turned to the pianist, and Blane took the opportunity to whisper in my ear.

"Tomorrow night. My studio. You in?"

The weight of his hands on my hips, the pressure of his fingertips against my skin demanded every bit of my attention. Nadia didn't matter. She could want him all day long, talk shit, threaten me. But in the end, Blane wanted me.

My smile threatened to take over my face at the thought. "Definitely in."

West

Sweat rolled into my eyes that afternoon as I dribbled in front of Patrick, who stood between me and the basket. The spring sun was high, though there was still that little chill in the air, like winter hadn't quite decided to let go. Not that I was complaining -- not after a couple of hours on the blacktop.

Patrick's arms were wide, his body low enough that

he would grab the ball if I didn't make a move soon.

"Come on, West. What are you gonna do? Stop being a pussy and take the shot."

"You sure are eager to lose," I panted just before I spun and took off around him. I made it to the basket and jumped, tossing the ball in a hook shot that bounced against the rim and through the hoop. "BOOM," I shouted, throwing my hands in the air as I jogged around Patrick. He bent over and wiped off his face with the hem of his shirt, shoulders heaving, shooting me an amused smile as sweat dripped off his hanging hair.

Cooper laughed as he got up off the bench. "Live it up. That was your last win." He picked up the ball and dribbled, somehow looking determined and lazy all at once.

"In your dreams, pretty boy." I walked over to my water and took a long drink, pouring some on my face. I sloughed the excess off my beard and pulled out my hair tie, knotting it up fresh again.

Patrick hung his hands on his hips and walked over to the bench. "Don't talk shit, Coop. He's got four inches on both of us."

Cooper smiled, dribbling between his legs. "Yeah, but I'm lightning fast." He spun around and made a practice shot.

I chuckled as the ball dropped into the hoop.

He jerked his chin at me. "You ready for this, bitch?"

I grabbed the ball as it bounced and shrugged, dribbling. "I dunno, you're not gonna cry if you lose or anything, are you?" I made a shot of my own, and it banked into the hoop.

Cooper scoffed as he trotted around and grabbed the ball. "One time. It happened once, and there was something in my eye." He shot and missed.

Patrick snorted.

"Right." I snagged the ball and ran to the three-point line to shoot. The chain hoop clinked when the ball passed through.

Cooper grabbed it and dribbled low. "Game to seven. Check." He tossed the ball to me, and I tossed it right back before he took off.

He made it to half court, and I turned, putting my back to the hoop, arms out, bobbing in front of him. I watched his eyes and knew what was coming. When he faked, I headed him off and stole the ball, dribbling back to the three-point line to make a shot. It bounced off the rim.

I groaned, and Cooper and Patrick laughed.

"Streak's over, stretch." Cooper recovered the ball, and we made our way around the blacktop. I covered him until he broke away, running up the court to shoot. The ball sailed through the air, but I jumped, stretching to tip the ball before it could get far.

"Told you, Coop," Patrick called from the bench as I recovered the ball.

I dribbled back to the three-point line, laughing. Cooper wasn't amused.

His eyes were narrow as he covered me. "I can't wait to see Maggie on Thursday."

I dribbled lower, brow dropping with my stance. "You don't stand a chance, dick."

"You sure about that?"

My answer was a shoulder to his chest as I charged past him and went for a layup. A layup that I made. I spun around and pointed at him. "You keep your hands off my sister."

Cooper laughed. "You're too easy, man."

I grabbed the ball and dribbled back to the three-point line with Cooper all over me. He stole the ball at the first opportunity and tried for a jump shot that I palmed, turning once I hit the ground to make a jump shot of my own.

I crowed when I made it. "How's that for easy, motherfucker?" I threw my hands up. Cooper grabbed the ball and tossed it to me.

"Goddamn you, you tall son of a bitch."

I leered, dribbling. "How's Astrid? I saw your picture in *Us Weekly* at the grocery store last week."

He covered me. "What's the matter, Shakespeare

getting a little tedious? We were on page twelve, so I'm glad you took the time to flip through it in the checkout line."

I tried to juke around him, but he stayed in my way. "I don't know how that's worse than you knowing what page you were on."

Patrick laughed, and I spun around and took off, only a step ahead of him but with enough room to take a bank shot. I missed. Cooper ran for the ball as I watched on.

I bent over, resting my hands on my knees. "Now's your only chance, so make it count."

Cooper smiled as he dribbled toward me, shifting to keep me guessing. I moved with him to the line. "Since you asked, Astrid's just as exciting as always. But it's getting old."

I met him step for step. "Time to cut it off?"

"Maybe I'll get with Lily instead."

Annoyance prickled my nerves, but I stayed on him. "You wish."

"Lily always has a special smile, just for me. I mean, damn, those Thomas sisters are *hot*."

Anger flared in my chest at the thought of Cooper and Lily, and I faltered. Cooper took the opening, cutting around me to run up the court to make a hook shot. I fumed as I recovered the ball and stopped next to the hoop. And then I nailed him with the basketball.

"Your ball, fucker."

"Ow, man," he said with a laugh when the ball hit him in the hip. He was lucky he moved — I was aiming for his nuts.

"Four to one." I got in his face as he dribbled, keeping my hands low and ready, on a mission. "Look at you, up bright and early at the crack of three in the afternoon. What's the matter, couldn't get laid last night?"

Cooper snorted dribbling between his legs. "I think we both know that's not a problem for me."

I watched, waiting for an opening. "Must be nice being rich and jobless. Until your dad pulls the plug on your bank account, at least. When's that happening again?"

His smile wavered. "Ask my mom."

"I already did last night." I snatched the ball and charged up the court, jumping for the rim. I slammed it into the hoop and hung on, dangling off the ground. "Slam dunk, motherfucker." I let go with one hand to flip him off.

Patrick and I laughed as I hit to the pavement, and Cooper hung his hands on his hips, huffing. "You're a regular fucking comedian today, West."

I grabbed the ball and spun it on my middle finger before dropping it and dribbling back to the three-point. Cooper didn't talk shit this time, and I stayed behind the line, ready to end the game, shifting back and forth as I dribbled. I faked, and he was so focused on keeping track of me that he bought it. I twisted around him and went for a jump shot, holding my breath when it hit the backboard.

I sank it.

I'm not gonna lie. I totally rubbed his fucking face in it.

But Cooper wasn't so easily razzed, even when I got in his face to laugh at him. He just shook his head. "Every goddamn time."

Nerves fired in my muscles, sending tiny shocks down my thighs and calves as I walked over to the bench and grabbed my water again to take a drink.

Patrick rested his forearms on his knees. "Four games in a row. You going for five?"

I took a seat next to Patrick, who sat on the back of the bench. The minute my ass hit the seat, I knew I was done. "Nah. Why press my luck?" I leaned back, trying to catch my breath.

Cooper stopped in front of me. "Going to Habits tonight?"

I shook my head. "I've gotta put a dent in these papers before I get too behind to catch up."

"You're such an adult." He smirked.

I snorted. "Compared to you, maybe."

He shrugged and bent down to dig in his bag for his

water and a couple of towels. "I'm a responsible drinker. That counts, right?"

"In some circles." I folded my hands behind my head and smiled.

Cooper took a drink. "Any news on your doctoral application? When do you find out if you made it?"

"A couple of weeks. I'm trying not to think about it." He handed me a towel, and I wiped my face.

"How's that working out?" The question was heavy with sarcasm.

I laughed and poured some water on the towel before hanging it on my neck. "Like shit. And I've got Simon Phillips around every corner hassling me about it as a reminder."

Cooper just scoffed and rested a foot on the bench, leaning on his knee. "Don't let that little prick get to you. There's no way Columbia is going to accept him over you."

I wanted to believe him, but I shook my head. I knew better than that. "You say that, but he's got status and money that I don't."

"But you've got brains and wit that he doesn't."

"That's not always the deciding factor, and you know it. But if I don't get in, I'll figure everything out. It's not the end of the world if I have to get my doctorate somewhere else."

He eyed me like he knew better. "Right, not the end

of the world. It's just the end of everything you've wanted since Blackwell took you under his wing first year."

I gave him a small salute. "Thanks for helping me forget all about that in case it doesn't work out, Coop. I knew I could count on you."

He put up a hand. "Hey, man. I'm just saying. You work your ass off. You deserve it."

I sighed. "Well, thanks for the vote of confidence."

"Anytime." Cooper jerked his chin at Patrick. "How are things at work? Tattoo any sweet asses lately?"

Patrick smiled sideways. "No, but I did a hip tattoo yesterday that wrapped down and around this chick's thigh, so she had no pants on for the entire session. We have two more sessions scheduled to finish it."

Cooper smirked. "Was she hot?"

"So hot."

"Hotter than Rosie?"

Patrick threw a towel at his face. "Fuck you, Cooper."

Cooper batted it away, laughing. "Just tell her you still love her, man."

Just like that, Patrick's eyes were dark, lips pressed tight. "It's not that simple, and you know it."

He shrugged. "Seems pretty simple to me."

Patrick's eyes were narrow. "Says the guy who avoids responsibility like chlamydia."

"Better to avoid chlamydia than the girl you love," Cooper volleyed.

Patrick huffed. "Says the guy who's never loved anybody."

Cooper made a longing face and sighed dramatically. "Not true. There was a girl in Saint Lucia who I loved *deeply* for twelve hours."

A laugh burst out of me. "You're fucking impossible."

Patrick leaned back with a slight air of superiority. "You don't get it, man. One day, you're going to meet a girl who you can't live without, and it's going to fuck you up. Joke all you want, but when it hits you, it's going to be like a glass door to the face."

But Cooper was as unflappable as ever. "Which is exactly why I'll keep avoiding it."

Patrick shook his head. "You're missing out."

"Am I? You just compared it to getting hit in the face. Hard pass, man. I'll stick to my empty relationship with Astrid and an endless supply of booty calls. No expectations. Dates when I want them. A bed to climb in if I'm lonely. West gets me. He's got Christine."

I rankled. "That's different."

He raised an eyebrow. "Enlighten me."

"Chris and I only hook up. That's all there is to our relationship."

"And how's that different from me and Astrid, or

anyone else for that matter?"

I rested my elbows on my thighs and looked up at him. "Maybe it's not all that different on paper, but I'm not scared of falling for somebody. I just haven't found that somebody yet."

"Who says I'm scared?"

Patrick and I laughed.

"What?" he asked genuinely. "I'm not afraid. I'm just not interested."

Patrick shook his head. "Because you haven't found that girl yet."

But Cooper's face changed, hardened. "You don't know that. Maybe I have, but I know better than to get involved with her. I'm a fucking mess, man. I can't be there for somebody else."

His unexpected honesty stunned us into silence.

Cooper pushed away from the bench and grabbed his bag. "You guys think you've got everybody figured out."

"Hey, man. We didn't mean--"

But his face softened, and he waved me off. "It's fine, really. Can we at least get a beer on our way home? I think West owes us a drink, Tricky."

Patrick smiled. "Agreed."

I stuffed my water bottle and towel into my bag, still curious as to what Cooper was talking about. He'd never mentioned any girls to us before, not with the emotion we'd just caught a glimpse of. Relationships were mostly a joke to him, something to pass his long days -- days he loved to act like were full of living but I knew to be lonelier than he'd admit. "All right. Drinks on me for being a better baller than either of you could ever hope for."

Cooper picked up his bag and snorted. "If you weren't a giant, we wouldn't be having this conversation."

"Don't hate on my dunk, Coop."

"Fucking showboat."

TOE-TO-TOE

Lily

"FIFTEEN MINUTES UNTIL THE SECOND ballet of the evening, Balachine's *Apollo*. Dancers to the stage please." The intercom cut off with a pop.

My nose was as close to the mirror as it could get that night as I lined up the fake eyelash and held it on my lid for an awkward five seconds, taking the opportunity to just breathe. The dressing room was empty — Jenni, who sat next to me, was already downstairs warming up. Who knew where Nadia was. There were eight dancers to a dressing room and a hundred dancers in the company, but when Jenni and I were promoted, they moved us in with her.

None of us were thrilled with the arrangement.

Once the lash was firmly in place, I blinked, fanning them to make sure they didn't slip. The big bulbs framed the mirror that was taped with ticket stubs and photos from shows, a box of flower petals on the counter amongst and explosion of makeup. I dug through the mess for my favorite lipstick, getting to work as Nadia entered the room and sat behind me, eyeing me in the reflection of her mirror.

Stone cold, Lil.

My eyes were glued to my reflection as I lined my lips, even though I could feel her watching me. It's impossible to ignore someone at times like that, when every molecule in the air is charged with tension and your fight or flight kicks in, anticipating the confrontation. I could *feel* her, even though she hadn't moved, hadn't spoken a word.

But the last thing I wanted to do was get into it with her minutes before a show — especially one where we'd be dancing together. I tried not to rush through finishing my makeup, not wanting her to know she was in my head, but I hurried anyway, anxious to get away from her. When I stood, she stared at me in the mirror, the façade of sweetness over the face of poison.

"Break a leg, Thomas."

I smiled back. "Eat a dick, Anderson."

I grabbed my open bag, stuffing my shoes a little deeper before blowing out of the room and trotting down the stairs. I was in warm up booties to keep my muscles hot, sweater on over my costume, and I dumped my things by the wall near the practice barres

just off stage, grabbing my toe pads and shoes to head
to the sewing table.

Our costumes for Apollo were simple — white
tights, leotard, and skirt — practice attire, really. They
were meant to be stripped down and bare, with nothing
to compete with the music and dance, the story. Jenni
was already at the table, hair in a tight, dark bun, long
neck bent as she used the spiked roller to scuff up her
shank for better traction. I set down my new shoes —
already sewn for the show — and grabbed the other
shank roller.

"Hey, Jen."

Her eyes were bright and twinkling "Hey, Lil. How
are you?"

"It doesn't matter how many years we've been doing
this. It never gets easier."

She nodded. "There never seems to be any less
pressure. In fact, I think every show is harder than the
one before." She set down the roller with a thump and
sat to pull her shoes on.

"I know what you mean. And I hate dancing with
Nadia."

Jenni snorted. "You and everyone. Although she
doesn't usually terrorize anyone but you."

"I guess I'm just the lucky one." I sat next to her
and pulled on my first shoe, wrapping the ribbon
around my ankle and tying the end, slipping the knot

into itself. I reached onto the table for needle and thread to sew the knot to my tights.

Jenni's eyes were behind me. "Looks like they're going at it again."

I followed her gaze to see Blane talking to Nadia at a barre where he was warming up. Neither of them looked happy, which probably shouldn't have filled me with satisfaction, but it did. His face was hard as he said something to her that made her cheeks turn hot pink, easy to see even from across the room. He turned and walked away with her eyes lasered on his back. And then she turned the fiery beams on me.

"Shit," I muttered and looked away, flustered.

"What do you think happened between them?" Jenni asked, pretending to look busy with her shoes.

My brow quirked. I wished I knew, but Blane and I didn't exactly do a lot of talking. "I don't even know. I've heard different things, that she dumped him, that they got in a big fight and just separated mutually."

"If it were mutual, I don't know if Nadia would be so ... well, so ragey. I actually heard they broke up because he found someone else."

My heart pumped a little harder. "Oh? Any idea who?"

She shook her head. "Who knows. Pretty sure almost anyone would bang him, guys included."

I laughed, mostly out of relief that the secret was

still safe. "I don't know what it is. Maybe that flash of blond hair. It's almost too long, but somehow it's just perfect."

She sighed. "What I wouldn't give to run my fingers through that. I want to know how he's so tan and if he's that tan *everywhere*."

I snorted, unwilling to respond.

"Maybe he fake bakes. You think he has a little Playboy bunny on his hip?"

I giggled. "I'd put my money on cherries."

She laughed. "Ugh, so douchey."

The orchestra began to tune, and Jenni and I hopped up, leaving our sweaters and booties with our bags before making our way to the edge of the stage. The lights went down. The crowd quieted. Blane brushed past me, smelling clean and fresh, walking to the center of the stage to pick up his prop lyre and pose as the prelude music began.

I felt Nadia behind me and shifted so I could see her out of my periphery as we waited for our cue. I don't know what she might have even done to me — maybe trip me as I tried to enter the stage or do something to my costume. Maybe nothing. But I trusted her about as much as the taserbait who rode the train with me late at night.

The curtain went up, and the violin solo began. Blane strummed the lyre, representing the birth of

Apollo as he discovered music. We watched his solo, the massive height in his jumps, the tightness of his turns and form. And then our cue came, and nothing in the world existed outside of that dance.

The crowd disappeared as I made my way onto the stage. The four of us were one unit, particularly the three women as we moved with a precision that I sometimes wondered if Nadia and I would ever find. But all we wanted was to be perfect, to honor the piece and the audience who had come to see it. Even Nadia wasn't immune to that. Plenty of the dancers hated each other, but in the end, it was forgotten for the sake of a performance.

My body was almost on autopilot — the culmination of years of practice and hours of rehearsals —but every single component of my mind was focused on the performance. Shows were always a blur. Sometimes I didn't remember them at all. Sometimes I only remembered the bad. And sometimes it didn't matter what I'd screwed up because the reaction from the crowd wiped everything away. Those were the moments I lived for.

We wove around each other, our dance steps exactly the same but timed in intervals as we wound through each other and around Blane, using each other for balance until the muse solos began.

Blane sat on a box on the stage as we danced,

performing the arts that we lorded over as muses. Nadia was first, and Jenni and I watched the diva dance her dramatic solo to represent poetry. She really was a beautiful dancer, but there was something anxious, urgent, about the way she danced that showed a bit more of her soul than I think she intended. Jenni was next, her dance for the muse pantomime cheery and bright, well suited for her. She smiled and bounced around Blane, long arms fluid. And then, it was my turn.

My part in the story was to introduce Apollo to dance, so I jetéd and arabesqued, pirouetted my way around the stage as he watched on. Every step was for Apollo, every attitude and battement wooing him until he stopped me, and I turned to make my way off stage once more.

I grinned at Jenni once I met her backstage, and she gave me a small hug, the two of us high on adrenaline. Nadia couldn't be swayed, only stood near us, scowling. I rolled my eyes at her. We were just one, big happy family as we turned to watch Blane perform his solo — Apollo's transition into manhood. His ridiculous vertical was the one thing we could at least all agree on.

After a moment, I hurried around to the other side of the stage to meet him on stage for our pas de deux where he was on the ground, arm extended, finger pointed at me. I touched my finger to his as the music changed. We danced through the pas de deux, and he was my support, always there to catch me, always there to lift me, balance me. I couldn't deny that we were a good pairing for more reasons than our height.

The pas de deux was almost over when I felt the ribbon on my left foot give way on a turn. It was too loose, and every twist of my ankle made it worse, but I wasn't in trouble until the end of the lively coda when my stitches gave way completely. The ribbon hung off my ankle where it was sewn to my tights, but I just dug in and held on, doing my best to avoid stepping on the dangling ribbon, thanking all that was holy in the world that the elastic in my shoe's casing was tight and that I'd made it to the apotheosis where there was almost no pointe work. If there had been, I would have been fucked.

We held the final formation, and the music ended to a roar of applause. We smiled and bowed, made our way off stage to the congratulations from other dancers and masters, everyone asking me about my shoe, commending me for finishing the performance. But it wasn't until after the curtain call that I really had time to deal.

I pulled off the double-crossing shoe and inspected it, grateful that I hadn't hurt myself, almost wishing I'd abandoned the performance to switch them out. I hadn't had a ribbon fail since I first started pointe and didn't have a system. But I *did* have a system. A damn good one. It didn't make any sense. I took the other one off and checked the ribbon. One of my stitches was cut.

Jenni stood next to me as I stared at the ribbon, trying to make sense of it. Had I accidentally cut it? I couldn't figure out what I'd done wrong. I had to have made a mistake.

I looked up and found Nadia staring at me from across the stage. Her smile said one thing.

She'd done it.

Rage shot through me like lightning, and I marched across the stage, not even seeing Blane until he stepped in front of me.

"Hey, Lily."

I tried to side-step him, but he grabbed my arms.

"Hey," he said softer, and I met his eyes. "What happened to your shoe? Are you okay?"

My nostrils flared. "No, I am *not* okay. She fucking cut my ribbons, Blane."

His eyes widened, and he glanced over his shoulder at Nadia, then back to me, jaw set. "Let me talk to her."

"If you think I'm letting this shit go, you're crazy."

He leaned down to get eye-level with me. "She's not going to listen to you, but she'll listen to me. Let me handle it. Otherwise, this is going to end in a fight, and that makes you look just as bad. Okay?"

I was so pissed I could barely see straight, never

mind trying to form sentences that weren't peppered with expletives.

He looked to Jenni. "Get Lily out of here. I'll deal with Nadia."

Jenni touched my arm, eyes searching my face. "Come on. She's not worth your reputation."

They were right. I knew they were right. But all I wanted to do was take a shank roller to that bitch's face.

I took a deep breath and addressed Blane. "You let her know that she'd better back off, or I'm coming for her. This is bullshit, Blane, and I'm not going to put up with it." I hoped he heard the threat to him in there — it wasn't just Nadia who would feel the consequences. By the look on his face, I think he got it. "Would you grab my things, Jenni? I'll meet you in the dressing room."

"Of course."

I gave Nadia a long look that I hoped transmitted my thirst for blood. The smirk she had on her face made it nearly impossible to walk away, but somehow I picked up my feet and left the stage with shaking hands, making my way to the changing room where I paced in front of the mirrors.

My mind went a million miles an hour and was no closer to slowing down by the time Jenni got there.

"Hey." Her voice was soft, like she was trying to approach a wild bear. She wasn't far off.

I turned to span the room again. "There's nothing I can fucking do about it, Jenni."

"I know." She set down our bags and leaned against the counter.

"Telling Ward would start a war. She would deny it. I would look petty. I can't confront her, or we'll end up in a fight, and I could end up fired. I can't believe she did this," I rambled. "I mean, I believe it, but fuck my life."

"Blane was talking to her when I left. I caught a little bit of it when I went to pick up your bag. When do you think she did it?"

I let out a breath, feeling stupid. "It was in here all night. She could have done it at any time."

"At least Blane stuck up for you."

The statement nettled me, and I felt like I had to make an excuse. "It's just because we're partners. No one wants someone they have to work with daily being terrorized by their ex. God, she's so fucking unprofessional. Trying to make me look bad in rehearsal is one thing, but to sabotage a performance?"

"Worse than that — you could have really hurt yourself."

I rubbed a hand over my face, pulling it away like it was on fire. My hand was covered in makeup, and I looked in the mirror to see that my eyeliner had smeared. "Ugh." I reached for my bag and dug around for my makeup wipes. Jenni grabbed one too, and we went to work, scrubbing off the warpaint.

"I'm sorry, Lil."

I sighed. "She's always been like this, but she's crossed the line. If she does something like this again, I'm going to Ward. Will you back me up? Even if Blane won't, if I have you, that should be enough."

"Of course I'll back you up." She scowled. "I hope he would, too."

"I hope he would too. But I can't pretend to understand the dynamic between the two of them." The realization that his loyalties might not be with me after all — the reminder that I was the new girl up against the one he'd been with for years — didn't sit well.

"Promise me you'll tell Ward if she does it again, for real."

"I promise." I smiled at her in the mirror, our faces pink from scrubbing. "Should I plot a revenge tour?"

"I'll help." She reached into her bag for her clothes.

But I shook my head. "I wish I had that in me. I'll do the right thing and wait for her to fuck up again. And then I'll bury that bitch proper."

Jenni smirked. "I'll grab my shovel."

West

I recrossed my ankles on Lily's coffee table late that night and sighed, glancing up at The Bachelor when one of the contestants threw a champagne glass at a wall.

What? Don't judge me. You have your vices, I have mine.

The room was mostly dark, with only the small lamps on the end tables lit. I sat near one of them with an essay in my hand, trying to make progress on my Herculean stack of terrible papers. Rose was at work, and Lily was at a show, so I'd opted to work at their place instead of mine for a change of scenery.

We all had keys to each other's apartments, as close as we all were and since we lived down the hall. It wasn't unusual to come home to find one of the girls in our apartment, though Patrick and I were at theirs more often, on account of the cable. Plus, their apartment was more comfortable. Nicer things, softer couch. It even smelled better, which — thinking about it — I guess isn't that surprising.

I heard the key in the door behind me, and I glanced over my shoulder to find Lily walking in, looking exhausted with her bag slung across her chest. Her blond hair was down and loose, still damp from her shower at the theater, blue eyes dull and lids heavy. She dropped her bag with a thump next to the door.

"Hey, West," she said wearily as she kicked off her

flats.

I watched her toss her keys into the dish on the table and take off her denim overshirt, worrying over her a little. The slope of her shoulders and tightness in her cheeks told me plenty. "Hey, Lil. Long day?"

She shuffled around the couch, falling into it with a flump. Her feet found their way into my empty lap, and I rested a hand on her ankle. She sighed. "Definitely very long."

I laid the essay down on top of the stack. "Want to talk about it?"

Her bottom lip slipped between her teeth, and she nibbled on it for a second. "So you know about Nadia, right?"

I frowned at the mention of her. "Queen Bitch?"

She rested her hands on her stomach over the pink fabric of her tank, threading her long, white fingers into each other. "The very one. She cut the ribbons on my shoe before the show."

Thoughts blew through my mind, fanning my anger with images of her falling, or of that dancer intentionally harming her. My chest was tight. "Are you all right? You're not hurt, are you?"

"No, no. The shoe didn't actually fail until the end of the piece, thank God, but I was so worried. I should have left stage and gotten a new shoe, but we were almost through the end, and I didn't want to abandon the performance. I knew I could hang on. As much as I can absolutely believe Nadia would do something like that, I still can't believe it actually happened to me."

"How do you know it was her?"

"My stitches were cut, and my bag was right next to her while we were getting ready. It was no accident — there's almost no chance that I could have done that. She just cut one stitch on each shoe, so it loosened up until it gave completely. Nadia's the only person who would do something like that to me, and she was watching me with this *look* on her face. It was her, I'm certain."

I was mostly calm, though my grip on her ankle was a little tighter than it had been a moment before. "Did you tell anyone?"

She shook her head. "I can't prove that she did it, and I don't want to take the rivalry to that level, you know? I feel like if I call her out, it's just going to make it worse. But if she keeps it up, I'll tell Ward."

I searched her face, wishing she weren't so noble and respecting her for it all at the same time. "Dammit, Lily. I'm so sorry. Why would she do something like that?"

I didn't miss the flush in her cheeks. She didn't want to talk about it, but admitted, "She's Blane's ex."

Disdain seeped through my thin façade of indifference to Blane. "Does anyone know you're …

rehearsing in your free time?"

"No. We haven't told anyone, or at least I haven't."

"Can you really count on him to keep his mouth shut?"

She shrugged with lips in a slight pout. "He seems intent on keeping things just between us, and I know Nadia doesn't know. If she did, she wouldn't even consider covering her ass or pretending not to be involved in harassing me. She'd straight up come after me, openly and with no fear."

I shook my head. "She's crazy. What are you going to do about her?"

She sighed again. "Part of me wants to do something horrible to pay her back, like put magnesium in her water bottle so she'll shit her leotard during rehearsal, or at least get a solid shart in. I'd even be happy with uncontrollable gas. My standards aren't high."

I couldn't help but laugh, and Lily smiled, wide eyes a little brighter.

"Whatcha working on?" she asked and nodded to the stack of papers.

It was my turn to sigh. "Grading undergrad papers, also known as everything I hate about being a TA."

Lily glanced over at the TV as one bleach-blond contestant cussed the other out. It was just one, long, continual beep, punctuated by aggressive finger pointing.

"Oooh, Celeste is *pissed*. Do they get kicked off if they fist-fight?" she asked.

"Nah, I think it's encouraged."

Lily shook her head. "I mean, with all that booze in the house, who could deny that? They should rename the show *Drunk Bitches Catfight over Some Asshole*."

I chuckled. "A little wordy. And obvious."

Her eyes were still on the screen as Celeste yanked her dress strap back onto her shoulder where it belonged. "You know, it's just so funny that people watch it thinking these asses are actually going to find real love. I mean, they start out with him being unfaithful. I feel like that's the worst possible way to begin a healthy, loving relationship."

"True. He always bangs them on their getaways."

Lily snorted. "Oh, my god. Can you imagine? They're probably like, 'The sex we have in the hot tub in Arruba will decide my fate and the fate of my children. Better give him my anus.'"

A laugh shot out of me. "Seal the deal with anal and blow jobs. Smart girls."

She giggled. "And yet, I still look forward to this show every week."

"It's vicious. There's something about seeing people act so base that really makes you feel like you've got your shit together."

"Amen to that." A commercial came on, but the DVR remote was out of reach, and neither of us made a move for it. She settled back into the couch, turning her attention on me. "Read me your favorite line from your paper."

I knew just the one and skimmed back to find it. "Ah, here it is. '*Iago was like a chess master. He totally set Othello and everyone up just to be a dick. He's like a super genius, like Machiavelli or Tupac or something, except in the end, he just ended up getting stabbed.*'"

She busted out laughing, and I laid the paper down next to me. "At Columbia? I mean, Jesus Christ. How is this kid surviving?"

I shrugged. "It's a low-level undergrad class, just something engineering kids take to get the English credit. The quality of his paper doesn't surprise me, since he usually smells like that hippy mixture of weed and patchouli. When he shows up to class, that is."

"Classic."

"He won't last long. Kids like that always end up getting weeded out."

She snickered. "Ha, ha. *Weeded* out?"

I laughed.

She yawned and stretched, settling a little deeper into the cushions. "Anyway, not every slacker gets cut out. Cooper lasted, didn't he?"

"Yeah, but he was smart enough to at least put in

the bare minimum needed to pass. A degree is a degree. Doesn't matter what your grades are as long as you get that piece of paper, if you're not going to grad school. Plus, his IQ allowed him to coast through Columbia with almost no effort."

Lily shook her head. "Smart bastard. Maybe someday he'll apply himself."

"We can hope." I set the paper back down on the stack. "How's *Swan Lake* going?"

"Well, I rehearse it at least once every day, six days a week, and I honestly don't know that it'll be enough. It's so difficult, so taxing. I could get hurt … I mean, I have to take care of myself. I've been going to the physio room more than ever, spending extra time stretching, even getting more massages than usual, though I guess I can't really complain about that."

I smirked. "Not really."

Her eyes were on her feet in my lap. "It's the hardest thing I've ever done. I don't know if I'll ever be good enough to really pull it off. I almost wish I hadn't been picked." Her eyes snapped up to mine. "Don't you dare repeat that either. God, I sound so ungrateful."

"I'd never tell anyone, Lil. And you're not ungrateful. It's an enormous amount of pressure."

"It really is. I know I'll get through it, but it's sort of looming over me. I'm sure I'll feel better once I survive a dress rehearsal."

"You'll do more than survive."

Her lips stretched into a smile. "Well, if you say so, then it will be."

I chuckled. "I'm not sure my words have the power to devise anyone's destiny, but I believe in you. This is the fire you're forged in. As scary as it is, you'll make it through, and you'll be stronger for it."

"I hope so."

"I know so." My hand moved down her foot where the balls and edges were red and angry. Two toes were taped together, and she was missing a toenail on one foot. I pressed my thumbs into the arch to knead the thick muscle with my fingers splayed across the delicate bones along the top.

She sighed, but I felt her tense. "Ugh, you don't have to touch my ugly feet."

"They're not ugly."

"Don't patronize me," she said flatly, lips pursed.

But I didn't stop what I was doing, only gave my head a shake as my eyes followed the line of her toes up to her ankle. "Your feet are the only visible sign of your love for ballet. Every mark, every callus and wound is a symbol of your pain, of thousands of hours of sweat and blood and work. You call them ugly. I call them art."

She didn't say anything, just watched me, but I kept my eyes on her feet as I worked on her arch and into the ball of her foot. After a minute, she relaxed under my touch.

"Thank you, West," the words were sleepy and slow.

"Any time, Twinkle Toes."

But she didn't respond, and by the time I looked up, she was asleep, her small face turned ever so slightly toward the television, all the lines of worry gone, swept away to leave only soft curves.

I smiled and grabbed a throw from the arm of the couch, laid it over her and shifted to lay a little lower on the couch. Her feet were a comforting weight in my lap, and I sighed at the simplicity of the moment before picking up the Idiot CliffsNotes on Othello once more.

OGLING 101

West

I SAT BEHIND DR. BLACKWELL as he conducted his lecture on Hamlet, discussing Polonius' speech to Ophelia as I organized my spreadsheet full of grades and notes. The lecture hall was packed, as all Blackwell's classes were, and full of rapt faces. The man knew how to command a crowd, that was for sure.

He strolled up and down the stage with his hands in his chino pockets, gray hair combed back, thick framed glasses resting on his nose. "You see, this moment is pivotal in Hamlet's story because, although Ophelia knows in her heart that she loves and trusts Hamlet, she feels compelled to listen to her father and brother — the patriarchy — as they forbid her from seeing him. Her mistake is in the assumption that their experience is her naiveté, and it's Polonius' mistake as well. The rift between the lot of them — created by this speech — is never repaired, and Hamlet and Ophelia won't know a happy moment again. And Polonius' own bumbling interference ultimately leads to his demise. The moral to take from this is: Mind your own business."

A soft chuckle rolled through the class as Blackwell glanced at his watch. "All right, that's it for today." The room immediately filled with the sound of shuffling papers, murmurs, and zipping, or unzipping as it were. "Next time we'll discuss Hamlet's downfall in detail, and don't forget to prep for your quiz on Polonius' speech. Here's a hint — take a close look at the metaphors and their hidden meanings."

Blackwell sat on his desk facing the class as he did after every lecture while most of the students streamed out, though a handful of girls and one guy waited in line at the platform to speak to the professor. I shook my head as I closed my laptop and slipped it into my leather messenger bag.

A dark-haired girl was speaking to the professor, books clutched to her chest, eyes darting to me every few seconds as she stumbled through a weak excuse to talk to him. The blond behind her wasn't even pretending to be interested in Blackwell, just stood there nearly gaping at me. The guy who walked up with her — also staring — elbowed her, and they looked away, for a second at least.

Blackwell just smirked and humored them. I pulled

my phone out of my pocket, feeling uncomfortable, trying to look busy so I wouldn't have to endure the attention from the undergrads. The minute it was in my hand, it buzzed with a text from Christine.

Hey, handsome. Out of class yet?

I smiled. Christine was a TA in the sociology department, and we'd been … well, there's no delicate way to put it. We'd been banging on the regular for months. I couldn't call it dating — I'd never met her non-Columbia friends, and she'd never met mine. We'd never gone out, unless you'd call the back of her Jetta 'going out.' Don't get me wrong. She was gorgeous and smart, funny. I just didn't want more from her, and she didn't want more from me.

Or at least I was pretty sure she didn't.

Chris seemed content with our setup, and we'd been going on this way for months. She was bold enough to approach me, direct enough to tell me what she wanted, so I gave her the same courtesy. She'd known from the beginning that I didn't date and had agreed to the arrangement wholeheartedly. But that didn't stop her from talking about us. I'd walked up on more than a few groups of our peers and heard my name, but the second they saw me, the girls scattered like blushing, giggling birds.

I hadn't always been such a loner. I met Shannon, my ex, freshman year, and we dated all through undergrad. We were happy enough, but I never thought to take it further than what it was. As in, it never actually occurred to me to ask her to move in, never mind getting engaged or married. She wanted to move to Washington and asked me to commit. Said she'd stay if I did.

She moved just after graduation.

It wasn't that I was afraid to settle down. I just never wanted to settle down with her. And when it was all said and done, I decided I wouldn't date anyone until I found a woman who moved me. Shannon had been crushed. I just didn't want to be the cause of that again.

I'd been mostly single ever since. Maybe I'd read too many books, too much Shakespeare to ever be content with someone who didn't make me *feel*. Until I found that girl, I was content to date my degree.

My general disinterest didn't stop women from trying. Maybe it was the man-bun like Lily said. Maybe I should cut it.

I laughed to myself. *Nah.*

I texted Christine back. *Almost finished here. You?*

Waiting for you in your office.

My eyes widened, and I sat up a little straighter. It wasn't *my* office — it was Blackwell's. Wouldn't be the first time we'd hooked up there, but it didn't make me any more comfortable with the idea that she was waiting for me. I hoped to God she wasn't naked.

The last of the students had walked away, throwing longing looks at me over their shoulders. One of the girls almost tripped on the stairs, her face beet-red as she hurried out. I pursed my lips to stop the involuntary laugh.

Blackwell turned to pack his things. "How are the papers coming?"

I stood and picked up my bag. "Ah, well, they're coming. Slow and steady, right?"

He chuckled. "You're doing a great job."

"Thank you, sir," I said with a nod. "I've enjoyed being a part of your classroom very much."

Blackwell smirked. "Seems they're enjoying you quite a bit too."

My ears heated up. "I'm sorry about that."

He waved a hand as he hung his bag on his shoulder. "Don't be. Believe it or not, I was once in your shoes. I even had a sociology colleague of my own." He waggled his eyebrows.

See? I hadn't told a soul, but somehow the entire department knew the details of my love life. I wondered just what Christine had said and to whom, since even Blackwell knew. I was surprisingly unruffled by her talking about us — it kept the others from openly hitting on me like they used to. And she was happy with the bragging rights, it would seem. President of the creepy fan club. Knowing Chris, she'd have T-shirts made that said something like *I conquered the West,* complete with a cartoon cowgirl wielding a lasso.

"Well, sir, I appreciate your understanding."

Blackwell sighed. "Ah, to be young again." He shook his head wistfully. "Well, I'm off to lunch. Keep an eye out for the quiz questions in your email, if you would, and print them out for me before the next lecture."

I relaxed a hair knowing he wouldn't be going to his office. "Yessir. See you in a couple of days."

We waved goodbye, and I headed out the back exit and toward Blackwell's office, texting Chris on the way.

Get yourself ready, girly.

My phone buzzed again in my hand. *Honey, I was born ready.*

I made my way through the halls and to the office smiling, glancing over my shoulder to make sure the coast was clear before opening the door and slipping into the dim room.

Christine was stretched out on her stomach on top of Blackwell's worn, wooden desk, which he kept unnaturally clean, for an English professor. Thank God, because Chris was naked as the day, long hair in a bun on top of her head, glasses perched on her nose as she thumbed through Blackwell's first edition *Anna Karenina.*

I smiled as I locked the door and dropped my bag, untucking my shirt as I strode over to her. "Nothin' like a little Tolstoy to get the blood pumping."

Her lips drooped into a mock frown. "What, nine hundred pages on doomed affairs and the Russian feudal system never turned you on? It's like I don't even know you."

I chuckled as I unbuttoned my shirt. "That book costs more than my first car."

She raised a dark eyebrow. "I'll put it down as soon as you're not wearing any pants."

I shook my head as I pulled off my shirt. "The objectification of men is a real thing."

She shrugged. "Tell me you don't like it."

"It's weird, Chris. You should see how some of the undergrads look at me. Makes me feel like a side of beef at a meat market." I unbuttoned my jeans and dropped them. I didn't have on underwear.

Chris sucked in a breath as she sat up and swung her legs over the edge of Blackwell's desk, crossing her dangling ankles, openly appraising me.

I gestured to her. "See? Like that."

She looked me up and down with a small smile playing at her lips. "It's just … appreciation. That's all."

"Mmhmm. I'll remember that." I smiled back anyway.

She met my eyes. "So Amanda's throwing a party this weekend for the TAs and a few grad students. Let's go."

I made a face. "Together?"

"Of course together, silly." She reached for my waist and pulled me to her. "Why, don't want to be seen with me in public?"

I flat-out frowned at that. "It's not that, it's just—"

"I mean, we're friends, right?" she backpedaled, trying to mask the hope in her voice, looking up at me innocently.

"Right. Yeah, let me see what I've got goin' on." I was suddenly uncomfortable and chased the fleeting thought of leaving. I couldn't help but wonder if she was asking me out. But she knew what I wanted, and I trusted her to be honest with me if her feelings had changed, especially if they'd grown.

Surely she really did just want to go as friends. I felt presumptuous for assuming otherwise.

"That's all I wanted, *West.*" She dragged the word out into a hiss before making it her personal mission to make me forget the conversation all together.

Lily

The pianist played Tchaikovsky's Elegy in rehearsal that afternoon, and I leaned back, eyes closed, arms extended while Bastian, Jared, and Seth carried me away.

"Good, good." Ward's voice echoed off the mirrors

and floor. "Let's back up and take it from the Dark Angel."

The corps girls and Nadia made their way to their bags along the walls to get a drink as Bastian, Jenni, and I posed in the center of the room and the music began again. Officially, there was no story in *Serenade*, but it was impossible not to watch without feeling one unfold. In the Dark Angel piece, Jenni and I would battle for Bastian, and in the end, the Waltz Girl — that was me — would lose him forever. I always felt like it was his death, and that at that point, the Waltz Girl is defeated, gives up. The segment after was where I would pick myself up and move on.

I loved *Serenade*. I'd loved it since the first time I danced it in the corp — it was one of the few ballets where Balanchine let the corps *dance.*

Jenni and I danced, the push and pull between the three of us carrying us through the piece until the music slowed, and I dropped in his arms and arched. He laid me down, and Jenni placed her hands over his eyes and led him away.

"Beautiful. Thomas, I want you to feel your loss when the Dark Angel takes Bastian from you. I want to see it on your face, in your arms, your hands. He's gone forever and he's left you here alone. You can't go on without him. The audience needs to feel it. *You* need to feel it."

I nodded, internalizing his words, feeling them burrow into my psyche.

Ward clapped. "Well done, everyone. I'll see you all tomorrow."

Everyone chatted as we bowed and curtsied to Ward and headed to our bags. Nadia glared at me from across the room, but I only rolled my eyes.

Bastian snorted, glaring back at her. "She should have been the Dark Angel instead of the Russian Girl. She's got that evil temptress look down."

"Ugh, no." I pulled on my warm up booties over my shoes. "I'd like to dance with her as little as possible, thanks."

Bastian ran a hand through his black hair, smiling. "Good point. Plus, Jenni's a better Dark Angel, anyway. It requires confidence that Nadia just doesn't have."

Jenni fawned dramatically. "Aww, thanks, Bas."

His blue eyes twinkled. "Anytime, Jen."

I shook my head. "I don't know if I would say Nadia isn't confident."

Bastian raised an eyebrow. "Confidence and arrogance aren't exactly the same thing. Really, she's insecure, and it shows when she dances. The Russian Girl is perfect for her. She brings the egomaniac to that piece like nobody's business."

We giggled.

"Seriously, she's the worst," he continued as he

packed his bag. "And somehow, since she and Blane broke up, she's even more conniving than usual. I mean, she's always bordered on sociopathic, but she pulls it off with the poise and judginess that only a ballerina can muster."

Jenni picked up her water and gestured with it. "I totally agree. And she's got it out for Lily."

My face tightened. "She's *always* had it out for me, that's nothing new. But after her stunt last night, it's all-out war."

Bastian's lips were flat. "Please, girl. She's just jealous."

I sighed. "She's got seniority over me, and she's danced more lead roles than I have. Bigger roles, to boot. The masters love her, and they'll keep loving her as long as they think she's checking her baggage at the door. I've got nothing she wants." My brow dropped. *Except Blane. But she couldn't know that.*

But Bastian leaned in, shaking his head. "You've still got a better standing than her. They can see through her ass kissing — they're not blind. You're genuine, easy to work with, take direction well. You're not *desperate.* When she dances, you can smell the urgency, like she's going to lose everything if she isn't better than everyone else. But here's the truth. Secretly, she doesn't think she's good enough. She just thinks she deserves it more than anyone else." He took a drink of water. "Entitled.

That's what it is. She and Blane deserved each other. Have you heard why they broke up this time? I can barely keep track."

Jenni's voice dropped as she leaned in too. "This time has been the longest. I heard they got in a huge fight, and he dumped her. I also heard he moved out this time and has been crashing at a studio he rents."

Bastian raised an eyebrow and glanced at Nadia across the room. "I heard something else." His eyes darted to me.

My cheeks were instantly warm, and I dug around in my bag for nothing to look occupied.

Bastian pressed on. "*I* heard that she didn't like that Blane had been paired with Lily for *Swan Lake*. She and Blane have performed it together two years in a row, so I guess she felt like she had a claim on it."

"And him," Jenni added.

I waved them off. "I don't know why everyone makes a big deal about it. We're only partnered because of our height."

Bastian leaned back against the mirror and raised a knee, propping his arm on it. "Doesn't matter to Nadia. How's *Swan Lake* going, by the way?"

I zipped up my bag and sighed. "Terrifying."

Bastian's smile brought me more comfort than I'd been expecting. "You're going to kill it, Lil."

"I hope so. I'm more freaked out than I've ever been

about an injury. About doing it right, doing it well. This … this is the role of my life." My voice had dropped with my gaze, locked on my hands in my lap.

Bastian tipped my chin up. "You are going to own it. I can't think of another dancer who I'd rather see dance Odette. Plus, you get to dance with Blane Baker and the ass of the century."

I had to laugh at Bastian's starry eyes.

"Oh, how I wish he weren't straight."

"I can't say the same," I volleyed.

Jenni chuckled and hopped up, grabbing her bag. "All right, guys. I've got to jet if I'm going to make it to *Four Temperaments* rehearsal in time. See you later." She twiddled her fingers at us.

"Bye," we chimed. Nadia left right behind her, bun as tight as her face, eyeing us the entire way out.

Bastian leaned in, instantly serious. "I know about you and Blane."

My head swung around, eyes bugging when they connected with his. I felt like I'd been slapped. "How?" I hissed.

"Don't worry. Your secret's safe in the vault." He tapped his temple. "I overheard the two of you talking in the hall the other day."

I scrambled through my memories, trying to figure out where we were and what we'd said.

"You didn't say you were together, but I could tell

where it was going. I mean, I can't say I didn't suspect it after sitting in on your Black Swan pas de deux. The two of you could make surviving sexual tension an Olympic sport."

I dropped my face into my palms, partly wishing I were dead, even though I was glad it was Bastian who figured it out and not Nadia. "Fuck." The word was muffled, sounding more like a groan than a swear, though I guess it was a little of that too.

He tried to comfort me. "Trust me, no one knows."

I looked up at him with my face steaming. "How could you know that? If you know, who's to say someone else didn't overhear us?"

"Because I'll hear about it if anyone finds out. People just tell me things. It's a gift and a curse." He shrugged.

I was way too far gone to be amused. "I'm under enough pressure as it is. Can you imagine what Nadia will do if she finds out? I can't handle the full-on assault from her over this. I don't even know what *this* is. We only hooked up once, and we've never gone on a date or anything."

His face was soft, eyes big and kind. He wouldn't betray me, not to anyone who would hurt me. All I could do was hope whoever he told wouldn't spill to someone who would.

"Whatever it is, just be careful. I don't trust Blane,

and if he goes back to Nadia — which he could, you should be prepared for that — if he *does*, he might tell her everything."

I nodded. "I'll talk to him about it tonight."

"And I'll keep my ear to the ground."

I sighed. "Thanks, Bas. It hasn't been easy to keep this a secret, not with us rehearsing together all day, every day. I swear, they keep pairing me with him, which is awesome and shitty all at once."

He made a duck face. "No way would I call that luck shitty. It got you boning Blane Baker."

I chuckled. "I mean, how the hell?"

Bastian smiled conspiratorially. "Is his ass as perfect naked as I imagined?"

"Uh, yes."

Bastian closed his eyes like he was eating an éclair. "Tell me he has a giant hammerhead."

I deadpanned. "He has a giant hammerhead."

His eyes were still closed as he grabbed my wrist. "Christ almighty, Lily Thomas. Don't you toy with my emotions."

I burst out laughing. "I wouldn't lie about something so serious."

He grinned and opened his eyes. "You have just made my year. Tell me it was hot."

I made a face. "Kind of?"

Bastian's mouth popped open. "No 'kind of.'" He

leaned in even closer. "Is it possible someone that gorgeous could be a bad lay?"

I blustered. "I'm giving him a pass. You know how the first time can be."

"No, I don't." One dark eyebrow was jacked.

I slapped his arm. "Ugh, that's exactly what my roommate said. I know you know what I mean."

But Bastian shook his head. "Just make sure it's worth it."

"I've wanted him forever. It's worth the shot, you know?"

He patted my arm. "I know. Just make sure."

The door opened, and the next round of dancers came in. Bastian winked at me as we stood and walked down the hall, parting ways when we reached the next studio. But the unease that had wriggled into my brain was forgotten when I found Blane waiting for me.

ANTICI....PATION

Lily

IT WAS LATE THAT NIGHT, but even though I was exhausted from a full day of rehearsals and performing *Serenade*, I was wired. I stepped out of the steaming shower and reached for my towel, rolling through my list of things to come. I'd washed off the grime from the day, shaved all the bits. Knew exactly what I'd wear to Blane's studio and exactly how I'd fix my hair.

Our first time was less than magical. This time? Well, this time was going to be magical, dammit. I was mentally prepared and ready to give it a hundred percent. Butterflies flitted around my stomach at the thought of him kissing me. And then I pictured myself laid out on the dance floor in the near dark with Blane's face between my legs, and the butterflies exploded into poofs of glitter.

Epic, guys. Knee-shakingly, thigh-quakingly epic.

I smiled to myself, humming as I stepped onto the rug and finished drying off, fueled by the excitement of seeing Blane. I toweled off my hair as steam climbed across the glass like a curtain, and I opened the door, watching it recede almost as quickly.

I glanced over reflection at my wide eyes and sopping blond hair, catching a glimpse of the tattoo on my ribs. The watercolor vines climbed up my side, sprinkled with roses and lilies, a Tricky Evans original piece, and Rose had one to match. I smiled to myself shaking out my roots as I walked into my bedroom — maybe tonight Blane would see it for himself.

My clothes were on my bed waiting for me — a low-cut black tank and jersey booty shorts. The pink, thigh-high leg warmers would go in my bag, and a sweater and leggings would stop me from having to use my mace on the train. But I had to at least keep up the pretense of rehearsal. Felt presumptuous to show up at his studio in heels and a little black dress.

I frowned when Nadia popped into my head uninvited. I wondered how many times she'd gotten ready for him just like this. Wondered what she'd think if she knew I was on my way to meet him. At some point, everyone in the company could know. The thought upset and excited me.

It was something I needed to talk to him about eventually, but I didn't want to talk. I just wanted everything to work itself out without any resistance. Was that too much to ask of the universe?

Probably. But I made my wish anyway and headed back into the bathroom where my phone sat next to the sink, lit up from a message I'd just gotten from my older sister, Astrid.

Hey, meet me at Habits. Just want to say hi.

I sighed and glanced at the clock — it was ten. Of course she would decide to come out tonight, not that I needed to be at Habits for her to feel at home. My big sister could look bored and starving pretty much anywhere, a trick of the modeling trade, I supposed. She'd always been quiet and a little judgy, but modeling had kicked her aloofness up to the next level.

Everyone knew her, though I didn't know if they'd hang out with her if it weren't for me, other than Cooper. They dated, or something — I'm not sure what you'd actually call it. Basically, they hooked up and took each other to events they needed arm candy and paparazzi bait for. It was a relationship of convenience, one that was necessary in their social circle. The comfort of a person who they knew was safe in a world where someone was always trying to take advantage of them.

I texted her back. *Sure, can't stay long. Got a date.*

Oh, is that what you're calling it? Bastian told me about Blaney.

So much for the vault. I scowled. *You're the worst, Astrid. And don't call him Blaney.*

Don't get your leotard in a bunch. Come on, I'll buy you a water on the rocks before your 'date.'

You're too generous. See you in a few.

I tossed my phone, and it hit the counter a little harder than I meant to. I didn't get why everyone was giving me crap about Blane. Okay, I guess it wasn't everyone, but between Rose, West, and now Astrid, I'd had it. I never commented on their dates. *Maybe* I used to make fun of West's ex, but that chick was about as interesting as a bag of wet hair. He could do so much better. The guy was gorgeous and smart, funny, driven. And with *manners*. A total catch. If he wasn't my best friend, I'd be all over that.

In fact, the first time I met West, Rose and I were trying to get my armoire up the stairs to move me in. We'd powered that beast up two flights and were halfway up the last, but we were worn out. I felt it slip in slow motion, and then bam — there was West, tall, dark and handsome, catching it before it smashed into a trillion pieces. That was before the beard and man bun, but let me just tell you, it didn't hinder the hotness. I'm pretty sure my undies melted on eye contact. Not gonna pretend like I wasn't bummed when I found out he had a girlfriend, but I put him in the friend compartment, and before long I'd forgotten all about that first meeting.

Mostly.

I sighed and put on a little lip gloss, just enough mascara to keep me from looking like an albino, and a tiny bit of blush — the bare minimum amount of makeup to make me look fresh and together. Effortless. You know, like I hadn't been thinking about the date for thirty-six hours straight or something.

I glanced at myself in the full-length mirror, tugging at my tank and inspecting my backside. Perks to being a pro ballet dancer? The body. Some dancers were never happy with the way they looked and took being thin way too far, like when they'd get that weird, pointy shoulder bone that sticks up. Two places where I drew the line on skinny — creepy shoulder bones and ankles so thin that they look like they'd snap when you're en pointe.

People always thought it was weird when I told them that almost every ballerina I knew smoked like a chimney to suppress their appetites and exorcise the stress that came with our job. I probably would too, if I hadn't puked my guts up at sixteen when I smoked for the first time with Jenni. We all drank too, though we had to be careful around big performances. Mostly we danced shorter shows, around thirty minutes each with a few scheduled each night, though we'd usually only dance in one. Each piece would run for several weeks on multiple nights, and then we'd cycle some out and rotate new ones in.

I didn't smoke, but I *did* love to eat. As long as I had clean lines in a leotard — it was virtually impossible not to, given the number of hours I danced every day — I was happy. Once I went on a week-long hamburger bender. One glorious week full of pickles and mushrooms and bacon and cheese. And then it hit my hips, and I made the disagreeable decision to only have one burger a month. Giving them up completely just wasn't an option.

Everybody thinks ballet dancers are a bunch of uptight dance robots, but the truth is that unless we had something big coming, we led pretty normal lives for people in our twenties. Besides the sixty-plus-hour work weeks.

I walked through the apartment, slipped on my flats, and hung my bag on my shoulder, and within a minute, I was heading toward Habits in the cool spring evening, trying not to walk too fast and failing. I know I looked like a woman on a mission, but I couldn't help it — I reached the front door in no time, pulling it open with a whoosh before blowing inside.

Everyone sat at the bar except Astrid. I cursed her, reaching for my phone to bang out a text. *I'm here, where are you?*

Almost there.

You said you were here!

No, I didn't. I said for you to meet me there. Read the text back, betch.

I scrolled back through. She was right. *Well, hurry up. You have ten minutes!*

Sir, yes, sir!

I huffed and stuffed my phone back in my bag. Astrid couldn't be on time to save her life. Seriously. If she were in a movie where she had to show up at midnight with the money, the bad guy would totally blow up the building just to prove he wasn't bluffing.

Everyone was lined up at the bar, and their faces swung around when I approached. "Hey, guys." I took a seat next to West.

Rose raised an eyebrow at me. "What are you doing here? I thought you had a '*date?*'" She made air quotes with her fingers.

I rolled my eyes. "Yes, I do have a *date*, but Astrid said she was coming and wanted to say hi."

Patrick groaned.

"I know, I know," I said as I took off my bag. "I just hope she hustles. I'm leaving in ten minutes either way."

Rose set a glass of water in front of me. "What are you guys doing tonight?"

"Oh, you know, just a little *rehearsal.*" I wiggled my eyebrows.

West gave me a look. "Has he ever taken you on a proper date?"

I gave him a look of my own. "No, but we're a little busy."

One dark eyebrow raised. "Not busy enough to stop you from 'rehearsing,' it would seem."

I gaped dramatically. "Are you judging me, Weston Williams?"

He picked up his beer, feigning indifference, that liar. "Not at all, just observing." He took a drink.

I sniffed and picked up my water.

Rose just smiled at me from across the bar. "Oh, don't let LumberWest get to you. I think his bun's too tight today."

I laughed, and West rolled his eyes. "Ha, ha, Rosie."

"Really, though," she continued, trying to rally me, "as long as you're happy, we're happy for you."

I smiled back even though the seemingly harmless statement shook me up a little. Did Blane make me happy? I mean, I was giddy and overwhelmed, was that the same thing? It was too soon to tell. Maybe after tonight I'd know for sure.

"Thanks." I nudged West in the arm, eager to change the subject. "Maggie flies in tomorrow. Exciting!"

West leaned on the bar and smiled at the mention of his sister as Cooper and Patrick chatted and Rose made a lap down the bar. I looked West over — dark hair tied back, the small strands curling against his neck and that one piece in the front that would never stay put. His eyes were so blue, with the longest lashes, and I shifted, feeling a little strange. My gaze caught on his bicep where his T-shirt stretched around his arm, then followed the lines of his tattooed sleeve, the dark swirling words that wrapped around pages of books that turned into origami cranes and flew away.

I blinked and met his eyes again when he spoke.

"It'll be good to have Maggie close by, especially after everything that happened in Jackson. She needs a fresh start."

"New York is one of the best places for that. We'll make her forget all about that jerkburger."

He smiled wider from behind his dark beard. "I'm sure you will. Getting away from home will be the best thing that ever happened to her. You two ready for another roommate?"

"We are. I made her some space in the bathroom, and our room is set. Hopefully she likes everything."

"Nervous about sharing a room?"

"Nah. If I could survive Astrid through junior high, Maggie will be a piece of cake." I pulled out my phone again and glanced at the time. "Ugh. She's such a pain in the ass."

"In a hurry, Lil?" Astrid said from behind me, completely unapologetic.

I turned in my seat and rolled my eyes at her. "Said

the girl who's too busy being popular to be bothered with such things as punctuality."

Astrid took off her black designer bag, and I cringed when she set it on the sticky bar top. That bag cost more than three months of my rent. She sat on the other side of me and crossed her long, skinny legs. Somehow she made black jeans, a white tee, and a leather jacket look like couture. As far as I knew, they could have been.

"I love you too, little sister." She smiled and turned to the bar. "Hey, Rose. Can I get a vodka soda?"

"No prob, Astrid. What's new?"

She ran her fingers through her blond hair. "I have a shoot for Barney's tomorrow, so it's the old liquid diet until tomorrow night." She held up the glass that Rose passed her and shook the contents.

"That's so bad for you, Astrid." I shook my head, openly judging her. It was my sisterly right. "You can't just starve yourself."

Astrid took a sip. "Remind me about that after you've been on a forty-foot billboard in Times Square."

Cooper spun his seat around and leaned back against the bar to address us. "While I've got you all here, I'm on the list for Noir Saturday night, want to go?"

Rose lit up. "Oh, man. Everybody's talking about that place. I heard it's like Gatsby meets Blade Runner."

West perked up at that. "Sounds interesting. It's hard to get into?"

Cooper's lips bent in that smarmy half-smile he wore so often. "For most people."

Astrid looked unimpressed. "Gretchen went last week. Said they do an aerial show every hour with dancers they snagged from Cirque du Soleil."

Rose beamed. "I'm down. I think I can get Shelby to cover my shift. Come on, Lil. You have to come."

It really did sound fun, but it also sounded like a long ass day of rehearsals and a show on Sunday. "I don't know, guys. I've got *Serenade* on Saturday and rehearsal all day Sunday."

"Ugh," Rose groaned. "This isn't an opportunity you'll have again any time soon."

I shrugged. "I'd rather sleep than wear heels."

She made a puppy dog face.

I sighed. "I'll think about it."

Rose smiled like she knew she had me. "I'll take that. I swear I won't get you wasted."

Cooper looked down the line. "West? Tricky?"

I didn't miss Patrick watching Rose. "Yeah, I'm in."

But West shook his head. "I don't know. Sounds like a good time, but I've gotta see where I'm at with work."

"Astrid?" Cooper's brow was up, and I couldn't tell if he really wanted her to go or was asking out of obligation.

"Sounds like a good time."

"Good. I'll reserve a table, then. And maybe we can convince Mom and Dad here to come with us."

Astrid smirked. "I'll work on Lily. You work on West."

He smirked back at her. "Deal."

Cooper leaned over to talk to Patrick as Rose made another trip down the bar, and Astrid took the opportunity to turn to me, eyeing me like she knew a thing or two. "So, Blaney, huh?"

I smiled despite the fact that she used the nickname again. Rose snickered from a few feet away as she poured a drink, but I didn't care. I hunched toward my sister, feeling like a teenager. "I know, right? I couldn't even believe it. Blane Baker." I shook my head, awestruck all over again.

"How did that even happen?"

"It started when we found out we were partnered for *Swan Lake*. He and Nadia broke up like a week later, and he turned the charm up to eleven." I'd dropped my voice, feeling like West was listening from behind me. "He asked me to rehearse with him, which I was hoping was code for something. It totally was." I giggled.

Astrid looked amused. "Look at you."

"I know!" Excitement washed over me again. "It's so crazy. I've wanted him forever, and now we're seeing each other."

"Naked," she leaned in, smiling as Rose leaned across the bar to get her head in the quiet conversation.

I laughed. "God. I don't know how to handle having something I've idealized for so long."

Astrid's smile faded into something softer. "Well, nothing's what it seems. Modeling isn't what I imagined it would be. The reality of being a professional dancer isn't what you pictured when you were a little girl. When you look behind the curtain after dreaming about something for that long, there's a lot of room for disappointment. You never find exactly what you were looking for. So just be careful, okay?"

And that right there was one of the many reasons why my sister was amazing. "Thanks, Astrid. I'll keep my eyes peeled."

"And your drawers, while you're at it," Rose said with a laugh, a little louder than I would have liked.

I threw a paper coaster at her. "I'm not wearing any, Nosy Rosie."

I didn't realize everyone was listening until they all laughed — everyone except West, who gave me a look I couldn't quite place, one that made me feel like I owed him an explanation. But I shook off the thought and stood, hanging my bag on my shoulder. "Anyway, I've got to run. Have fun, guys." I kissed Astrid on the cheek. "Thanks, Astrid."

"Any time. Don't get into any trouble."

I waggled my brows. "No promises. Bye, guys."

A chorus of goodbyes washed over me, but my brain was already rolling toward Blane and what I hoped would be the bang of the decade.

West

I watched Lily walk away as annoyance twisted around in my guts like snakes, though I couldn't figure out why. I'd only caught bits and pieces of the conversation, straining to hear what she was saying while trying to look inconspicuous. It wasn't easy.

I didn't like that she was worked up again, and hearing her whispering about this Blane guy irritated me. I tried to ignore the fact she didn't have panties on.

My mind hung on the whole thing like a snag in a sweater that I couldn't leave alone. I wanted to know what made this guy so special that she'd break her long-held oath of staying single for him.

Astrid shook her head as she moved a seat closer to me. "I don't know about all of this."

My brow dropped, and Rose shot her a look. I was so anxious to get the dirt that I took the opening without a second thought. "You mean Blane?"

Astrid leaned on the bar, the quintessential supermodel. She and Lily looked a lot alike — tall and blond, with long arms and legs, small faces and big, almond-shaped blue eyes. Astrid usually had an air of apathy about her, but it was times like this when I knew it was a show.

"Yup, good old Blaney Baker." The words were heavy with cynicism, and as she took a drink, I felt my heart sink.

"What's the deal with him?" I asked, and Patrick leaned forward to try to listen. I moved my stool back so he and Cooper could hear.

"You guys know about Nadia, right?"

We all grumbled our assent.

"Right. So she's always been a bit ahead of Lily in the company, until now. Now Lil's getting the roles Nadia has or wants, since I guess the Master in Chief of the company likes Lily paired with Blane. Blane who just dumped Nadia, maybe for Lily."

Something flared in my chest — jealousy? I pushed the thought away, telling myself I was just worried for her welfare.

"So part of the issue is Nadia, but the rest is that Blane is a total douchebag."

"How do you know?" Patrick asked in challenge. "You don't know the guy personally, do you?"

"No, but Sebastian Ames and I are besties, and he's been in the company with them since they were at SAB. The stories I've heard over mimosas and eggs sardou would make your head spin. Like Blane thinks Jager

Bombs are 'tight,' and Bastian said he uses this special lotion made for strippers that's like part baby oil, part self-tanner. And Nadia is like next-level. One time, she soaked a sock in fish oil and stuck it in the bottom of one dancer's bag for flirting with Blane. Or another time when she and Blane broke up, she made a fake Craigslist ad for 'male company' with his phone number on it. The instructions said to only call between nine at night and six in the morning, no voicemails. I'm telling you guys, this has the potential to blow up in Lily's face."

Rose stared Astrid down. "I don't know if Lily would appreciate this conversation happening without her here."

Astrid waved her off. "Please. I don't think Lily sees what's really going on, and she needs somebody to look after her. Bastian's watching her from the inside, but she's going to come to all of us for advice, and we need to know what we're dealing with."

I had a million questions, but I was torn between wanting to know everything and wanting to respect her privacy. "Lily's a big girl. She can take care of herself. Why shouldn't we let her make her own choices?"

"Because she's blinded by his douchesparkle. This guy is trouble for Lil, and she doesn't see it. Blane and Nadia break up all the time, so chances are, it's only a matter of time until he goes back to her. And when he does, he could tell her everything. I can't imagine that knowledge would make Nadia happy, and she's already got it out for Lily."

I fumed. "She cut the stitches in Lily's ribbons at a show last night."

Rose's eyes shot wide. "She *what?*"

I nodded. "Lily said she couldn't prove it or she would have told Ward."

"That bitch." Rose muttered.

Cooper spoke up, face tight with concern when he asked Astrid, "What do you suggest we do about it?"

Astrid shook her head with her eyes on her drink. "No idea. She's not going to hear us if we try to convince her, so I guess we just prepare for the end of it. Nadia is ruthless, and I think she's jealous of Lily. Plus, she knows about Lily's crush and loves to make her look bad, especially in front of Blane. If she figures out they're hooking up, it's going to get ugly."

I picked up my beer, but my stomach turned at the thought of someone hurting her. I set my glass down again. "This sucks, Astrid. What the hell are we supposed to do with this information? How are we supposed to watch her back?"

"Arm yourself with knowledge, Weston. She's fulfilling a fantasy right now. I mean, she's been about Blane since she was fifteen. Just the ultimate crush of her entire life. No big deal." She shook her head. "You don't just walk away from that. She's going to have to see it through. I don't doubt she'll figure him out — she's too smart not to — but I can't imagine a scenario in which there's a peaceful ending for Lily and Blane."

I rubbed my face, wishing things were different. Lily deserved to be loved, not dicked around by some beef-headed asshole. "Are you saying there's absolutely no chance he could care about her?"

"There's always a chance, but from what Bastian's told me, the guy's a self-absorbed narcissist. Throw Nadia in on the whole situation, and it's a time bomb."

Rose and I glanced at each other, the worry on her face mirroring my own. "All right," I started. "Then we'll be there for Lily and try to help without getting involved."

Cooper nodded. "You guys try to steer her without her realizing. Maybe there's some way to head off the train wreck."

Rose sighed. "Maybe it'll work out. Maybe he really cares about her."

The thought made me feel even sicker. "Maybe. We've just got to try to trust that she knows what's best for her."

Astrid drained her drink and set it on the bar with decision written all over her. "What if I can convince her to come to Noir and to bring Blane with her? Then we can judge for ourselves." She picked up her phone with bright eyes as her fingers flew. "I'll tell her to ask him to come. If he says yes, she'll definitely come with us."

Patrick picked up his drink. "It could work."

I hated this plan. "Or maybe her 'rehearsal' tonight will be a mess, and the whole thing will work itself out."

Astrid looked a little sad as she put her phone down. "We can hope."

SPIN OUT

Lily

I PULLED OUT MY EARBUDS as I approached Blane's studio with my nerves all over the place. The building had been converted from apartments to private studios that the owner rented out for classes and lessons and was beautiful in its own right — lofted ceilings, big windows, old, polished wood floors. I'd been thinking nonstop about this moment, the one that approached with every stair I climbed, and when I reached the door, I took a deep breath, smoothing my sweater.

I hesitated with my knuckles hovering in front of the door.

Do it, Lily.

I held my breath and knocked.

Blane opened the door, blond hair in disarray, and I caught the crisp scent of soap. I stood there staring at him for a moment, eyes on his full lips, teeth bright when he smiled at me. He looked so good — tank stretched across his broad chest, straps lying over the thick muscles of shoulders, jersey shorts hanging low on his hips. I smiled back up at him innocently, adjusting my bag on my shoulder, and he shifted out of the way to let me pass, closing the door behind me.

The studio was nearly dark, just like the last time, and I walked across the room to set down my bag. I pulled off my sweater and lost my pants, leaving me in my booty shorts. I turned when I felt his hands on my hips.

"Hey," he said, smiling.

"Hey." I slipped my arms around his neck.

"So, I'm sorry we haven't had a chance to talk about everything."

I shrugged and lied. "It's okay."

"And I'm sorry about last night with Nadia. It won't happen again."

I raised an eyebrow.

"No, really. I know how to get what I want from her. If she messes with you again, let me know. I'll take care of it."

The sentiment made me feel better. "Thanks, Blane."

His arms tightened around my waist, bringing my stomach flush with his. "Thanks for keeping this between us. I know you get how complicated it is."

"I do." The words were a little sad.

"And who knows what Nadia would do if she found out."

My chest tightened at the mention of her name. "What did she say when you talked to her?"

He glanced away, shaking his head. "She denied it, but I know it was her."

I mustered the courage to ask him *the* question. "What happened between you two?"

My arms on his shoulders rose and fell as he shrugged. "She didn't like us partnered together, and I'm sick of being bullied by her. The combination of the two ended in a fight where we both walked away." His hand found my ass, and he smiled. "So now I just want to have fun, you know? Nothing complicated. You're into that, right?"

The explanation was enough for me, and optimism washed over me. I could have fun and be not-complicated with Blane. "Works for me." I remembered Astrid's text and smiled up at him. "Oh! So, Saturday night, we were thinking about going to this new club. My friend got us in VIP. It's called Noir, or something."

Blane's face lit up. "I keep hearing about it. The lead singer of Paper Fools started it. Apparently, his wife is an artist and designed the whole place, set it up as an investment." He shook his head in disbelief. "Who got you on the list?"

"Cooper Moore."

He gaped. "You're *friends* with Cooper Moore?"

I chuckled. "Yeah, Astrid Thomas is my sister, remember?"

"Man, I totally forgot they dated. I'd love to go."

"Sure. I thought it might be fun to go out. But," my smile fell, "with Astrid and Cooper, there might be paparazzi. I don't know how much of a secret we'll stay."

His brow dropped for a split second before he wiped the look away. "No worries. We'll play it by ear." He kissed my cheek and walked across the studio to the stereo. I felt like I was drunk as I sat down and pulled on my leg warmers — we were going on a date this weekend, and we were about to get freaky, for real this time.

I wondered what kind of music he'd turn on. Maybe Tchaikovsky or Chopin. Schubert — I loved Schubert.

Thankfully, the studio was dark because my face bent in a frown at the sound of the experimental electronic music, a trancy, repetitive loop of atmospheric sounds that made me feel like I was on drugs. Or at least I imagined it would be something like that, since I'd never done any myself.

No, not even weed. I know, I know. Professional ballerina, remember? Goals. Aspirations. Eyes on the prize and all that.

I shook off my disdain. Blane's lame taste in music couldn't bring me down — I could be flexible in more than my hips.

He strutted over to me like he knew he was hot, and I pushed away the fleeting thought that he sort of put out a patronizing air, like he was doing me a favor. But that was silly — he wouldn't have invited me over if he didn't want me. I think.

He didn't stop until he was so close that I couldn't breathe, and my lids fluttered closed when he slipped a hand into my hair and pressed his lips to mine.

God, it was so nice. My only complaint was that it didn't last long enough.

He pulled me down to the ground until we were kneeling, held me against his hard chest as his hands roamed my ass. Within seconds, his hand was in my shorts, to my disappointment. Look, I know my boobs aren't the biggest, but they're not bad for a ballerina, and they really, really wanted his attention. But Blane didn't seem to be interested in much above the waist.

I almost forgot about the slight entirely when he slipped a finger inside of me.

I sighed, leaning into him, rolling my hips against his hand. This was definitely better. Last time, he'd gone straight for the gold.

"Lie down," he ordered.

Oooh, bossy. I like it. I smiled, biting my lip as I did as he asked. He grabbed my shorts and pulled them off, leaving my leg warmers on. My brain went crazy, hoping to God he was going to go downtown like I'd imagined.

Magical.

And then, he pulled a condom out of his pocket and dropped his pants.

Thirty seconds of foreplay. That's what I got.

So not magical.

I was so surprised and disappointed, I wasn't even sure what to do other than lay there like a limp noodle, staring at the ceiling as he tried to prime my poor, neglected vagina to the sound of bad techno. He straightened his arms, locked his elbows so he could watch our bodies meet with each thrust. I tried to get in the zone. Thought about the too-short kiss, but it pissed me off because that's all I'd gotten before he took me to Pound Town. Next thing I knew, he was about to come and glanced up to watch himself in the mirror.

After he slowed down, he finally looked down at me, smiling. I'm pretty sure my expression read something like, *You've got to be fucking kidding me.* But my lady bits wouldn't take that as the end.

I put a hand on his chest and shifted to roll us over, and thank God he complied because I didn't really want to fight about it. I'd been revving up my libido for days, and it was my turn. I settled in on top of him, hands on his chest as he laid there looking sort of … *apathetic* was the best word I could find in the moment. I guided his hand to my boob and tried to concentrate.

Blane Baker would get me off, goddammit, or I'd do it myself.

He gave it minimal effort, squeezing it gently, neglecting my nipples all together. I closed my eyes. *There, that's better.* I put every ounce of concentration that I had on that spot, working and working until I finally I felt it coming, and then I let that hard-earned orgasm go.

Things I learned: My middle finger is a much better lover than Blane Baker.

My heart slowed down, but I was already ready to leave. I was disgusted — he'd used me, and I'd used him right back. I needed to think. I needed to talk to Rose. And I most definitely needed to get out of Blane's studio.

Another shower wouldn't hurt, either.

I dismounted, wishing I had the cheer of a gymnast as the word implied, and grabbed my shorts, tugging them on before I walked over to my bag. The leg warmers came off in a flash, and my sweater and leggings were on before Blane had even finished getting rid of the condom.

I picked up my bag, and when I stood, he sidled up

behind me, nuzzling into my neck. "Thanks, Lily."

"Mmhmm," was all I could manage. I didn't know if I was mad or hurt or what. All of the above. Too many things to verbalize in that moment.

"I'll see you tomorrow." He kissed my forehead and turned away, dismissing me.

I stared at his back, not even sure why I was surprised. But instead of giving in to the impulse to throw my bag at him, I gripped it tight, charged out, and ran down the stairs and to the subway with my mind spinning like a pirouette.

West

I leaned on the bar, laughing at something Cooper had said, but my smile fell when I saw Lily walk into Habits. I felt like she'd just left, and I checked the time. She hadn't even been gone an hour. Her face was tight, lips flat, body coiled up and ready to spring. She wasn't just annoyed or angry — she was pick-up-a-bar-stool-and-chuck-it-through-a-window pissed.

Rose hauled ass around the bar to the door, and we watched with no idea what was going on. Lily's hands flew, cheeks red. Rose grabbed her by the shoulders and pulled her into a hug, and Lily closed her eyes, nodding at something Rose said in her ear. Rose let her go, giving instructions before Lily nodded once more, eyes on the ground as she turned and left the bar just as quickly as she'd entered it.

Rose ran a hand through her hair as she walked behind the bar again, and a barrage of questions came from all of us at once.

She held up a hand to stop us. "She's fine, okay?" We all shut up and waited. "Thank you. Her date didn't go well, and she's upset. I can't leave right now." She turned to me, eyes pleading. "Will you go talk to her?"

I was already getting up. "Of course."

She relaxed a hair. "Thank you."

I nodded and blew out of the bar, hoping for Blane's sake that he didn't hurt her. The street was dark and busy enough that I couldn't see her until I was almost on her, despite my anxious scanning. She'd been walking fast enough that she was almost to our building.

"Lil," I called.

She turned, looking a little confused, then annoyed as it dawned on her that I'd followed her from the bar. "Ugh, dammit, West. Did Rose send you after me?"

I searched her face. "She's worried about you, and so am I." I pulled her into my side, hanging an arm on her shoulder as we started walking again, trying for calm, even though the question burned in my chest. "Did he hurt you?"

"Not like that," she mumbled.

I let out a breath. "What happened?"

She huffed. "I don't want to talk about it."

I smiled over at her, but she kept her eyes on the sidewalk in front of her. "I know you better than that. Just tell me what happened."

She was quiet for a second. "It's embarrassing."

We reached our building, and I pulled open the door for her. "I'm not gonna judge you. You know that."

She was quiet again as we climbed the stairs.

"Lily?" I prompted.

"I know, I know. I'm getting there. Just … maybe a tiny drink would help."

"Fair enough." I pulled out my keys and unlocked her door for her, since she was too distracted to have gotten her keys out.

"God. Thanks, West." She stepped in and flipped on the light, tossing her bag by the door.

"No prob," I said as I closed the door. "What are you drinkin'?"

"Just a tiny bit of gin." She sat down at the table and picked at the placemat hem, looking crestfallen.

I opened the cabinet for a glass, then made my way to the fridge for a little ice and a lime to twist, just how she liked it. I snagged the bottle, taking it with me to the table where I sat next to her and poured a shot. She took it gratefully, knocking it back without flinching.

The second she swallowed, she blurted, "I slept with

Blane."

I'd already known that was where she was going, and that it wasn't the first time, but hearing it from her lips stopped my heart for a split second. Somehow, I kept my face straight. "And this is a bad thing?"

Her cheeks were so red, her blue eyes were electric. "Well, I hoped it wouldn't be, but it was. It was a *very* bad thing. Like, an epic fail of epic, horrible proportions."

I relaxed considerably, even though I felt like a traitor for it.

She wouldn't meet my eyes, just looked down at the ice in her glass. "It's just … I mean I don't know whether he's that inadequate in bed or if he's just not that into me."

I poured another shot, but drank it myself.

She chuckled and reached for the glass to pour herself another drink.

I watched her knock it back. "What exactly is going on between you two?"

Lily sighed. "He said he just wanted to have fun, which I assume also means no commitment. But whatever that was, it certainly wasn't fun."

I shifted in my seat. "You know that means he's probably seeing other people, right?"

She looked uncomfortable. "Yeah. I hadn't really entertained the thought before tonight. I knew he wasn't trying to get into another serious relationship, but in the back of my mind, I hoped he would be so into me that he would want more. Now I don't know if I even want more, not if he's not genuinely into me."

"If he's not into you, he's either blind or stupid. And if he's either of those things, you should dump him. If he's bad in bed, you should *definitely* dump him."

She snorted, rolling her eyes as she leaned back in her chair. "So basically I just need to dump him."

I shrugged, hoping I seemed nonchalant. "Sounds that way to me."

Lily sighed and rubbed her forehead, looking exhausted. "It's more complicated than that. I've wanted this forever, you know? I don't know what to do. I mean, if he's just that bad in bed, maybe I can … I don't know. Train him, or something."

I leaned on the table and met her eyes, looking for answers to give her. "Maybe. You really like him?"

She looked away, chewing on her lip for a second. "I don't know. I … I think so. I can see how it makes sense with our schedules and careers and all. We understand each other's lives that way, which is the hard part of ever dating anyone outside of the industry." She sighed again. "I just *want* it to work so bad, you know? And I feel like if I don't give him a chance, I'm giving up too easy. But, at the same time, I don't want to be with someone who doesn't want me."

"And you shouldn't be. Not when there are a million guys who would treat you right. If this joker isn't giving it his all, then he doesn't deserve you."

Her lips turned into the smallest smile as she spun her empty glass around. "Thanks, West. I guess that's what I need to figure out, which sucks because right now, I don't even want to see that assface, but I've got to get through a full day's rehearsal with him tomorrow."

"Are you gonna talk to him about it?"

Her face hardened. "Not tomorrow. I need time to cool off, or something. I'm too fucking mad."

I eyed her, realizing there was more to it than she was letting on. "Sounds like it's worse than him being a bad lay."

Her lips screwed a little tighter. "He just … he didn't pay a lot of *attention* to me. I don't know if I can be with someone who doesn't at least pretend that they want to have sex with me."

The thought blew my mind, and I blinked from the impact. "Well, that explains why you came home so fast."

She dropped her head into her hands. "God, it was so bad. I felt used, and so I used him right back. Doesn't that make me just as bad?"

I hated seeing her hurt and confused. "No, because you were holding out hope that there was more to it."

Lily shook her head, touching her fingers to her lips,

staring off at nothing. "I don't know why, honestly. I really don't know him at all."

I knew what to say, but I watched her for a moment, not wanting to encourage her, but needing to give her some hope. So, I let it loose. "Maybe you should try to get to know him." I regretted it as soon as I'd said it, until a ghost of a smile passed across her lips.

"Maybe. It'd be nice to go on a date, at least."

I scowled to say that should have already happened, and she gave me a look like she knew I'd say that.

"We really *are* busy. You know how our schedule is."

I put my hands up in surrender. "I know. Maybe just make a little time."

She made a disapproving face. "If I decide to ever speak to him after tonight."

"Yes, in that case."

She laughed. The sound made me smile, especially knowing I'd been the reason for it.

"Feeling better?" I asked.

Her shoulders relaxed with a sigh. "Loads. Want to watch a movie?"

I smirked. "*Ten Things I Hate About You?*"

"It always cheers me up."

"You're not tired?"

Lily folded her hands on her stomach. "I'll regret it tomorrow, but I'm not ready for bed yet. I don't think I could sleep."

"Well, I'd be glad to keep you company, so long as you keep your promise never to tell anyone how much I love this movie."

"What's not to love? It's got everything — laughs, love, dancing, sonnets, and Shakespeare. Of course you love it."

Lily stood and walked into the living room, and I couldn't help but admire the curves of her calves and thighs, up to her hips and what had to be the nicest ass I'd ever seen in person. The ass that Blane Fucking Baker had the privilege to have for his very own — a privilege he squandered. I tried not to think about finding him and punching him in the eye socket.

I followed her to the couch, taking the seat next to her. She was already curled up and working her DVR, and I pulled the blanket over us, propping my feet on the coffee table. I rested my arms on the back of the couch, and she leaned into me as she turned on closed captioning.

I shook my head. "Nu-uh. No distracting subtitles. I don't care if you've had a shitty night. I'm putting my foot down." I reached for the remote, but she held it out of my reach.

She stretched her arm as far as she could. "No way. I love them, and I need them so I don't miss anything. My house, my remote, my rules."

"Not this time, Twinkle Toes." My reach was longer

than hers, but she shifted away, giggling.

"Mine!" she said with a laugh, and I reached over her, laughing back.

"Gimme it, Lil." My fingers found her ribs and wiggled, and she squealed.

"Oh, my god, stop it!" She shrieked and squirmed underneath me.

"Not until you give it." I stretched a little further until I grabbed it from her hands, and we lay there laughing. It took me a second to realize I was lying on top of her with the blanket twisted around us and one of her legs around my waist. Our noses were inches apart. She blushed, and I could barely breathe.

"Told you it was mine tonight," I said with a smile as I backed off of her.

Her laugh this time was breathless. "You win this time, Williams. Soak it up."

She nestled into my side as I hung my arms on the back of the couch. "Oh, I will."

THE WAIT

Lily

IT MIGHT HAVE BEEN THE best dream ever.

I watched Blane cup my bare breast, eyes closed as he performed full on titty-worship. My hands were in his blond hair, and he hummed as his lips closed around my nipple like I was the most delicious thing he'd ever tasted, moaning a little louder when I wrapped my legs around his waist and squeezed to get our bodies as close as they could get.

I wanted him so bad, my body ached. He broke away and looked up at me. "You're so beautiful, Lily. I've always wanted you, ever since the first time I saw you. Nadia was just a distraction. I never thought I was good enough for you."

I sighed and touched his cheek. "Oh, Blane."

He smiled up at me. "I owe you something special. Something *extra* special." He moved down my body, and my heart went ballistic when he disappeared under the fluffy, white covers.

I reached up for my headboard and hung on as he hooked my legs on his shoulders, feeling his breath first, then his hot mouth as he closed it over me. My eyes rolled back in my head, breath frozen. His hands gripped my hips, pulling me down into him. It was everything. His tongue traced patterns, flicking and circling until I was panting, and he broke away just before I could come.

"Ah, ah, ah. Not yet, Lil."

My heart stopped at the sound of the rumbling Mississippi accent. And then the covers shifted, sliding out of the way to reveal West climbed up toward me, eyes on fire, dark hair loose and messy.

I didn't have time to respond, not before his lips were on mine, the scratch of his beard against my skin as he kissed me so deep. I wound my arms and legs around him as he guided himself to press against my opening, and I squeezed, forcing him in with a long, satisfied sigh.

"Tell me you want me, Lily," West said against my ear.

"I want you," I breathed.

He pulled out and slammed back in. "I've always wanted this. I've always wanted you." He slammed into me once more.

"God, West, please," I begged, and he gave himself to me again and again.

My body flexed just as my eyes flew open. I pressed my hips into my mattress, gasping as my heart clanged and pulsed with the release, still feeling the weight of his body on mine, his lips, the way he felt inside of me.

And then, I freaked the fuck out.

I rolled over and stared at the ceiling, trying to figure out what the hell that was. The feeling was still so strong, the *need* for him, that I couldn't even handle it. I kept trying to push it away, thinking about Blane and how great that was before it took a hard left into Whatthefuckville.

I thought about what I'd eaten the night before. Surely it had to be a case of bad shellfish. Maybe it was triggered by West tickling me, because I swear to God I almost kissed him right then. He smelled so good, and he was looking at me like … I don't know. It was crazy. All of it was crazy.

My brain was a traitorous slut for giving me a West wet dream over a Blane one.

I threw off my blanket and marched into the bathroom, cranking the shower to cold and stripping my clothes, hoping I could sanitize my dirty ass mind so I could get through what was already shaping up to be another horrible day.

West

After fighting to stay awake for the last hour, I tried to stifle my yawn the next afternoon as Blackwell finished his lecture. I'd stayed at Lily's until Rose came home, and even then, I didn't want to leave. She was unhappy and confused — I could see it all over her. But all I could do was hold her as she leaned into my side through the movie, and I wished I could somehow take her pain away through transference of my arms around her.

I'd been lost in my thoughts, and when I looked up, the last of the students streamed out of the classroom. Blackwell glanced at me as he packed up his things.

"You holding up okay, West?"

I smiled and packed my bag in a rush. "As well as can be expected, sir."

"You seemed a little absent today."

I grabbed my bag and hung it on my shoulder. "Sorry about that, sir. Late night."

"Ah," he said with a nod as I followed him to the back door of the auditorium. "I was concerned it was about your application. Debates in the committee are winding down. Won't be long now. I know the waiting isn't easy."

"No, sir. It's not."

He pushed the door open. "I've been doing this for long enough now to know how the committee works. I don't want to get your hopes up, but I want you to try not to worry too much. I think it would take something serious to stop you from being accepted."

I looked down with warm ears, humbled. "Thank you, sir. I appreciate it."

We stepped into the hallway and made our way toward his office. He smiled over his shoulder at me and paused, waiting for me to catch up. "My pleasure. I've enjoyed being a part of your success, ever since you were a freshman. I'd like to think that someday we'll be colleagues."

"I could only hope for such an honor."

"Your proposal for the program was fascinating. Women's power in Shakespeare? It's a topic that's been covered hundreds of times, but not usually with your take. It's typically the pseudo-feminist angle. Shakespeare: killer of the female spirit."

I chuckled. "More like Shakespeare: everybody dies."

He nodded, amused. "That's more accurate."

I stuffed my hands in my pockets and shrugged. "I just never saw Shakespeare that way. The women in his works held tremendous power, even though they were sometimes treated with very little respect by the other characters. They were always strong, always trying to muck through life just as well as any man. And how many men died for the love of one of those women?" I gave my head a shake. "Personally, I find it fascinating and moving. The thought that you could find someone who held the power to ruin you or rescue you. And that in the end, you could die — especially if The Bard had anything to say about it — so when you have your moment, you've got to take it and live it as fully as you can."

Blackwell smiled. "And that's exactly why the doctoral spot is yours to lose."

A thin, nasally, very British scoff came from the hallway in front of us. "Well, well, well. If it isn't Blackwell and his little pet."

I looked ahead to find Dr. Aldous Cox stopped a few feet in front of us, hands in the pockets of his too-large pleated pants. He was a small man with wireframe glasses perched on his hawkish nose, sparse hair combed over a generous bald spot. The look on his face could only be described as prickish. Simon Phillips was at his side, tall — at least by comparison to Cox — dark eyes twinkling and smile stretched in a leer.

Blackwell smirked as we came to a stop. "And how are you, Aldous? I hope you're finding your

Composition 101 lectures enriching."

They both scowled at us at the dig — Comp 101 was the bottom rung of the Lit department.

I felt like we were in an academic Spaghetti Western. All we needed was a tumbleweed made out of crumpled up Kafka pages to roll between us to the tune of a harmonica interlude.

But Cox's scowl slid back into a greasy smile. "Oh, shaping young minds is an enriching profession, don't you think? And how are the two of you? Preparing for Mr. Williams' denial letter, I presume?"

Blackwell chuckled. It was an easy, charming sound, and Cox's smile pinched until it looked like he'd smelled something dank. "I think we both know that's unlikely, Aldous."

Simon shifted, squaring his shoulders. "There's no way Williams will make the program, not if my father has anything to say about it."

"Your *father* won't *have* a say, will he?" Blackwell asked, calm and mildly amused, speaking to Simon like he was a child.

Simon folded his arms across his chest. "They listen to him. He *matters*, unlike Williams here." His voice was heavy with contempt. "He's got nobody on his side."

Blackwell's eyes narrowed at his lack of eloquence and the implication that I was somehow less than Simon Phillips. "West has *me* on his side. Or are you suggesting that my standing at Columbia isn't equal to *Phil Phillips*?'"

I pressed my lips together to keep from laughing.

Simon's nostrils flared like a racehorse.

Cox glared at Blackwell as he spoke to Simon. "Don't let James get to you, Simon. They always squeal the loudest just before they're tossed into the slaughterhouse." They started walking again, and we all stared each other down until they'd passed by.

I shook my head as we walked down the hallway. Blackwell turned to me.

"Cox has always been a real dick."

We both busted out laughing.

"Whatever happened between the two of you?"

Blackwell sighed. "Well, it's been a long rivalry, I'm afraid. We both went to Cambridge, in the same class, though he never did like me much. We always seemed to be neck-and-neck, ended up in the same master's program. I actually beat him out for the doctoral program there, and when I came to Columbia, he followed within a year. He's a brilliant man —in another universe, we'd be friends. But in this? He's just too bitter, unable to live without comparison, sadly. I'm just a masthead at which to aim his worldly rage."

"The face of evil."

We reached his office, and he opened the door. "I really couldn't tell you how it began. Aldous has never been what one might refer to as cuddly, even in his youth. I'm a natural extrovert, an orator — I've always been sort of fearless in that way — and for whatever reason, that challenged him." He walked behind his desk and set down his bag. "In any event, the battle is long and fierce, and I don't know that it will ever end. He uses anything he can for ammunition, too — reviews, student grades, grad students. I choose candidates based on merit. He chooses candidates based on who he thinks will beat me."

I set my things on my small desk against the wall. "And Phillips was his choice?"

Blackwell nodded as he unpacked his laptop. "Simon's smart and driven. But he's arrogant. I sometimes feel that Aldous and I are fighting our own battle through our students, over and over again to no end." His eyes were down, pensive as he opened his laptop. "My only comfort is that I try to help students whom I believe in."

"Well, sir, I hope I can live up to your legacy."

He gave me a comforting smile. "You already have."

West

A couple of hours later, I sat on my couch, staring at an essay without seeing a single word. I'd been home for a half an hour, and Maggie would be there any minute, but I was jittery, hating that I couldn't be there to pick her up. Her flight landed just as I was getting out of class — there was no way I could get there in time, and she said she wouldn't wait for me, not wanting me to go to any trouble. Stubborn girl. Must have been genetic.

I checked my phone again to make sure she hadn't called before opening my messages to text her, but I put it down again. She'd call if she needed me. Plus, she was with Cooper. He'd take care of her, or I'd take care of him.

Patrick walked into the living room to drop into an armchair and prop his feet on the coffee table, crossing his legs, clad in black skinny jeans. He was wearing a purple V-neck which should have made him look like the obnoxious brand of hipster or the Joker, but Patrick pulled off the look like he'd invented it.

"Hear from Maggie or Coop yet?"

"Not since her flight landed an hour ago. They should be here soon."

He smirked. "You ready to have your little sister down the hall again?"

I tossed the paper on the coffee table with a chuckle. "All the better to keep an eye on her."

Patrick folded his hands behind his head. "She's a grown woman. Pretty sure she can take care of herself."

I eyed him. "You stay away from my sister, Tricky."

"Hey, don't get me wrong. Your sister's hot—"

"Watch it."

"—but she's not exactly my type."

I relaxed a little. "No, I guess she's not. Not like that's ever stopped you before."

He made a face at me and scoffed. "Come on. You think I'd nail your sister?"

"I'd hope not. I don't want to have to mess up that pretty face of yours."

He chuckled and sank a little lower in the chair. "Speaking of pretty faces, what happened with Lily last night?"

I hung my arms on the back of the couch, shaking my head. "She confirmed most of what Astrid said. I don't trust that he's for real, but she's mad as fuck at him right now. Hopefully that's the end of that. She can just let it fizzle the rest of the way out, fade away into the night." I twiddled my fingertips.

"I can't say I'm not curious about the guy. I want to meet him — see what he's about."

"Well, no offense, but I hope we don't have the chance. I'm not interested in meeting the guy, not after the douchebaggery he's pulled on Lil."

"What happened?"

I shook my head. "No details, but you wouldn't approve."

He frowned. "You can't drop that on me and then not tell me what happened, man."

"Sure, I can. Look, I'm doing it right now."

My phone rang on the coffee table, and I snatched it up to answer. "Mags, you all right?"

"I'm *great*, are you kidding? I'm in New-York-Fucking-City!"

I chuckled. "Did Cooper make it there?"

Her voice was flat. "Sure did. Thanks for the warning, ass."

"Well, you wouldn't wait for me at the airport, so I had to take measures, Margaret."

"Ugh, Weston. You're worse than Dad."

I smiled. "Thank you."

"We're downstairs. Come help with my gigantic suitcases."

I was already pulling on my shoes. "On my way." I hung up and slipped my phone into my back pocket.

"Need a hand?" Patrick asked.

"Knowing Maggie, I probably need four."

Patrick laughed, and we hurried down the stairs to get my little sister.

We found her sitting on one massive suitcase, chin-length, curly blond hair a contained mess, freckles smattered across the apples of her cheeks as she grinned at me. Three more gigantic suitcases stood behind her next to Cooper, who smiled as he leaned up against the black Town Car he'd picked Maggie up in.

I hung my hands on my hips and shook my head at

the sight of her. She hopped up and bounded into my arms.

"Good to see you, kiddo. How was the flight?"

She stepped back and pushed her hair out of her face. "Long. I sat next to the cutest little old lady, but she drank like four of those tiny bottles of vodka, and then she just wouldn't stop talking, not until she passed on me out mid-crossword puzzle."

I laughed.

"Seriously, on *me*. My arm fell asleep."

Patrick gave her a side hug. "Hey, Maggie. Glad you're here."

"Thanks, Patrick. Me too." She took a deep breath through her nose with her hands on her hips like an explorer. "Smell that? Change is happening, boys!"

"Cooper behaved himself, right?"

She shot him a look. "Perfect gentleman."

Cooper shrugged, smiling crooked. "What?"

I eyed him. "Grab a suitcase, Casanova. Let's get all this upstairs." I picked up the bigger one and made a face. "Damn, Mags. Is mine full of books?"

"This is the twenty-first century, West. I have a tablet. That suitcase is full of shoes."

Patrick snorted as we walked into the building and up the stairs, none of us talking for the strain of my sister's suitcases. I couldn't even imagine how much they cost to fly.

We stopped in front of Lily's door, and I knocked. Rose answered after a second. It was two in the afternoon, but she looked like she'd just woken up. Her black hair was in a sloppy knot on top of her head, and mascara was smeared in little rings under her eyes. Somehow, she still looked amazing, even in a loose T-shirt and sleep shorts. Patrick noticed, too. I could tell by that expression he always wore when he was around her, like his heart was full of shrapnel.

"Hey, Maggie. Welcome back." Rose gave her a hug.

"Thanks, Rose!" Maggie bubbled. "I can't believe I'm actually here. I mean, this is *New York*. Like, for real. I *live* here!"

Rose smiled. "You sure are chipper this morning."

I shook my head at her. "It's two."

She pulled open the door to let us in and narrowed her eyes at me. "Like I said, *morning.*"

We rolled the suitcases full of bricks into the living room. "Where do you want these?" Cooper asked.

"In Lily's room is fine. We got you a bed and decked it out for you, Maggie, but we can take the bedding back if you don't like it."

Maggie beamed. "Oh, I'm sure I'll love it."

I followed Cooper and Patrick into Lily's room and asked over my shoulder, "You hungry, Mags?"

She touched her stomach. "Starving. Let me get

cleaned up and we can go eat, yeah?"

"We can go to Habits. Get Rosie some breakfast."

Rose made a face. "Ha, ha."

We lined up the suitcases along the wall, and I turned to see Maggie looking over her half of the room in wonder. Her bed was pushed against the far wall in the corner, decked out in fluffy, white bedding that was ruffly and girly while still looking somehow sophisticated. Lily's was almost exactly the same, but in a soft pink.

Rose leaned on the doorframe. "Your dresser is over there, and there's room under the bed and in the bathroom. Just make yourself at home, Maggie."

Maggie bounded over to Rose and hugged her around the neck, eyes shining. "Thank you, Rose. Thank you so much for this."

Rose's eyes widened from the surprise, but she smiled and hugged Maggie back. "We're just glad we can help out."

Seeing Maggie happy was a huge weight off my shoulders and heart. I couldn't help but smile. "Want to unpack first or eat?"

"Eat, for sure."

"Give me five minutes." Rose turned for the bathroom.

Maggie pointed in her direction at the bathroom door. "Is she for real? Five minutes?"

Patrick chuckled. "Oh, she's for real. Rose requires very little maintenance."

Maggie shook her head. "Well, that makes me feel like a narcissist."

I laughed and hooked her neck, pulling her a little too hard to ruffle her hair.

"Hey!" She batted me away. "I know it looks like a mess, but it actually takes a long time to tame."

We walked into the living room and stood near the door waiting for Rose. "So, you're officially here. What do you want to do first?" I asked.

"Hmm." She looked up at the ceiling. "Well, we didn't get to go to the Met last time I was here. And I want to see Lily perform, for sure."

I smiled. "*Swan Lake* starts in a couple of weeks. You should hold out for that."

Her eyes went wide with excitement. "I had no idea she was in *Swan Lake*. We have to see her."

"We already have tickets to opening night."

Cooper had been standing quietly behind me, unusual for him. He stuffed his hands in his pockets. "I've got a thing, so I'm going to head out."

"All right, man."

He glanced at Maggie. "Good to see you, Maggie."

Her face tightened. "You too, Cooper."

Cooper gave the slightest of smiles before ducking out of the apartment. I eyed Maggie. "What's the deal with you two? He didn't make a pass at you in the car, did he?"

She sighed and waved me off. "No, bossy. It's nothing. You know how Cooper can be. He just gets under my skin." Rose walked out from the bathroom ready to go. "All right, now feed me before I turn into a monster."

I snorted. "More like an angry bunny rabbit."

Lily

I was right. My day had been a disaster, and I still hadn't shaken my weird-ass dream.

It didn't help that Blane's stupid hands were all over me through rehearsal that afternoon as we went through the Black Swan pas de deux again and again. Black Swan had always been harder for me than White — the pop and snap of her movements as she tricks Seigfried, the desperate, cold-hearted nature of her character … it just wasn't me. Unsurprisingly, Nadia danced a stellar Black Swan.

Today, I was channeling my inner Nadia.

He rested on one knee at my feet, looking up at me with longing as he brought my hand to his lips. But I smiled wickedly down at him and snapped my hand back, pirouetting away from him so he couldn't touch me.

It was the only way I wanted to dance with Blane after last night.

West had stayed until Rose came home, and once he was gone, I told her everything, including all the stuff I couldn't bring myself to talk to West about. She had been surprisingly quiet, just listened without offering any advice past suggesting he wasn't worth it.

Part of me agreed. But today, as I was stone cold, Blane seemed confused — like he genuinely didn't get why. He kept asking me if I was all right, not that I would give him a clue. I was still too pissed to have that conversation with him. He definitely earned points for trying. But I only smiled curtly and carried on, trying to ignore him as much as possible, which was difficult, given the fact that our bodies were touching for hours on end. I'd rather have been curled up in a vat of sardines or a hamper full of dirty jock straps.

As soon as the music stopped at the end of rehearsal, I put distance between Blane and myself.

Ward assessed me, impressed. "Well done, Lily. That was the best Black Swan I've seen you dance. Whatever you used to get you there, bottle it up and keep it on hand. Fantastic job."

I curtsied. "Thanks, Ward."

He nodded, and I turned to walk across the studio to my bag with Blane on my heels.

"Hey, Lily. You sure you're all right?"

I didn't even sit to take off my shoe, just untied the ribbon and pulled it off as quickly as possible, stuffing it in my bag.

"Yup. Fine."

He leaned against the barre and crossed his arms. "You don't seem fine."

Because you know me so well. I pulled off the other shoe and shoved it in my bag that I zipped with a rip. "No, really. I'm perfect, Blane." I slipped my feet into my flats and grabbed my bag, whirling around. "Gotta run. Bye, Ward," I called across the studio and blew out without looking back.

The door closed behind me with a thump, and I glanced up to find Nadia leaning against the wall with her arms folded across her chest and a twisted smile on her face.

"Ugh, not today, Nadia." I stormed past, and she pushed off the wall and followed.

"What's the matter, precious? Bad day?"

"I'm not kidding. You don't want to fuck with me right now." I reached the elevator and hit the call button. She put her back to the wall to face me, looking satisfied with herself.

"I just want to make sure you're okay, Thomas." The words were saccharine.

I glared at her. "I'm sure you do. Everyone seems to be really interested in how I'm doing today, even

144

Blane." I couldn't help goading her — I was ready to fight after an already shitty day, with or without her in my face.

Her eyes narrowed, shoulders squared. "Stay away from him."

"Or else what?" I spat. "You don't own him, and he obviously doesn't want you anymore."

"That's not what he was saying last night."

Rage flashed through me. Had he gone over there after I left, or was she bluffing? I thought of the two of them together in the studio and wanted to scream. But I shook it all away. It didn't even matter — I wasn't even sure I wanted him anymore. "Nice try. Just keep telling yourself he's still in love with you, if it helps you get off at night."

The elevator doors opened, and I stepped inside. She spun around and gave me a look that would have withered me on any other day, but I stood my ground, giving it right back to her.

"Watch your back, Thomas." The doors closed, and as she disappeared behind them, I leaned against the rail and sighed, feeling a million years old.

"Already on it, bitch."

FLOWERS FIX EVERYTHING

Lily

A HALF-HOUR LATER, I threw open my apartment door and slammed it shut behind me. I'd showered at the studio to wash away my agitation, then blared my rage mix the whole way home, but it did little to help calm me down. I know it seems weird, but there's something really comforting about music that makes you want to smash things with a baseball bat. But nothing could help me today.

I dropped my bag next to the door with a thump, and Rose stuck her head out of her room.

She looked me over. "Uhh, you okay?"

"No, I am *not* okay." I tossed my keys in the dish, wishing I had something else I could make noise with besides my mouth. Like maybe a chainsaw. "That was a fucking disastrous day." I dropped into a chair at the table.

But Rose didn't ask questions, only made her way into the kitchen to get a glass, fill it with ice, and pour me a vodka tonic.

I slumped into the chair and accepted the drink gratefully. "I really shouldn't drink this."

"Just have one. Maybe two. You'll sleep like a baby tonight." Rose hopped on the counter and waited for me to explain.

I took a long drink and set the glass down. "My day was a complete shitshow from the second I woke up until I walked out of the theater."

"What happened when you woke up?"

I made a face. "I had a weird dream."

Rose raised an eyebrow. "About what?"

I tried to think of a way to ask without giving anything away. "Have you ever had a dream about one of the guys? I mean, besides Tricky."

She laughed. "Oh, my God. Who did you dream about?"

Epic fail. "Blane."

"Liar."

My cheeks were hot. "I'm not lying, Rose! He was in it."

She eyed me.

"And then he turned into West."

She shook her head and burst out laughing.

"Don't mock me! It was very upsetting, and it might

have ruined my whole day. I almost woke you up to tell you this morning."

"I wish you had."

"Now who's the liar?"

"You're right. I probably would have sleep-punched you."

I sighed. "Anyway, I was in rehearsals all day with Blane — an entire day with his dumb paws all over me, looking at me like I was a box of contraband donuts at fat camp."

Rose snickered.

"I just don't understand. I mean he looks at me like he wants me, but when we're together, I don't get the feeling he's all that interested. And last night was terrible, Rose. Terrible. I don't want to do that again, not like that."

She crossed her dangling ankles. "Well, you could either break it off or try to make it work. Maybe he's just bad in bed. Maybe he really does like you. Or maybe he's using you."

It was true — it could have been any of that. My relationship status was about as clear as a serial killer's cellar window. "I don't get what this game is. I don't know how to play it, Rose." I dropped my head to my hands. "What the fuck am I doing?"

"You're confused, and with good reason. You expected him to be everything you imagined."

"He so wasn't. Isn't." I shook my head. "I don't know if I can keep seeing him. I felt so *used* last night."

Her face was soft.

"I just wanted to believe that us hooking up was the first step to something more, but I'm starting to think that was one hundred percent unrealistic. He just gave me the hot beef and sent me on my way." I took another long drink, nearly draining the glass.

I glanced up when Maggie stuck her head out of our doorway with pink cheeks, looking sheepish. "Hey, Lily."

I gasped and hopped out of the chair, having totally forgotten with all the drama that Maggie was moving in today. "Oh, my god. Maggie! I'm so sorry." Shame washed over me as I gave her a hug. "You made it okay? Get settled in?"

She waved me off. "Oh, I'm fine. I was just unpackin' and heard you come in, but I didn't want to interrupt. And then I felt like a creep." She chuckled awkwardly.

"I'm glad you came out." I hooked an arm in hers and we walked back to the table to sit. "I feel like I should ask you more questions, but I can't think of a single one. I don't know if I'm emotionally equipped to see outside of my shitstorm today."

"Really, I'm fine. Just excited to be here more than anything." Maggie's smile was soft and sweet. "So, who's this Blane guy y'all are talking about?"

Rose slipped off the counter and poured three drinks this time — one for each of us.

I took my nearly empty one to the dome and grabbed the fresh one. "So Blane is the guy I've wanted ever since I was old enough to want one."

"But…" Maggie prompted.

"But, he's a raging jerkhole who apparently only wants me for my ladyhole." I took another drink, wishing I could wash away the knowledge. "Be glad you weren't here last night when I came home. *Not* okay."

Rose snorted. "When I came home from work, she was watching *10 Things I Hate About You,* cuddled into West's side like a sloth."

"What? It always makes me feel better. I'm not ashamed that teen comedies from the 90s do it for me."

Maggie laughed. "West loves that movie."

"Shh, that's supposed to be a secret," I snickered. "I was up way too late, and exhaustion is definitely not helping my mental state. One more of these pretty babies, and I'll be out like disco." I shook my glass. "So, Blane is also my partner a lot of the time, which was super awkward today. It's so strange that a couple of days ago, I thought having his hands on my body was the sexiest thing ever. Now they're like meathooks." I sighed, shaking my head. "Ugh, how am I going to get through rehearsals every day with him?"

Rose gave me a sympathetic look. "Well, you're going to have to find a way to let it go and move on."

I eyed her like she'd sprouted an extra arm.

She shrugged. "I didn't say it would be easy."

I groaned and buried my face in the crooks my arms on the table.

Someone knocked on the door, but I didn't move. I was giving up. Problems? What problems. No comprénde, amigo.

I heard Blane's voice when Rose answered the door, and my head shot off the table like I'd been hit with a cattle prod. Pretty sure my eyes looked like golf balls as I glanced at Maggie, who seemed confused. *Blane*, I mouthed at her, and her face stretched in surprise, her lips in a little 'o.'

I smoothed my hair and hopped out of the chair, turning to the mirror hanging on the wall. At least I hadn't cried. It could have been worse.

I took a deep breath and walked around Rose and into the doorway.

Blane stood in the hallway with a dejected look on his face, holding a bouquet of calla lilies, my least favorite of the entire lily family. But still. Dude brought me flowers, and his eyes were so sad. I kept my chin up, but I could almost hear myself agreeing to whatever it was he wanted. He'd been chasing me around all day trying to talk to me, but I never imagined he'd show up at my door looking like he'd dropped his ice cream cone in the dirt.

I was too confused to be pissed at that point, but I could pretend with the best of them.

"Thanks, Rose," I said with a nod, and she gave him the hairy eyeball once more before turning back into the apartment. I heard her bedroom door close, then mine. "What do you want, Blane?"

"Can I come in?"

Ugh. "Sure." I moved out of the way to let him pass and closed the door behind him. When I turned around, I folded my arms, hoping I looked like I'd take no shit. I was pretty sure I wouldn't. Like, thirty percent positive.

"I know you're upset with me, and I think I know why. You know, when you left last night, I couldn't stop thinking about you." He took a step closer. "I was off my game, you know? And I wanted to apologize today, but you wouldn't talk to me. So I came here to say I'm sorry." He extended the flowers.

I stood there for a moment, playing through scenarios. Me taking them and beating him with them in an explosion of petals and leaves. Me accepting them before I jumped his bones in the kitchen. Both outcomes were equally satisfying, so I went ahead and took the flowers with a sigh.

"Thank you, Blane. They're beautiful."

He moved even closer and laid his hands on my arms, looking down into my eyes. "You deserve better than that."

"Damn right, I do."

Blane smiled, and my knees felt like jelly. How did he do that? That asshole. "Give me a do over. Let me make it up to you."

And that was it. My resolve dissipated like smoke, and I relaxed under his touch, smiling up at him. "All right."

My eyes were on his sultry lips as his smile stretched wider.

"On one condition."

His lips froze before they reached the pinnacle. "Which is?"

"I'm not having sex with you again until I know you're for real."

The smile started up again, and maybe I was just being paranoid, but this time I didn't fully buy it. "Of course. Anything you want." He pulled me into a hug. "So we're okay?"

His chest was warm and solid under my cheek. "Yeah, we're okay."

"Thanks for giving me another shot, Lilypad."

I cringed.

He leaned back and tipped my chin with his fingers to place a soft kiss on my lips. "Listen, I've got to run, but I'm really glad we're all right."

I hated to bring it up, but Nadia was still in my head, buzzing around like a hornet, and I couldn't let him go without asking. "Before you leave, I wanted to ask you something."

"What's up?"

I took a breath, still wrapped in his arms. "Nadia she said she saw you last night."

He shook his head, and I tried to read his expression, but it was blank. "I crashed at the studio after you left. Don't listen to her. She's just trying to get a rise out of you."

I didn't believe him, but I didn't *not* believe him either. "What's new, right?"

He chuckled, and the sound traveled through his chest and against mine. "Don't let her get to you. It only encourages her." He kissed me on the forehead. "I'll text you later, okay?"

"Sounds good," I said as he pulled away.

I opened the door and watched him walk down the hall to the stairs, waving once over his shoulder before he was out of sight. I sighed and closed the door, looking down at the lilies.

Rose bounded out of her room, eyes big. "Flowers? Are those calla lilies?" She took the bouquet. "You hate these."

I sighed again and found my way back to my drink.

Maggie poked her head out. "Is he gone?"

"The coast is clear," I said as Rose sat next to me and set the flowers on the table.

Maggie took a seat and nudged the bouquet. "Lilies, huh? Original."

I snorted, drink hanging in my hand. "Regular lilies are fine. I mean, it's a little obvious, but I like them all right. But calla lilies? It's what you send when someone *dies.*" I gestured to them with my drink. "What the hell kind of gift is that to bring the girl you're trying to get back? Plus, they look like vaginas."

Rose almost choked on her drink, and when she'd swallowed the displaced mouthful, she rubbed her nose. "Oww, that burns," she said, giggling.

"What did he say?" Maggie asked.

"He apologized and asked me to give him another chance."

"And you said no?" Rose encouraged.

"If by 'no' you mean 'yes,' then totally."

"Ugh, Lily," Rose groaned.

"Don't make me feel guilty, Rose! You didn't see his face. I really think he wants to try to make this work, and I'd regret it if I didn't see it through, so don't get all judgy on me. This is deep seated — like ever since my hormones activated. I'm willing to overlook a lot. So he sucks in bed. Maybe he's awesome otherwise."

"Probably not."

"Mean! I won't know for sure until I try, right? Gotta ride the Noah bike, Rose. I have to."

Rose put up her hands. "All right, all right. Fine. I get it. Regret's no easy thing to carry around." Her eyes were on her drink. "Sometimes I think about Tricky that way, you know? What if things had been different? Because it felt right at the time, but what if I'd made different choices? What if he had? What if I'd told him what I really wanted and how I felt about him? But I didn't. He didn't. And we're where we are. Things are too complicated to go back now."

Maggie leaned on the table. "Whatever happened between you two?"

Rose sighed before taking a long drink. She set the glass down. "For a while, it was perfect, you know? We had this agreement, since we'd been friends first. The only way we'd risk our friendship was to try to take the expectation out of it. If either of us wanted out, all we had to do was say so, and we promised not to ask questions. One day, he said it was over, and I had to agree. I thought it would be temporary, though. I thought what we had was more than we could walk away from. But the next night, he brought another girl to Habits to hang out with the group — while I was working. I couldn't even leave. Just had to sit there and watch."

Maggie shook her head. "What a dick move."

I gave Rose a look. "You know it's not that simple, Rosie."

She shrugged. "He told me the next day that he'd just been scared, that he wanted to try again. But by that point, it was too late — I was too hurt to go back." She shifted in her seat and picked up her drink again. "Anyway, I wish I'd said something from the start. Told him how I felt, put up a fight when it could have changed things. But now I'll never have the chance. There's no repairing that part of our relationship, not when we're still trying to patch up our friendship."

"Plus," I added, "you have to endure his smolder daily."

Rose laughed. "Ugh. That."

"He's so intense." Maggie took a drink.

Rose let out a breath. "You have no idea."

Maggie settled back into her chair. "I think I'll always wonder if it was somehow my fault, what happened with Jimmy. I mean, I know he's just an asshole, and there probably isn't anything that could ever change that. But no one wants to learn a truth like that on their wedding day by walking in on their fiancé boning the maid of honor an hour before the ceremony."

I shook my head. "That had nothing to do with you."

Maggie just stared at her drink. "What's sad is that

so many people knew he was runnin' around on me, but nobody told me. At least I found out before we'd gotten married."

Rose brought her knee up to her chest. "Here's the thing about guys like that — you could have been his dream girl, but he was still going to fuck around. And you're right about finding out sooner than later. Better on your wedding day than after you'd been married for ten years and had kids. Can you imagine?"

Maggie laughed, the sound laced with sadness. "Nailing my best friend behind the bounce house at a birthday party."

Rose snorted and twisted her dark hair over her shoulder. "Or the PTO president backstage at the school play."

I giggled. "Or the Girl Scout troop leader on a pile of Thin Mints. See? That would have ruined America's favorite cookie."

Maggie sighed. "You know what I'll never forget is the look on his face. He was in a goddamn tuxedo, and Laura had her bridesmaid dress hitched up to her hips. One thing I never thought I'd see on my wedding day was her vagina."

I took a drink. "I seriously can't even imagine. And then to have the reception anyway?"

"Well, Daddy had already paid for it, and we all needed to get drunk at that point."

"I just can't believe you kept that dress on and found a way to enjoy yourself like a badass."

Maggie chuckled. "Oh, well, believe me, I cried my fair share. I'm lucky I had y'all there with me. If it hadn't been for you keeping me laughing, it would have been an even darker day than it already was."

"It *was* a good party," I added.

Maggie raised her glass. "Even when the boys left to go hunt Jimmy down."

Rose shook her head. "Luckily they were too drunk to make it very far. West was gonna disfigure the guy."

"Nah," Maggie said and took a sip. "That's what Tricky and Cooper were with him for."

"As if they could have stopped him once he really got going."

Maggie smiled. "It feels real good to be out of Jackson. I couldn't run into Laura at the grocery store again and not want to bust open a pack of razors to assault her with."

Rose sneered. "Ugh, you really went to the same grocery store?"

"Only once, and then I vowed to never shop at another FoodTown ever again. Anywhere. If I ever go to Canada, and they have one, I won't step foot in the door. I swear to God." We all laughed. "And Jimmy … well I couldn't handle him trying so damn hard to get me back. You know, you make up your mind to do something, and you're dead set on it. And then that asshole sends you flowers. He cries. He begs. Gets on his hands and knees and tells you he wants you to mother his children and he'd made a mistake. He'll never do it again, he swears. Most of you just wants to kick him in the teeth. But part of you believes him. I just couldn't sit in the middle of that fight anymore. I had to get away."

Rose leaned her chair back to snag the vodka bottle and pour herself another drink, leaving the bottle on the table. "And now that you're away, how do you feel?"

Maggie's smile was full and genuine. "Like I'm brand spankin' new. Like everything that happened before was a bad dream, and now I get to start over. One thing I do know is that I don't want to fall in love again, not for a long time. Not until all my wounds heal up. For now, I want to have fun and be young and not worry so much about settling down."

"Cheers to that." Rose raised her glass.

We raised our glasses and took a drink.

"So," Maggie continued, "I have five months before work starts for real. I need to get certified to teach in New York so I can start subbing here and there and find a permanent job. I've got the refund on most of my honeymoon to get me by — Daddy also paid for that, by the way — and I have the savings I'd put together. My plan is to use this time to decompress before I get back to being an adult."

I nodded my approval. "That plan sounds like exactly what you need. You're so well adjusted for everything that's happened. I just don't know how you do it."

Maggie shrugged. "I might be in a little bit of denial."

We all laughed.

"Whatever, though, because that gets me through my days. It's only been a month, so I have a bad feeling I'm headed for a massive breakdown. I still haven't had a real one. It's weird because I can feel it just under the surface, like it's waiting to get out. But mostly I feel all right, so I'm just going with it."

"Well," I added, "Rosie and I are experts at getting drunk and losing our shit, so if you ever want to partake, just let us know."

She chuckled. "Deal. And I apologize in advance because when the top blows off my emotions, it's probably going to be ugly."

I raised my glass and clinked it to hers. "Don't worry, sister. We've got you."

THIS BITCH

West

THE FOUNTAINHEAD LAY HEAVY IN my lap that evening, the massive hardback as weighty as the words inside. The apartment was silent. Patrick was at work, and I'd been trying to keep my mind occupied since the excitement of Maggie's arrival, but I still couldn't concentrate on grading papers. So I'd picked up my favorite book, which I had a standing date with, reading it over and over again whenever the mood struck me, carrying on like I'd never stopped.

"Howard — anything you ask. Anything. I'd sell my soul…"

"That's the sort of thing I want you to understand. To sell your soul is the easiest thing in the world. That's what everybody does every hour of this life. If I asked you to keep your soul — would you understand why that's much harder?"

I looked away to my window where the city shifted

into night, the line from the book rolling through my mind as I sat in solemn silence.

A knock sounded at the door, and I glanced over to see Maggie walking in. She was a sight for sore eyes — even just having her close by for a few hours had brought me a lot of comfort, to have a bit of home in New York for good. And knowing we'd all be able to help her move on was the bonus.

"How's it going?" I smiled at her and laid my worn bookmark in the crease of the hardback before setting it on the coffee table with a thump.

"Good, finally unpacked." She flopped into an armchair. "Ugh, not Ayn Rand again." She nudged the heavy book with her toe, but it didn't move.

"Hater."

She dropped her chin, lips flat. "It's pretentious bullshit written by an uncaring, stone-cold egomaniac."

I shrugged. "Maybe at first glance, but that's not how I see it. It's about the power of self. It's about surviving against all odds, strictly on willpower and belief in your own vision. It's about succeeding — not because someone gave you their approval, but because *you* did what you set out to do. You created your success using only the power that exists between your ears, even though the odds were stacked against you."

Maggie made a face, ignoring everything I'd said. "Roark *rapes* Dominique."

"That was your big takeaway?" I shook my head. "It's consensual, Mags. It's not rape, it's surrender."

She folded her arms across her chest. "Pass."

"That's the beauty of books, little sister. What means nothing to one has a profound effect on another." I recrossed my ankles. "So I want to know where the hell you put all those shoes."

"Under my bed, along with most of my clothes in those rolling bins. Lily and Rose got me a cute thrift dresser, too."

"Yeah, I know. Guess who hauled it upstairs?"

She chuckled and perked up, face animated as she leaned forward. "Oh, man, so Lily's boyfriend, or whatever, came by." She made a duck face, shaking her head. "Man, he's *hot.*"

I felt myself frown. "Ah, so you met the infamous Blaney?"

She snorted. "That's what y'all call him? That's terrible. Anyway, I wouldn't call it an official meeting — I just caught a glimpse of him before I ran to our room to give them some privacy. He brought her flowers and apologized for bein' a weirdo."

My frown deepened. "Flowers, huh?"

"Yeah, calla lilies."

"She hates those." The thought made me feel better. Smug, even.

"I know. So obvious, right? I don't know if he's the

brightest Crayon in the box. And apparently, he's not the most, ah … considerate lover."

My brow dropped. "Yeah, I heard."

Maggie watched me for a second, eyes narrowed. "Does that upset you?"

"Why would it?"

"I don't know, West. Why would it?"

I scowled. "I just have a bad feeling about this guy."

"And what kind of man would you feel good about?"

"The kind who would respect her. Who would treat her like they know what they've got. The kind who'd do anything to keep her."

Maggie looked amused. "If she found someone who would love and respect her to your very high standards, would you feel better or worse?"

I made a face. "What's that supposed to mean?"

Maggie smiled at me like she knew something I didn't and leaned back in the armchair, putting her hands up in surrender. "Nothin'."

Irritation wriggled its way through me. "Listen. The guy's never even taken her on a date. So what if he brought her flowers — flowers that she *hates*, let's remember that. I don't trust a man who keeps a girl like Lily a secret."

"All right, all right. I get it."

But I just kept on going, unable to shut up and let it

go. "And she never dates, Mags. Never. If she's going to put her heart on the line, that asshole better take care of it. I trust her to make her own decisions, but I'm just worried she's too blinded by the crush to see him for what he really is."

She put her hands up. "Okay! I didn't know it was such a sore topic, jeez."

Me neither. My mood had turned foul, stinking with agitation that I wasn't quite able to sort out. My phone buzzed on the couch next to me, and I picked it up to a text from Christine.

Just checking in, still interested in going to Amanda's party?

Maybe in part out of spite, I answered, *I'm in. What time?*

Let's have a drink beforehand. Where do you want to meet?

I know just the place. I sent her the address to Habits and smiled.

Lily

The sweat on the glass of my third vodka tonic rolled onto my hand as I sat alone in my quiet apartment. Maggie had gone over to West's just after Rose left for work, leaving me alone to contemplate my relationship status, or lack of one.

The stupid death-lilies mocked me from the table, perched in the ugliest vase we owned as a joke. I should have been more grateful. It really *was* sweet of him — I couldn't even remember the last time a guy had thought to buy me flowers. But the whole thing had confused me just when I thought I was figuring out what I wanted. Namely, not him. Then he showed up being all sweet, and now I wasn't so sure anymore.

I was left wishing for him again, or wishing for a version of him that I wasn't sure existed. But that old image I had of him was so strong in my mind, so powerful, that I found myself a sort of slave to it. I wanted him to be that man so badly, I felt like I could nearly will it into existence.

I sighed, considering another drink, but I had to stop. Three drinks was well past my limit.

The door opened behind me, and I glanced over my shoulder to find Maggie striding in. "Have you moved from that spot?"

I looked back to my feet. "Nope."

"Well, come on, lazy bones. Let's go to Habits."

I made a stinky face at my socks. "I don't know. I have to get up early. Plus, I've already hit my drink maximum."

"Then you can go just to sober up. We won't stay long. West is meeting some girl there, so when they leave, I'll be alone."

This time, my stinky face was directed at Maggie. "A girl? What girl?"

She shrugged and grabbed her sweater off the back of the chair. "Christine, I think? Another TA." She disappeared into it, and her head popped out of the neck hair-first, curls bouncing.

"Never heard of her."

Maggie shrugged, but she was watching me like she knew something. "Weird. Let's go sniff her out."

I was already getting up. "Deal."

I made my way into my room and pulled on light gray jeans, my favorite dusty rose V-neck, and dark gray ankle boots, inspecting myself on my way out. My hair was a bit of a mess after air drying — not hot enough. I marched into the bathroom and grabbed the hairspray and a comb, teasing the length of it and braiding it into a messy fishtail that I left hanging over my shoulder.

Better. I smiled at my reflection.

Our jewelry hung on a series of hooks and wires on the bathroom wall, and I chose a few thin gold necklaces and one long gold locket that was my grandmother's. Then lipgloss happened. Then mascara and a couple of bracelets. And with that, I was all of a sudden fully dressed for going out.

I blamed vodka.

My boots clicked on the hardwood as I made my way out of the bathroom, still working the clasp of a last minute bracelet swap.

Maggie assessed me as I approached. "I didn't know

we were like *really* getting dressed."

I shrugged. "It was an accident." I grabbed my purse.

"Well, you accidentally look awesome." Maggie smirked, and her phone dinged. She glanced at her screen. "West is downstairs."

"Let's not keep the man waiting." I followed her out and closed the door behind us before locking it, though it took me a little longer than it probably should have. What? That hallway is dark. Also, I'm a lightweight.

I tried to sound nonchalant, but I was dying to know about this girl. Plus, vodka. Pretty sure my voice was a half-octave too high to be considered casual when I asked, "So, you don't know anything about Christine?"

We made our way down the stairs, and Maggie glanced at me. "Just that he's going to some party with her tonight."

"Do you know what department she's in at Columbia?"

Maggie smiled. "Nope. I know as much as you do."

My brow furrowed. "He's never mentioned her before."

"Not to me, either. Guess we'll see, huh?"

"Guess so." Our footfalls echoed in the stairwell for a moment as we walked in silence. "I wonder why he hasn't talked about her before. Couldn't be that serious, could it?"

"You're awfully curious about her."

I laughed, trying to sound light. "I mean, it's just weird. I thought West and I talked about everything."

"You didn't tell him much about Blane until the other night, right?"

"That's different," I scoffed.

"How so?"

"Because I don't know what Blane and I even are."

"Maybe Christine and West are the same."

I made a noncommittal noise and pushed open the door to the building.

West stood near the curb in a gingham button-down cuffed just above his elbows. Tattoos climbed down to the middle of his forearm, hands in his pockets. His dark hair was down tonight, thick and curling just at his collar with ruts in the top where he'd run his fingers through it. When he saw me, his blue eyes sparked, or maybe I just imagined they did.

I took a breath, feeling overwhelmed by the sight of him. Maybe I shouldn't have agreed to come after Rose's vodka tonics. I wondered just how much heavier her pour was than I'd noticed.

I smiled at him, trying to cover the fact that I was staring at him and that I was still butthurt about his keeping Christine from me. But I thought about how I wanted West to like Blane, or at least try. And so, I decided. I was going to like her, no matter what. I was boarding the supportive train.

"Howdy, friend," I chimed as we approached.

"Howdy, ladies." His voice was deep and rumbling. "I didn't expect to see you tonight, Lil."

"It's Rosie's fault," I said as we walked toward Habits. "She fed me drinks until I lost my ability to be responsible with my time. Plus, Maggie said she'd have me home before I turn into a pumpkin."

He glanced at me, smiling. "Drinking *and* staying out late? Who are you?"

I chuckled. "Apparently a whole new me, one who will probably hate myself at five when my alarm goes off." The conversation lulled for a second, and I fought the urge to mention Christine. At least I hadn't lost *all* of my inhibition. I had to play it off like I didn't care, even though curiosity was eating at me, scratching at my throat to get out.

"Do you work every day, Lily?" Maggie asked.

"Almost. My one day off a week is Monday, but I'll have the summer off, sort of."

"Wow. How many hours per day?"

"Well, I usually get to the theater early to go to the physio room, stretch, that sort of thing. Barre class starts at ten-thirty — that's our warmup until eleven-forty-five. Then we have rehearsals from twelve to six, and performances anywhere from two to five nights a week, starting around seven-thirty."

Maggie shook her head, gaping. "That's crazy. How do you stand working that much?"

"Easy," I said with a shrug. "It doesn't feel like work. The season is from September to the beginning of June, and then through the summer we have classes and tours and stuff, but it's much less rigorous."

"You're hardcore."

I snorted. "More like obsessed."

We approached the door to Habits, and West opened the door for us. I followed Maggie in, and when I passed West, he laid a hand on the small of my back. It was such a strange thing to notice, something he'd done a hundred times, but I'd never paid attention before.

Stupid vodka. Worst idea ever.

Rose waved from behind the bar, pointing to three seats near the end. We walked through the light crowd, and West took the farthest of the three seats. Maggie snagged the first, leaving the stool between them my only option.

Rose tossed her towel over her shoulder and leaned on the bar, smiling as I took my seat. The necklaces she had on lay nearly in her cleavage in the scoop-neck black tank she wore, and her black hair framed her face and shoulders. She even had red lipstick on tonight. The girl made a killing as a bartender.

"What are you doing here, Lil? I figured you'd be

passed out by now."

I shrugged and tucked my purse in my lap, only slightly annoyed. "I'm allowed one night of staying out until ten, aren't I?"

She poured me a water and shook her head, smiling. "Anything you want. What are you two drinking?"

"Makers and ginger," West answered.

"Same for me," Maggie added.

"Maybe I wanted a drink too, Rose."

She raised an eyebrow. "Oh? What can I get for you, princess?"

I smiled. "Water's good. Thanks for asking."

"Typical." Rose rolled her eyes, laughing as she set two rocks glasses on the counter and filled them with ice. "So what are you guys up to tonight?"

Thankfully Maggie answered because I wasn't even sure why I was there. "Just came down to say 'hi' and keep West company while he waits for a friend."

Rose poured whiskey over the ice. "Cooper or Patrick?"

"Christine," West said, and Rose's eyes shot over to him.

She made a face at him. "Who's Christine?"

God bless Rose. I waited for his answer, sipping my water.

West shifted on his stool, looking a little uncomfortable. "A sociology TA I know. We're going to a party that another grad student is throwing."

Rose's eyebrow climbed as she handed him and Maggie their glasses. "A Columbia intellectual boozer? I've always wondered what happens at those. Do you get wasted on cabernet and talk about Neitzsche?"

He brought his drink to his lips. "Don't be gauche. We drink pinot noir and compare margin notes on *Lolita*."

Rose snorted.

"Hey, guys." Cooper said from behind us. I turned to greet him as we all chimed our hellos. He looked fantastic, as always — like a rich motherfucker who didn't even care that he was rich. You wouldn't know by looking at the tall, dark, and stubbled playboy that he was loaded. It was in the little details. His Cartier watch. The Pierre Maheo coat and Massimo Dutti shirt that no one would know were designer, and pants that fit him like they were made for him, which they might have been. He was somehow elegant and casual all at the same time.

The dude was a walking vagina magnet.

Rose poured him a neat scotch, passing it to him between West and me.

"Thanks, Rosie." He raised his glass at her before taking a sip. "What are you doing out, Lily?"

I huffed. "God, is it really that surprising to see me out on a weeknight?"

They all looked at me.

I put a hand up. "You know what? Don't answer that."

Cooper smiled. "Don't get me wrong. I approve." He nodded to me and West. "Did you guys decide if you're coming to Noir on Saturday?"

Maggie's face lit up. "What's Noir?"

"A club you're not going to," West popped without missing a beat.

"You're not the boss of me."

Cooper shrugged. "It's true, you know. You're not the boss of her. She can come if she wants to."

Maggie bowed her head at him. "Thank you, Cooper. I'd love to. It'll be my first real New York nightclub. I am absolutely in."

West rested his elbows on the bar and sighed. "Guess I'm going too, then."

Maggie rolled her eyes. "I don't need you to babysit me."

He scoffed. "If you think I'm letting you go to that club with only Cooper to make sure you're all right, you're crazy."

I blurted, "I'm in too, and so is Blane." All of them turned to look at me. "What?"

West stiffened next to me, and Rose gave him a pointed look. "Nothing. We're all looking forward to meeting him. Aren't we, guys?"

At least Rose had my back. "Thank you, Rose."

She gave me a supportive smile, though her eyes darted to West once more before she made her way down the bar toward a drunk guy who was waving at her like he was drowning.

"Are we still on for the opera tomorrow night?" West asked, sort of snippy.

I gaped at him. "Why would we not be? We've been planning it for months."

He shrugged and looked into his drink, leaning on the bar. "I don't know. You sure Blane's going to be okay with it?"

My eyes narrowed. "I don't know, are you sure Christine will be?"

His brow dropped. "She's just a friend, Lil."

"Funny, I've never heard of her before tonight."

He opened his mouth to speak, but his eyes shifted to look behind me. I turned to see a tall, slender woman with long pitch-black hair walking through the bar, waving, eyes locked behind me. On West. I glanced back at him to find him smiling at her as he stood.

"Hey, Chris."

She approached and reached up to kiss him on the cheek. "Hey." She hooked an arm in his and turned to the rest of us.

I couldn't help but check her out — long, skinny legs in dark jeans, bangles on her arm, simple gold necklaces around her neck disappearing into the opening of her deep red button-down that was unbuttoned a little too far, if you asked me. From what I could see of her boobs — which was enough, by the way — they were amazing.

Every intention of liking her for West's sake jumped straight off the top of the Chrysler building.

Cooper's eyes roamed up and down her body, the action thinly veiled by his diversion of sipping scotch. Maggie's gaze bounced between me, her brother, and Christine. My face felt like a mask, and I realized my eyes were locked on the spot where her fingers grazed the skin of his forearm.

I looked up and put on my best smile. It must have been a homer because she didn't seem to notice that I pretty much instantly hated her.

I turned to Rose with that fake-ass smile on my face. "Can I get a vodka tonic, please?"

She gave me a look that told me to be nice, but she poured me a drink, which saved her from getting slapped.

West fumbled for a moment before speaking. "Ah, I'd like y'all to meet Christine. Chris, these are my friends, Cooper, Rose, and Lily, and this is my sister Maggie."

She waved. "Nice to meet you."

Cooper stuck out a hand. "You too."

Christine took it, blushing ever so slightly. "Cooper Moore?"

He flashed that pantybomb smile at her. "That's right. What are you drinking?"

"Rum and Coke, please."

I turned my back to Chris and West to give Rose the real *What the fuck* eyes, glad to see that she had her fake-ass smile on too.

"Sure thing," she said in her waitress voice.

"So," Maggie said with an edge to her voice, "West says you go to Columbia too?"

I turned back around and instantly regretted it when I saw her smile. It really wasn't fair for someone to be that pretty.

"I do. We're in the graduate program together. Hopefully we'll be in the doctoral program together, too." She was grinning, and her grip on West's arm tightened.

I took a long sip of my drink. I couldn't be sure, but it seemed like West wanted to pull away from her. The hold she had on his arm would have made dislodging her difficult without being rude, and West wouldn't be blatantly rude. It was against his genetic Southern code.

He was uncomfortable, which was oddly satisfying.

Cooper took the rum from Rose and handed it to Christine.

"Thanks, Cooper." She took a drink.

We stood in awkward silence for a beat. Christine looked around the bar. West's eyes were on the door. The rest of us watched each other, thinking a million things we couldn't say out loud.

"So, sociology, huh?" I said lamely.

She gave me a patronizing smile. "Yeah. Don't worry, no one really knows what exactly that means."

A laugh burst out of me. "What a pompous thing to say."

West coughed, and Cooper choked on his drink.

I kept the ball rolling, pretty sure I could recover it. "I actually love sociology. I find people fascinating — humanity and the patterns in human behavior. I read *What about Mozart?* by Howard S. Becker last year."

"Well," she stammered, "I, ah — his work on deviance has always been groundbreaking."

West pounded his drink, eyeing me.

"I think so too, Christine."

She smiled and turned to West. "You know, I don't want to be late. Maybe we should get going."

West's eyes were dark. "Good idea." He set the empty glass on the bar with a super-hot Christine still on his arm. "See you guys. Be good, Mags. Take it easy, Lil, okay?"

"Yup." I gave him a look that said I'd do whatever I'd want and took a drink. "You kids have fun now!" I raised my glass.

"Thanks, Lily. Nice to meet you. Hope to see you guys again soon." She smiled up at West like she'd won the goddamn lottery as they walked away.

"Oh, us too," I called after them, and Rose pinched the back of my arm as she waved the hand that wasn't assaulting me. "Ow, Rosie! What the hell?"

"That was so fucking rude," she hissed.

I crossed my legs. "I don't know what you're talking about."

"You called her pompous, you ass."

I shrugged. "Well, she was being really fucking pompous."

"She seems perfectly nice."

"I'm sure." I took another long drink, and Rose shook her head at me.

"What in the world is the matter with you?"

I huffed. "Nothing. She just wasn't what I was expecting, and I'm stressed and tired and dealing with Blane and I just wanted a goddamn drink. Why are you making such a big deal about it?"

Rose sighed and put her hands up. "Fine. We're talking about this tomorrow when you're not drunk. Maggie, please take her home after this drink."

I fumed. "Why does everybody feel like they can tell me what to do? I'm not a child."

"You're acting like one."

I set my drink down with a clink. "God, this is such

bullshit. I'm always the responsible one. I'm always the good one. I can't even have a couple of drinks without everyone acting like I'm shooting heroin. And anyway, *you* are the one who got me going tonight, Rose."

Even Cooper was eyeballing me. I glared at him. "You're the last person I thought would judge me, Cooper Moore." I reached into my purse and grabbed some cash, tossing it on the bar in front of me. "You guys all suck."

Maggie looked hurt.

"Not you, Maggie. Just these assholes." I jerked my head at Rose and stood up a little too fast.

Cooper caught me by the arm when I leaned. "Whoa, Lil."

I shook him off. "I'm fine. I just didn't eat dinner, and Rosie pumped me full of grain alcohol."

Maggie stood and grabbed her bag. "Come on. Isn't there a pizza joint on the way home?"

I was still mad as hell, but the thought of pizza perked me up. "Oh, I could go for that."

"Me too," she said conspiratorially. "Pizza makes everything better." She hooked her arm in mine, and I felt instantly better. "See you, guys," she called over her shoulder, and we headed out the door.

I was still bent, even at the prospect of a giant, cheesy slice of heaven, even with Maggie's arm in mine as we headed toward the street pizza counter. At least she wasn't judging me.

West crossed my mind again — seeing him with Christine made me feel backward. "How long do you think West's been seeing Christine?"

She chuckled. "Wow, straight to it, huh?"

My cheeks were warm. "It's just so weird. I haven't seen him with a girl since he and Shannon broke up, and that was almost two years ago."

"Well, I wouldn't take it too seriously. I didn't get the vibe that he was all about her."

I huffed, flustered. "That's not what I mean. West can date whoever he wants."

She smiled at me. "Sure."

Irritation flared. "Dammit, Maggie. What the hell does that mean?"

"Nothin', really. Just you and West are awfully wrinkled up about who the other one's seeing."

"Well, if he had told me about her, I wouldn't be annoyed."

She didn't say anything as we took a few more steps.

"I mean it. I wasn't prepared for that at all, so to go from thinking he's single to seeing smarty-pants hottie Christine on his arm blew up my brain for a second." I thought about the two of them standing in the bar again and shook my head. "I guess it's no wonder. They go to school together, they're at the same place in their lives. I can see the appeal. Plus, did you see her?"

"I saw her. Did you see when she was all googly over Cooper? She looked like she was ready to take her shirt off right then."

I giggled. "Well, at least their date would have been over if she showed everyone her boobs in Habits."

She laughed. "Ugh."

"So West is mad about Blane? I knew he was anti, but I didn't think he was *really* anti. Just like overprotective-friend-wary."

"Oh, not mad, I guess. He just doesn't like the idea of you with someone who doesn't treat you well, or his version of well, I suppose."

"Huh." I contemplated that as we approached the window that faced the sidewalk.

Maggie stepped up first. "Can I get a slice of supreme and…" she turned to me.

"Make it two, please." I reached into my bag for cash and passed it through.

The pizza boy nodded and winked at us before flopping our humongous slices on the crappiest paper plates ever and pushing them through the window.

"Thank you," we chimed and headed toward the building.

I folded my slice in half, salivating, and shoved the end in my mouth. "God, I love New York."

Maggie laughed with her mouth full.

"You were right, you know."

"About what?"

I adjusted my grip. "Pizza makes everything better." I took another massive bite.

"I'm glad you're feeling a little better."

What I felt was life-worn. "It's been a bad day. A really stupid, long, bad day." I started to take a bite, but lowered my hand. "I misbehaved tonight, didn't I?"

"Maybe a little."

I sighed. "I embarrassed West."

"Maybe a lot."

Guilt slipped over me. "Do you think he's very upset with me?"

"I don't know. He actually looked more worried about you than angry with you."

"I'll talk to him tomorrow, try to make it right. I shouldn't have mouthed off. The whole thing just threw me. Plus, vodka."

"Yeah, I'm gonna make a blanket statement and say that vodka does *not* make everything better."

I laughed, and every bite of cheesy goodness made my world a little more bearable.

WHERE'S THE WHISKEY

West

CHRIS CHATTERED ON AS WE walked to the subway, still hanging on my arm, but I was barely listening — my mind was on Lily. I'd never seen Lily belligerent before. I'd seen her weepy and sentimental when she was drunk, but mostly she was just adorable and hilarious. This whole thing with Blane had her sideways.

I added it to my list of reasons why I didn't like him.

We descended the stairs and were walking through the turnstile when I finally calmed down enough to think about Chris' performance. For her to be so public with me, grab me like she owned me? And in front of my friends? The whole thing made me uncomfortable, but I was the only one to blame. I never should have had her meet me at Habits.

In any case, it seemed that she definitely believed we

were on a date, despite our conversation specifically about going as friends. She knew I didn't want more, but here we were, boarding the train with her gripping my arm like I'd run away if she let go.

We took our seats, and Chris laid a hand on my thigh. A couple of teenage girls a few seats down giggled and whispered, looking in our direction. Chris was sitting close enough to me that I had to put an arm on the back of her seat to buy myself a little space. Except that seemed to be what she wanted because she immediately leaned into me. I leaned away, hoping she'd get the signal.

No such luck.

So we sat on the train with Christine still talking, requiring very little from me in the way of conversation. Had she always talked this much? How had I not noticed before?

I grappled with what to do about her. I didn't feel comfortable pretending, but I didn't want to upset her, either. My instinct was to get through the night and end it on the way home. If I said something now, she'd have gotten all dressed up for nothing, gone to all the trouble just to get dumped.

But I thought about the other side of it for another beat. Why end it? Maybe I could give it a try with her. On paper, she was everything I was looking for. We were in the same place in our lives, in our careers, shared the same group of acquaintances. It would be convenient. But as she pressed herself against me in the subway car, I knew. I didn't want to be with Chris — not like that.

All I could do was endure the night and try to let her down gently at the end of it.

I felt a little better having made a decision, finding it easier to participate in the conversation through the rest of the train ride and toward Amanda's apartment. We walked up the stairs to her building and through the open door to the sound of indie folk rock and the lingering smell of weed. There were hipsters as far as the eye could see, standing in groups with wine glasses and beer bottles.

Rose's fortune telling skills were bang on.

Chris tugged me through the crowd, stopping here and there, talking to everyone like she wanted to be sure they all saw us together. Someone brought us drinks, wine for Chris — noir, as suspected — and a beer for me, an IPA. I didn't even like IPA. Give me a stout or even a honey blonde. But if the choice was between the two, I'd take beer over wine any day. Some of the guys nearby were discussing little-known craft beers like some people talk about underground bands, and as I took a sip of the bitter ale, I wished very much that I hadn't agreed to come.

Christine wound her fingers through mine and

pulled me to the door, up the stairs and to the roof, and I was quick to grab the roof door for her, using any excuse to let go of her hand. She wasn't making it easy to play along, not with the parade and fanfare. The minute we were outside, she slipped an arm around my waist and dragged me toward her friends.

"Amanda!" Chris waved across the roof to Amanda, who waved back, dark eyes bouncing back and forth between us. I tried to give her a smile, but could feel the halfassery of it, and when we made full eye contact, I knew she knew it.

We — meaning *she* — talked to Amanda, and I sipped my tragic disaster of hops and barley. One thing was clear: the whole night was a charade.

I drained my beer. "Need another drink?" I asked Chris, needing to get away.

She beamed up at me. "I will by the time you're back."

I nodded and pulled away from her, feeling like I'd shed shackles. "All right."

"Hurry back," she cooed.

Christine didn't seem to notice my weak smile the way Amanda did — she grimaced at Chris' enthusiasm behind her back.

I let out a heavy breath as I headed down the stairs and into the apartment, working through an exit strategy as I headed into the kitchen.

Wine bottles were lined up on the counter, all reds, and I picked the noir with the most interesting label — it was called *Complicated*, which seemed appropriate — to pour her a glass. My next priority was to find something, anything else to drink. I would have even settled for rum. But there was nothing. I reached into the fridge and grabbed another IPA with a sigh, wondering just how the night could get worse.

"Well, well, well. If it isn't Weston Williams."

And there it is.

I turned to find Simon Phillips standing behind me, looking smug. He was a decent looking guy, shorter than me, but not exactly short in general. He looked rich, which was appropriate because he was. Rich, entitled, and an absolute asshole. Columbia's finest, people. One of those fifth generation kids who'd never had a real job, never had to work hard for anything.

It wasn't the fact that they had money that bothered me — I mean, one of my best friends was heir to a billionaire's fortune. It was that they expected the universe to *give* them all they wanted. The sad part? With the money they had at their disposal, the universe generally complied.

That privilege potentially included the delivery of the last spot in the doctoral program.

"Hey, Simon," I said. "How's life as Dr. Cox's favorite tool?"

"Funny, Williams. We'll miss you at Columbia next year. Tell everyone at NYU we said hello."

"Tell them yourself."

He smirked. "I saw you were here with Chris. I don't know what she's doing with you when she could have someone like me. You've got no standing at Columbia. My father—"

"No one cares, Simon." I stepped around him, and he grabbed my arm. I stopped and looked down at his hand, then back to his eyes. He let me go.

"You scholarship shits are all the same. I don't even know why they don't do away with the program all together."

"Who would've thought Columbia would actually give a damn about quality over bluebloods?" I shook my head. "No one likes nepotistic assholes except other nepotists. Two weeks and we'll know for sure. I'll be sure to send you a parting gift." I walked away.

"Fuck off, West."

I flipped him off over my shoulder without looking back.

My mood was deep enough in the gutter by that point that I found myself rolling through excuses to leave in earnest. Once I was on the roof again, I scanned the clusters of people looking for Chris, but I couldn't find her. I'd almost given up when I walked around a corner to see if she was behind the stairwell entrance.

"I swear, he's this close to committing," I heard Chris say.

I stopped dead.

"You think?" Amanda knew better by this point, it seemed. Her voice was heavy with skepticism.

"I *know*. We hooked up in Blackwell's office again the other day, and he did that thing where …" Her voice dropped off, and I leaned forward, straining to hear what she was saying.

Amanda giggled. "Oh, my god, Chris."

"I told you I'd woo him with my vagina." They snickered. "I mean it, though. This is our first real date, and I think there's a serious chance we're going somewhere."

"God, the whole department would be so jealous, even crotchety old Cox. I don't know how Simon doesn't see Cox has a boner for Blackwell. That's really why they're rivals."

Chris laughed. "Everyone's already jealous. Every time we talk about West, all those bitches gather around and eat up the details, but they walk away talking shit. I mean, tonight I met his friends, and even one of them, Lily, was totally jealous. I don't know how she couldn't see that we were together."

My blood boiled, and I stepped around the corner just as she said, "That bitch better back off, because I will not share."

Chris' back was to me, but Amanda's eyes flew wide the second she saw me. Chris turned, the sleazy smile melting off her face when she saw the look on mine.

"Could you give us a minute, Amanda?" I asked quietly, never taking my eyes off Chris.

"I, uh … of course." She hurried past us, embarrassed.

I glared at Chris. "I didn't realize I was so close to committing."

She smiled, trying to play it off. "That's just girl talk, you know? I didn't mean it like that. Like, I get that you want to take it slow—"

"I don't want to 'take it' anywhere, Chris."

She waved her hand, bracelets clinking together. "You don't mean that."

"I was going to end it as soon as we left this … *party*. How's that for committing?"

Her smile slipped, and she took a step toward me with a hand outstretched. "West, I—"

"And if I ever hear you badmouth Lily again, we're going to have even bigger problems." I handed her the glass of wine. "Have a good time, Chris."

And with that, I walked away, tossing my shitty beer in the trash without a second glance.

JUST SAY NO

Lily

I TROTTED UP THE SUBWAY steps the next afternoon during my break, heading to the burrito joint where I was meeting West for lunch. I'd been anxious to see him all day, worried about his reaction to my little show the night before. So I'd apologized via text and asked for his forgiveness, which he gave, then asked him to lunch. I owed him a decent lunch and a face-to-face apology after my behavior. When I pulled open the door and saw his smile as he waited for me at a table, my anxiety fell away.

He stood and walked toward me, that tall drink of water dressed in jeans and a button-down, hair in a messy bun. We met halfway, and he pulled me into a hug.

"How are you feelin' today?"

I sighed against his chest. "Meh, I've been better.

This burrito should help." He let me go, and we walked up to the counter. "So, tell me straight up — how mad are you that I was a huge ass last night?"

He smiled down at me with an eyebrow up. "Only a little. What are you getting to eat?"

I eyed the menu hanging above the girl behind the register. "I've got to take better care of my body before I hurt myself. So I'll go healthy — veggie burrito, sauce on the side. And a side of fries."

He laughed. "Healthy."

"My hangover demands carbs, Weston," I said with a shrug. "On Sunday, after we get through Noir, it's a full-on juice diet for me. Until then, I'm compromising."

"For you, sir?" The girl wet her lips as she looked him over.

He didn't seem to notice. "Double steak California burrito with extra avocado, please."

"Sure you don't want fries too, West? Jeez."

His lips bent in a lazy smile. "Nah. Mine's got fries *inside* of it."

I chuckled. "That's so excessive."

West pulled out his wallet, and I tried to block him.

"Stop it. This is on me."

"No way, Lily." He moved my hand and pulled out cash.

I tugged at his arm. "I owe you."

"You don't owe me anything. Here you go, miss."

He put the cash in her hand. "Keep the change."

"Thanks," she beamed at him, dreamy-eyed as she handed him the little plastic numbers.

I shook my head as we grabbed our drinks and took a seat.

I put my number on the table and fiddled with it, not wanting to meet his eyes. "So how did last night go with Chris?" Her name alone gave me indigestion. Could have been the hangover. Pretty sure it wasn't, though.

A shadow passed across his face. "It was enlightening."

"Oh?" I asked, hoping I didn't sound too optimistic.

His lips were flat. "Chris had the wrong idea about her and me."

"And what idea was that?"

"She thought we were together."

"But you weren't?"

He shook his head, eyes on his paper cup as he spun it around. "No, not really."

I waited for him to elaborate, but he didn't. "Well, what were you?"

He shrugged and picked up his number, leaning back in his seat to inspect it. "She was just somebody I knew."

"Knew in the Biblical sense?"

He laughed at that, which made me feel better.

"Yes," he said after a second, meeting my eyes.

"Oh." Even I heard the disappointment in my voice.

"Does that surprise you?"

I smiled at him, going for reassuring. "No, I guess not. I mean, I saw you together. It was pretty obvious that you were together in one way or another."

The girl behind the counter brought us our lunch and made extra sure West was comfortable, that he didn't need napkins or extra sauce or anything. I didn't care that she ignored me, because as soon as I saw the fries, I stuffed a steaming hot, salty potato in my mouth and moaned.

"Damn, that's good." I ate another one and took a drink of my water. "Listen, I'm really sorry about last night. That was totally inappropriate and uncalled for."

He snorted. "Yeah, it was."

"I don't know what got into me. I think I was a little hurt."

West's brow dropped as he unwrapped his burrito. "But why?"

"Well, I'll be honest." I watched him until he met my gaze "After our talk about Blane the other night, I was surprised to hear you were seeing someone."

He shook his head like I was being silly. "I wasn't really seeing her, though. If she'd been important to me, I would have told you about her and brought her around. I would have taken her on a *date* if I really cared about her." He shifted his burrito, trying to figure out where to start before taking a colossal bite.

"Ha, ha." The thought that he really didn't want her like that comforted me. "Well, I'd hope you would have told me if you felt something for her. I care about you, and I want to know what's going on with you. I really did walk into that bar prepared to like her, for your sake. Your happiness is important to me, so if she was what you wanted, then I'd have found a way to get on board. Even if she wasn't good enough for you." I smiled and took a rude bite myself.

He nodded as he swallowed and touched his napkin to his lips. There was some guacamole in his beard, and I laughed.

I pointed at my chin. "Missed a spot, buddy."

West pawed at his beard with the napkin, smiling. "So you met Chris for a grand total of five minutes and that gave you a good understanding of whether or not she was good enough for me?"

"Yeah, sound familiar, judgypants?" He laughed, and I shrugged. "It was just a gut feeling. I could see that you were uncomfortable, so obviously something was missing. What was the deal?" I took another bite.

He looked away, seeming to try to compose his thoughts. "She just didn't move me in any way, do you know what I mean? Like, it was fine, to be with her.

That was the most feeling I could muster about it. Sort of apathetic. But I've kind of always been like that. Whomever I end up with should make me *feel*. But then part of me wonders if I'm not equipped to feel more than that apathy. That's my fear, I guess."

I swallowed. "Okay, first, no one says 'whomever' in conversation. I feel like you should have a top hat and monocle on for that to make sense."

He smiled crooked. "Sorry, didn't mean to let my Lit show."

I chuckled. "Secondly, I don't think you have a problem feeling. Think about how you get about your friends. About Maggie. You're passionate about literature and learning. And you have to admit that you get a little ragey when it comes to people you care about."

"Maybe."

"I don't know, West. I think you feel very deeply." I took a bite.

He seemed frustrated. "Then why haven't I found that feeling with a woman? I mean, I was with Shannon for years and never felt really connected to her." He shook his head. "I'm better at friends. Although ..."

"Mmhmm?" I said around a mouthful of dry spinach and feta, eyeing the sauce with longing. Oh, the things I sacrificed for fries.

"Well, there was a girl in high school that I had a

huge crush on. She was one of the popular kids, while I usually had my nose in a book and hung out with the band geeks. I used to watch her in the lunchroom with her friends and daydream about what it would be like to be part of something like that."

"Sounds creepy."

"It probably was. But I used to think about her all the time, daydream about what it would be like. I *wished* for her."

"I get that."

"I know you do. I think what it boiled down to was that I was in love with the idea of her, not her as she existed, if that makes sense."

"I think I might know exactly what you mean." I took a long drink of water to wash away the lump in my throat.

He eyed me as he pulled down the foil on his burrito. "Speaking of crushes, how'd things go with Blane today?" He took a bite.

I sighed. "I haven't seen him much, and it's been a relief. I'm just not sure if I'm ready to deal. He's been texting me, brought me flowers last night … I mean, he's trying, you know? So what else can I do but ride it out?"

He made a face.

"You still think I should dump him."

West swallowed and set his burrito down, leaning

back in his seat. "Look, I'm not gonna tell you what to do. I just think that if you find someone you're meant to be with, there's no question. There's no maybe. You just want them. You *need* them."

I wished it were true, hoped it could be, but I just wasn't sure. "How do you know if you've never felt it? Your experience so far in life says it doesn't exist."

When he looked me in the eye, I saw his hope. "Because I have to believe that love isn't always a choice. That there's something about a love that deep that's chemical, molecular. That's the thing I'm waiting for."

His eyes were so deep, I had to look away. I pulled the foil back on my burrito to keep my hands busy. "So you're saying you don't think people fall in love? You don't think they just date and get to know each other? That it can be a gradual thing?"

West shrugged and picked up his lunch again. "Sure it can. But I don't think you should start a relationship with a foot out the door."

"Interesting," I said half to myself.

His eyebrow jacked. "What, you don't agree?"

"No," I conceded wholeheartedly. "I don't disagree. I just hadn't thought about it like that, that's all."

He took a bite, and we ate in silence for a moment while I digested my burrito and his words.

West broke the silence. "So, is Blane still coming

with us tomorrow night?"

"As far as I know, yeah. I think it'll be the last chance, for him and me, you know? Like, I have to see how it goes when we're on a date—"

"Still not a date."

I huffed. "Well, it's *almost* a date. I'm counting it. If things don't fall into place, I'm calling it off. You're right. I shouldn't be so on the fence."

"Say that again."

My brow quirked. "Uh, I shouldn't be on the fence?"

"No, the other part where I was right."

"Ha, ha." I threw a napkin at him.

He laughed, the sound deep and comforting as he grabbed the napkin mid-air and threw it back in my face.

"Dammit, West!"

His blue eyes twinkled at me. "You're gonna be okay, Lily. I believe that."

I smiled back. "Then I believe you."

Lily

By the end of rehearsals that day, I felt loads better, and not just because of the carbs. Lunch with West has done a lot to set my world to rights, knowing he wasn't upset with me, knowing he broke it off with Christine for good. It was a relief to know he hadn't even really liked her to start, not in the real, relationship way. She wasn't right for him — they even looked wrong standing next to each other. Equal levels of hot, but it just all felt *off.* I was glad to know I was right about them after all.

The lilting piano music played as we made our last pass across the studio, an all-female group working on several parts of *Serenade.* I was grateful Blane was in a different studio so I could concentrate. I needed every brain cell I could muster after slaughtering so many the night before.

The rehearsal ended, and I hurried to my bag with excitement flitting through me at the thought of the opera in a few hours. It was early enough that I still had time to get ready at home before West picked me up, and I had important primping to do. So I changed and blew out of the studio, waving at the girls over my shoulder.

Blane was waiting for me in the hallway, leaning against a crate labeled WIGS 197 with his hands in the pockets of his jersey pants. He gave me that sparkling Blane Baker smile, and I melted a little. "Hey, Lilypad."

Oh, god. Please, don't let that nickname happen for real. "Hey, Blane."

He pushed away from the wall, and we walked toward the elevator together. "How was rehearsal?"

"Good. Group practices are so much more fun than

solo. I sort of miss being in the corps, is that weird?"

Blane shook his head. "I think about that all the time. The whole time you're in it, you're waiting to get out. But the minute you're promoted, you realize just what you had. I missed the crazy schedule and camaraderie within a month. Dancing solos and principal roles isn't nearly as fun. Too much pressure."

"God, it's so true."

We walked for a bit in silence until we approached the elevator. He pushed the call button. "I wanted to swing by and say hi."

My heart flipped.

"Are you busy tonight? I thought we could hang out."

Then my heart fell flat on its face. I wasn't quite sure if he meant to hang out or *hang out,* which bugged me. The elevators doors opened, and we stepped inside. "I'm going to the opera tonight with a friend. But I'll definitely see you tomorrow for Noir, if you're still in?"

The door closed behind us, and he smiled, stepping toward me until my body was flush against the wall of the elevator and his lips hovered over mine. "Oh, I'm definitely in."

He kissed me, a hard, demanding kiss, and I was elated, heart racing as I wound myself around him. He took my submission as permission, deepening the kiss, one hand in my hair.

For one, long moment, it was glorious.

His free hand slipped into the back of my pants and between my legs. As good as it felt to be touched and as neglected as I'd been, I was instantly turned off. I turned my head, breaking the connection.

"Blane …"

He backed away, jaw a hard line, eyes almost accusing. "Yeah, sorry."

I reached for him. "Blane, I—"

The elevator door opened, and he walked backward for a few steps. "It's okay. I get it. Have fun at the opera, all right? I'll see you tomorrow."

I tossed my hand in a wave and exited the elevator as he turned and walked away. My throat was tight, my chest full of regret, then anger that he could make me feel regret for not letting him finger bang me in an elevator. To catch glimpses of what he *could* be, what I imagined him to be, then to have it ruined by what he actually *was* was maddening.

But I tried to shake it off. Tomorrow night, we were going out. It would be the final testament to our pseudo-relationship.

And tonight? Tonight, I'd go to the opera with my best friend. That thought alone helped me shed the rest of the day's bullshit like an empty shell.

BUTTERFLY

West

I RAN MY HAND THROUGH my hair again that night, inspecting my reflection. It wasn't the first time Lily and I had been to the opera together — in fact, it was a pretty regular affair. But this time, I was actually dressed for the occasion.

I adjusted the knot of my narrow tie, smoothing a hand down the buttons of my navy vest. I'd had the suit made for my application interview with the help of Cooper's eye and direction. I'd never understood the sentiment of having a good suit until I put it on for the first time. There's absolutely nothing like it, the feeling of quiet confidence and power. Like I could take over the universe, if I set my mind to it. Or the doctoral program at Columbia. Either, or.

I opened the medicine cabinet and picked up my beard oil, pouring a little into my hand before working it in. Don't make fun of me — thought it was excessive too. Maggie gave me some for Christmas a few years ago, and when I finally caved and used it out of curiosity, it was a game changer.

I didn't choose the hipster life — the hipster life chose me.

The familiar smell of cloves and oranges filled my nose, and I turned my head to check myself out once more, feeling a little vain while somehow fighting the urge to do more. I sighed. For once, I hoped I'd look like I was meant to be standing next to Lily, who always looked incredible, especially when we went to the opera.

I left my reflection behind and made my way through the apartment and into the kitchen. Patrick smirked at me from where he lay stretched out on the couch with a sketchbook.

"Looking fancy, man."

I held out my hands and spun around on my heel like Sinatra, tucking a hand in my coat pocket when I came full circle, ending in a snap.

Patrick laughed. "Save some suave for tomorrow night."

I frowned as I grabbed my keys and wallet. "I'm only going so I can make sure nobody messes with Maggie."

"Oh. So it's got nothing to do with Blane and Lily, right?"

My frown deepened. "Why would it?"

He shifted to sit up a little straighter, amused. "What, you're not even a little curious?"

"Of course I'm curious."

Patrick watched me for a second. "But you don't want to meet him?"

I eyed him. "What's your angle, Tricky?"

"I just want you to admit that you want to go tomorrow and meet Blaney in person."

"All right, fine. I want to meet him so I can kick him in the kneecaps."

Patrick smiled and closed his sketchbook. "I don't like it either, but you don't have a lot of room to judge, man. As much as he sounds like a dog, I get why Lily's into him. They have the same goals, same rules, same fucked-up schedule. I'm sure it's convenient. Sound familiar?"

Agitation bubbled under my skin. "Chris and I were different."

He shrugged. "You keep saying that. Maybe you were, maybe you weren't. I'm just saying."

I squared my shoulders to face him. "Listen, I'm just not convinced that he's good enough for her, that's all."

"To be fair, you don't think anyone's good enough for her."

"No, I don't," I shot. "Certainly not some dick who hasn't even taken her to dinner and bangs her in secret." The thought of him touching her made my stomach turn.

"You never took Chris on a date."

"But that's my fucking point, Tricky. I didn't care about her, so no, I didn't take her on a date. If Blane really cared about Lily, he'd fucking act like it."

Patrick looked at me like he knew something. "So they're just hooking up. Why does that piss you off?"

"I'm not pissed off," I snapped.

He laughed, and it fueled my aggravation. "My bad. You're *Blaingry.*"

I fumed. "Let's just see how this asshole does tomorrow night. Maybe I'm wrong. Maybe he'll be a fucking saint, and I'll eat a fat piece of humble pie."

"You'll feel even worse if you're right."

"Maybe so." I turned for the door. "I'm gonna be late."

"Should I wait up?"

I flipped him off over my shoulder and left, closing the door harder than I meant to. My brain was scrambled eggs as I walked the hall to Lily's door, pausing on her doormat, hesitating for a long moment before I knocked.

I heard her heels as she approached and unlocked the bolt, pulling the door open with a whoosh that stole the air from my lungs.

Lily stood in the doorway, tall and lithe, blond hair

twisted up, skin like porcelain against the inky black of her dress. The bodice was fitted, covered in sheer lace that stretched across her shoulders, and I followed the line of her ribs down to her tiny waist, then the bell of her skirt to the hem that hit in the middle of her long thigh. But that wasn't what stopped my heart.

It was her eyes, bright and blue behind thick, black lashes as she looked up at me, some emotion behind them that I couldn't place. Something in the pink of her cheeks that whispered a secret that I couldn't quite hear.

I don't think I could have told you my name in that moment, if you'd asked me.

Maggie cleared her throat from behind Lily, and I looked over at her with a smile, not sure how long I'd been staring. I felt like my world had been flipped, and it took every bit of energy I had to try to set it to rights. "Hey, Mags."

She came in for a side hug. "Don't you look handsome. That suit!"

"What, this old thing?"

Maggie laughed. Lily still hadn't moved — just stood in the entry way staring at me, stunned. I glanced over at her with my ears hot. "You ready, Lil?"

She blinked and nodded, snapping back into awareness. Her smile was soft and lovely as she picked up her clutch, and when I offered her my arm, she slipped her hand in the crook of my elbow. I tucked it into my side, a familiar feeling, something we'd done a hundred times. But this time was different, a change that was so slight, I couldn't put my finger on it. I only knew I didn't want to let her go.

Confusion and elation twisted through me, but I winked at Maggie, playing the charm to hide the free fall. "Don't get into any trouble, now."

Maggie laughed, hanging on the door. "Oh, no. I'm saving that for tomorrow night."

I made a face at her and shook my head as we walked out of the apartment.

"Have fun, you two!" she called after us, looking at us like ... well, I don't know like what. Like she was proud. Nostalgic. Sad and happy, all at the same time.

Lily and I walked in silence for a moment, and my brain kicked into overdrive. I was so overwhelmed by her, I couldn't concentrate — every place where she touched me, just the presence of her body next to mine as we walked down the stairs was too much.

I tried to make sense of it, wondering why now? After all these years, why tonight? The realization that Chris had been working an angle, trying to manipulate me, was still fresh. Maybe whatever was happening was some sort of rebound, emotional fallout from ending things with Chris. But that would mean that I had cared about Chris — the only discernible feelings I had for her were laced with surprise and disgust.

Lily would never do something like that to get what she wanted. She was an optimist, an honest, good-natured woman. She didn't hide her feelings, didn't skirt around her intentions. She didn't have to. Lily knew what she wanted and went for it with every bit of her heart. *That* was the kind of woman I wanted.

Shock ripped through me at the realization. With every step, I tried to push the thought away, but it clung to me like a magnet. Me and Lily? That had disaster written all over it, and the cost could ultimately be our friendship. Nothing was worth losing that for. I saw what happened to Rose and Patrick, and I never wanted to be the reason Lily hurt like that.

Lily hung on to my arm, her skirt flouncing with each step.

"You look beautiful. Thank you for accompanying me tonight," I said.

She laughed, her red lips stretching wide. "Thank you. You sound so Southern when you say things like that."

I smiled down at her.

She glanced over at me with approval written all over her face. "Where have you been hiding that suit? It looks like it was made for you."

I stood a little straighter, puffing out my chest. "I had to appear in front of a panel and present my doctoral proposal, and for that, I needed a good suit. So

I got one. There just aren't a lot of places to wear it."

"Well, the opera is a great excuse."

"That it is. I wish I'd splurged sooner. I'm never as well-dressed as you are when we go to the opera."

"Tonight, I think you have me beat."

I shook my head with my chest aching. "Not a chance. Not a chance in all of creation."

She smiled down at her feet as we descended the last flight.

"How did the rest of your day go?" I asked.

"Up and down. Rehearsal gave me a boost. *Serenade* is such a beautiful piece, and it's almost like being a part of the corps again, which I miss. I'm so glad we're performing it this week."

"Did you end up talking to Blane?"

She tightened her grip just a little. "Briefly."

We walked up to the door, and I pushed it open, holding it for her as she passed. "That bad, huh?"

She sighed as we walked up to the sidewalk. "I just don't get him, that's all."

"What happened?" I asked as I stepped up to the curb and threw a hand in the air, sticking two fingers of my free hand to whistle. A cab pulled up almost immediately.

Lily's brows pinched together as I opened the door. "One minute I feel like he really likes me, and the next …"

I took her hand to help her in. Part of me didn't want to know what she was going to say, but I spoke up anyway. "The next he what?"

She slipped into the cab, swinging her long legs in behind her silently.

I climbed in behind her and addressed the driver. "The Met, please." He nodded and took off, and I angled to face her. Her eyes were on the street beyond the window. "You don't wanna talk about it?"

Lily looked back at me. "It's not that. I just hate not understanding what's going on. I'm not used to this. I just want someone who will tell it to me straight, you know? I don't like being toyed with." She sighed. "The problem is, it's so bad with him that I don't even know if I'm being toyed with or not. I can't tell, and that makes it worse than anything." She gave her head a little shake and smiled. "I don't want to talk about him anymore, though. You didn't run into Christine today, did you?"

I leaned against the door. "No, but I admittedly hid in Blackwell's office most of the day. I didn't want to see anybody, not after that party, which was a nightmare, by the way. Complete with a Simon Phillips dream sequence."

She groaned. "Ugh. Not that guy. What happened?"

"Nothing, really. He just mouthed off, but I was

already pissed because of Chris. She was dragging me around that party like a show pony. By the time Simon got to me, he didn't stand a chance."

"I'm sorry, West," she said sincerely.

I smiled. "Don't be. In a few weeks, we'll know for certain who made it. If it's him, he'll never let me live it down. Ever. He might even defile my tombstone with something like *Columbia's Second Finest.*"

Lily made a face. "Is there seriously a chance he'll beat you for a spot?"

"There's always a chance. A lot of factors play into it, and I can't pretend to know where I stand. Simon's an old money legacy, with generations of alumni in his family tree." I sighed in an attempt to relieve the bit of stress that had crept into my chest. "I did my best, and that's all I can do."

She nodded. "The waiting is the hardest part. Until I was offered a contract with the company, every rehearsal was pumped full of anxiety. I felt like I had to push myself as hard as I possibly could, because if I didn't, I'd lose. I'd fail. Every rehearsal was driven by the absolute need to get a contract, to get asked to stay. In my apprentice year, I was a mess. I couldn't sleep, barely ate … making it into the company was everything I'd worked for. Every one of my eggs was in that basket. Who knows what I would have done if I hadn't made it."

"You would have gone to Juilliard and landed a prestigious job somewhere just as important as the New York City Ballet. There's no way that your talent would have gone unnoticed."

"Thank you, West." She blushed. "Anyway, I hate that you have to wait so long to find out about your application, especially while getting hassled by that shit-for-brains."

"Oh, don't you worry about me. I can handle Simon just fine."

We pulled up to the Met, and I paid the cab driver before opening the door and climbing out, offering a hand again to pull her out and onto the sidewalk. We were quiet as we walked up the gradual steps, Lily on my arm, soaking up everything. The fountains in the courtyard were lit up, as were the massive arched windows of the Met Opera House. It looked like a chapel. In a way, I supposed it was.

I snuck a glance at Lily as we walked, struck by her once again. Her face said what I'd been thinking about the buildings around us — her eyes full of wonder and lips in a small smile — and I followed the line of her jaw to the nape of her long neck where small tendrils of her blond hair curled against her skin.

"I love this place at night," she said as we walked past the bustling Lincoln Center on the west side of the courtyard. "I never come through this way, you know, *especially* at night. It feels like we're walking into something spectacular, doesn't it?"

"It does," I answered quietly.

She smiled over at me as we walked around the fountain to the entrance, all while I tried to make sense of whatever malfunction my brain was in the middle of. Things with Lily had always been easy, until a few days ago.

Now I felt everything slipping away and rushing toward me all at once.

I pulled open the door, and we walked the plush, red carpet, through the ticket master, and to the bar.

An older woman and her husband approached us as we were waiting for our drinks. "Excuse me, miss?"

Lily turned to her. "Yes?"

"Forgive me for the intrusion, but are you Lily Thomas?"

She smiled graciously and extended a hand. "I am. It's nice to meet you."

The woman beamed and took her hand, placing her free hand on top. "Oh, I just knew it. I saw your debut principal performance of Firebird last fall, and it moved me, truly. You are an exquisite dancer."

Lily's cheeks were flushed, her eyes sparkling. "Thank you so much, ma'am. It means the world to me that you would take time out of your night to come say hello."

I thought I might burst from pride.

The woman glanced over at me as she let Lily go. "Oh, is this your boyfriend? What a lovely couple you are."

Lily's cheeks flushed. "This is Weston, a very dear friend of mine."

I extended a hand, and she took it. "Pleasure to meet you, ma'am."

"You as well. Miss Thomas, we have tickets to your *Swan Lake* opening show, and I must say that I'm thrilled to see you perform. I'll be bringing my hanky."

"I only hope I can do it justice."

The woman patted Lily on the arm just as the bartender passed me our drinks. "Oh, I have no doubts, and neither should you. It's so very nice to meet you both. We'll leave you to your evening."

"Enjoy the show," Lily said with a smile.

The woman waved, smiling back. "You too."

Lily took a breath, blushing up at me as I handed her a glass of wine. "I swear, that's the best feeling in the whole world."

"Better than performing?"

"Okay, second best." She took a sip, and I just watched her for a moment while she opened her program. Every move she made was poised and elegant, moving with absolute grace. Her hands were perfect, like a doll's, even as she turned the pages lazily and took another drink of her wine.

My thoughts skittered around my head too quickly to catch a single one. I didn't know what to say, so I sipped my scotch and listened as she talked. The difference between listening to Lily talk on and listening to Chris was in high relief, the contrast of the two women almost blinding. I cared about every word that left Lily's ruby-red lips.

It wasn't long before we made our way into the theater and took our seats behind the pit just as the house lights dimmed and the opera opened. I could feel her next to me — every breath, every movement of her body — her presence alone occupying all of my senses. I couldn't sort it out, not through the first half of the show, not through intermission where we had a few more drinks. And as I sat through the final scenes of the opera, I couldn't comprehend what had changed, when it had shifted. But I wasn't the same. She wasn't the same.

All those years, I thought Lily was out of my reach. We'd always been affectionate, always been close, but the boundaries were firmly in place — we were *friends*. I shared every victory and defeat with her, and she did the same. We were a part of each other's lives and experiences, and we always had been.

She was my friend, and I loved her.

Butterfly was on the stage, singing with all of her

heart about the love she'd lost, the love she'd never truly had to begin with. Singing of the sacrifice she would give, that she had to give for the sake of her son. She gave the tiny American flag to the boy and said goodbye, walked behind the curtain with her seppuku knife to take her life. But my eyes were on Lily.

Her eyes were wide, brow bent with emotion, fingers on her lips. The tears in her eyes were illuminated by the stage lights, and when the music reached the apex, the lights flashed red. She blinked from the shock, and the tears she'd been holding back rolled down her cheeks, chest shuddering as she drew in a breath.

I wanted to reach for her, pull her into my lap and hold her, kiss away her tears. The beauty of her emotion held me dead still, watching her feel. I couldn't disturb that. And if she looked me in the eye in that moment, she'd know what I'd only just realized.

No one was good enough for Lily. But I could be. I wanted to be.

I loved her.

My own emotion took over, my chest aching like a Lily-sized bomb had detonated in my ribcage. I was in love with Lily. How I'd made it all that time without realizing it, I'll never know.

I reached for my pocket square with shaking fingers and passed it to her, and she gave me a grateful smile before blotting her cheeks and nose, turning her gaze back to the stage. Her free hand slipped into mine and squeezed, and I ran my thumb over her knuckles, knowing she didn't know what the motion meant to me. I willed her to understand without words, willed her to realize that she loved me too. Imagined her turning to me with her eyes full of hope and finding recognition in them.

Part of me wanted to drop to my knees at her feet and beg her to say she felt the same.

But logic reared its ugly head, sprinkling dissension like the beginning of a rainstorm. *What if she doesn't feel the same?* Drip. *What if she really wants Blane?* Drip, drop. *What if I ruin everything?* Drop, drop, drop. And then, the deluge of self-doubt began. I pictured her pitying me, the awkward hand patting and sympathy that would follow before our friendship drifted away. I imagined her angry and hurt that I would throw something like that at her after all these years.

Was telling her worth the risk? Could I lose her forever?

I couldn't be sure, not until I'd sorted it out for myself.

The music ended, and the curtain dropped as the crowd flew to their feet in a roar of applause. Lily was still crying — smiling and crying, like sunshine in the rain. We clapped and cheered until the cast had come and gone and the house lights went all the way up. Lily was still beaming as she took my arm once more, and we followed the crowd out of the theater.

I had no words. None that I could say out loud.

She was quiet at first, still reeling from the performance as we made our way slowly toward the exit behind the crowd, my hand over hers where it curled around my bicep as she leaned into me. It wasn't until we'd stepped out into the cool night that she found her voice. And then the conversation didn't stop as we went through what we'd seen together, the moments that struck us in the performance. She cried again in the cab talking about the ending, hand to her chest, long fingers clutching my handkerchief. It was beautiful. She was beautiful.

The walk into the building was quiet once more, the only sound in the stairwell our echoing footfalls until we reached her door.

"I can't wait to get these shoes off," she said with a laugh as she dug through her purse. "Heels are about a million times worse than pointe shoes."

I only smiled down at her, standing close enough that I barely had to raise my hand to cup the back of her arm, shifting my thumb against her soft skin. Her hand stilled in her purse, and she looked up at me, her eyes so open I could see her heart. Overcome, that's how I felt, as if nothing in the world could stop me from wanting her. The pull of her was so strong that I couldn't deny it. I leaned into her just as she leaned into me, lips on an achingly slow track to connect. But before I could reach those lips, she blinked and stepped back, cheeks flushed.

"Oh, my god. I'm so sorry. I must have had too much wine."

My hand dropped as I straightened up, crestfallen, palms damp out of nowhere. I tried to smile past the ache in my chest. "Must have. Sleep it off, Twinkle Toes."

She pulled out her keys and smiled. "You too. Thank you. That was ... it was amazing, as always."

I slipped my hands into my pockets, clenching my fist tight. "It was. I'll see you, Lil."

Lily opened her door and looked back over her shoulder at me. All I wanted was to stop her, push her up against the door and kiss her until she was breathless.

"Night, West."

I watched the door close, putting distance between us that was instantly flooded with my thoughts, rushing in my ears, louder than they'd been all night. I peeled my feet off the ground and walked to my door, fumbling with my keys, unlocking my dark apartment and stepping in with my mind everywhere but where I was.

I didn't even see Patrick sitting on the couch, not until he spoke. "You all right?"

I jumped. "Jesus Christ. What are you doing sittin' in the dark like a goddamn serial killer?"

"Reading." He held up his phone.

I rubbed my face and reached for the light switch, flipping it on before pacing through the living room.

Patrick watched me with dark eyes. "What happened?"

"I don't know." I turned to span the room again, dragging my fingers through my hair.

"Is it bad?"

I loosened my tie. "Yes. Whatever this is, it's definitely bad."

He folded his arms across his chest as I struggled with where to start. I turned and made a lap around the room once more.

"So," he prompted, "you went to Lily's to pick her up, and then…"

"…And then, we left. And nothing was different, but *everything* was different. She … I …"

Patrick seemed startled and somehow entertained. "You're speechless."

I shook my head and sat on the couch, elbows on my knees, fingers in my hair, staring at my oxfords. There was only one way to explain it. "I think I'm in love with her."

He nodded and said simply, "I think you are, too."

I eyed him, confused. "Why do you not look surprised?"

"Because I've known for years. Did you really only just figure this out? I honestly thought you knew."

I pinched the bridge of my nose and squeezed my eyes shut. "No. I didn't know."

"You need a drink." He rolled off the couch and strode into the kitchen while I tried to get regain my composure. He came back with a bottle of bourbon and two glasses, set them on the coffee table, and poured us each a shot.

I took it graciously and slammed it. "What the fuck, Tricky." I hung the empty glass between my knees. "What the fuck."

"Did you tell her?"

"I can't, not until I figure it out myself."

He shrugged and leaned back in the couch. "Seems pretty simple to me."

I glared at him, annoyed at the minimization of my crisis. "Says the guy in love with Rosie."

His brow dropped at the dig. "Hey, man. Not fair."

I sighed. "It's not that simple. You know that better than anyone."

"It is, and it isn't. Can you see yourself with her? Do you want to be with her?"

I imagined what it would be like to be with her.

Pictured her curled up in my lap with my lips on hers. Saw her face graced with a smile full of love, long body stretched out in my bed in the shadows of night. I thought my heart might explode. "Yeah," I answered, my voice rough.

"Then you have to tell her."

I huffed, wishing I could. "Not without a plan. Doesn't matter that I want to knock on her door right now and tell her everything." I scrubbed my hands down my face. "Tell me not to do it, Tricky."

Patrick leaned forward, resting his elbows on his knees. "Just go tell her. Don't make the mistake I did and keep it to yourself."

"But what happened with you and Rose is exactly why I don't want to just go over there, guns blazing. I've got to be careful and do this right. The timing is bad, Patrick. Really bad."

He poured us each another drink, considering it. "I guess she is seeing somebody. Is she really that into Blane, though?"

His name hit me like a baseball bat to the face. I'd forgotten all about him for a minute, forgotten that I was supposed to spend a whole night with him and Lily. "Fuck, man. I don't know. She wants to be. Tomorrow is supposed to be the last shot."

"Look, you have to tell her, eventually. Can we agree on that?"

There was no way I could keep it to myself forever. I nodded.

"Do you think you can wait until after tomorrow night?"

I picked up my drink. "If I have to." I knocked it back and set the glass on the table again.

He rubbed a hand on his jaw. "I don't know. Maybe you should talk to Rose. She'll know how to handle this better than anyone."

I sighed, shaking my head with my eyes on the empty glass. "How did this happen? When did this happen?"

"It's been happening for years, West."

"I didn't know. All this time, I didn't know. I didn't think I could have her, and I now don't even know if she wants me. But I want her, Patrick. Right now, I'll tell you that for a fact. I want her more than I've ever wanted anything." It was clarity I'd found, as subtle as a bucket of ice water down my back. "How can I get through a whole night watching her with someone else? How can I keep this from her?"

"Maybe you should stay home."

My brow furrowed. "And leave Maggie and Lily alone to deal with a bunch of drunk assholes? No way."

He shrugged. "Then you've got to suck it up. Buy yourself some time so you can do this right. You've only got one real shot at it. Don't fuck it up."

Don't fuck it up. No pressure. "Maybe I just shouldn't ever tell her." I knew it was an empty threat as soon as I'd said it.

He gave me a pointed look. "You really think you can keep your mouth shut forever? Because that's not as easy as it looks."

I sighed again.

Patrick leaned forward. "Listen. Cooper and I will keep your mind off Lily tomorrow night while we're out. You can be there to check everything out without having to deal with it all alone. We've got your back. And tomorrow morning, talk to Rose. She'll know what to do. If you can catch her early enough, you might end up with enough time to see to Lily before she leaves for the day."

Patrick poured me another bourbon as I rubbed my face. I sat back on the couch and sipped it, feeling like I'd aged ten years. "And for now, I wait."

He nodded. "You wait."

"And I have to tell her."

"You do. But not yet."

"I can't not tell her." I stared at a spot on the wall.

"Nope."

"And she might hate me for it."

"Yup."

I glanced over at him. "How have you been doing this with Rosie for all this time?"

He let out a heavy sigh. "Because she knows how I feel. I have no choice. I fucked it up, and this is my punishment. There's no talking about it, and there's nothing to be done."

"But you're still friends. So there's hope for Lily and me."

"There's always hope. That's what keeps you going."

I nodded. "How the fuck am I going to ever go to sleep?"

But Tricky only laughed. "This will help," he said as he raised his glass, and we drained them together, pouring another without hesitation.

SCHEMES

Lily

I SIPPED MY COFFEE THE next morning with my eyes out of focus, staring in the general direction of the kitchen cabinets. I'd barely slept after the opera, tweaked out and unable to make any sense of the end of the evening.

I'd almost kissed West.

Embarrassment washed over me again at the memory. I didn't know what had come over me — if it was just latent emotion from the opera or some mental sabotage connected with Blane. The opera had just been so overwhelming, not only because of the performance, but because of West. When he showed up in that suit and looked at me like … I don't even know what. That look hit me in a way I couldn't sort out. All night long, I kept catching myself falling into him, into his eyes, into his words.

I didn't know what was the matter with me. When he touched my arm in the hallway and I looked up at him, I hadn't wanted anything else in the world but for him to kiss me, and the feeling didn't leave me. I lay in bed half the night staring at my ceiling, contemplating getting out of bed to go over there. If I'd have thought of anything to say, I probably would have. But I didn't know what I even wanted from him. Besides his lips.

The thought was so upsetting. Here I was again, wanting something I shouldn't. Maybe I only wanted things I couldn't have, things that were impossible. Mental masochism.

I felt like an ass for putting West in the position to have to deal with my crazy. He was my best friend. I tried to make sense of it all, find some reason that would explain why I'd lost my mind. I mean, everything *was* coming to a head. The pressure of *Swan Lake*. The mess that was my relationship with Blane and the backlash of Nadia. I told myself I was just overwhelmed. Stressed.

Everything with West *had* to be a byproduct of that.

I smiled to myself, feeling relieved. Almost kissing West was just wine and stress and the comfort of a familiar face. West wasn't interested in me like that, and I was with Blane — sort of.

Blane was trying, he really was, from sweet texts to the flowers. I was still determined to give it one last shot because I couldn't take that kind of regret to the grave. I'd be an old lady in a nursing home, lamenting over canasta about 'what if' and doodling his name on the edge of my bingo card. So, if Blane was going to try, then so would I.

Third time's a charm.

I pictured us all dressed up, arm in arm, and my stomach fluttered. VIP with Cooper was always fun, if not a little overwhelming. To live the life of the rich and famous for a few hours was a thrill, but I was glad I got to walk away from it at the end of the night. I couldn't imagine living like that all the time, with everyone in your business, people trying to take advantage of you, cameras following you around. Even being remotely connected to that life through Astrid was enough for me. It was part of the reason why Cooper and Astrid were closed off to newcomers, and outside of our little group, stuck to others in their social circle.

I took another sip of my coffee and checked the time. My day was packed — rehearsal all day and a show that night. Luckily *Serenade* was short, and we were performing first. There would be plenty of time to get back here and get ready before we left. My hot-ass dress and a glass of gin would be waiting for me to prep for a night that had the potential to be one for the books.

Self-made magic. I was all about it. Maybe tonight would be the night that Blane would actually give it to me in the bedroom, because if he played his cards right, I'd let him. I wanted it given to me so badly, I could almost taste it — the sweet, sweet taste of satisfaction.

I smiled to myself and turned my attention back to my book. Everyone was still asleep, which wasn't a surprise. I loved weekend mornings, those few hours where the world was still quiet, the day full of possibility, just me, a cup of coffee, a book, and the golden, early morning sunshine. That right there is happiness.

Rose's door opened, and she stumbled out, a mess of hair and legs as she headed for the bathroom, swearing under her breath when she bumped into the doorframe. My brow quirked, wondering why she was awake. I hadn't expected to see her until I came home from the show.

When she reappeared a second later, she looked more together by only a degree. Her hair was a little less drunk lion and a little more tipsy llama. She mumbled to herself as she wandered into her room briefly, coming back to the living room with jeans on and her combat boots in hand.

"Where are you going, Sleeping Beauty?"

"Breakfast." The word was a curse if I'd ever heard one.

I eyed her. "With who?"

"Tricky." She sat on the couch and pulled on her

boot.

My eyebrow jacked, and I smiled at her. "Oh?"

"Don't *oh* me," Rose huffed. "It's nothing."

"It must be something if it's got you up before ten." I gave her a look and took a sip of my coffee.

She shoved her other foot into her boot. "I'm not equipped to talk about it without coffee."

"There's some in the pot."

"No time." She grabbed her purse and keys and headed for the door.

"Well, take a nap when you get home because I need you on your game. Blane Baker is happening tonight!"

Rose pulled on her jacket and shook her head, her voice gruff. "You sound awfully excited about it."

"Well, this is the last shot, and I'm feeling really good about it. I'm getting on the bicycle one more time, and I have a feeling it's going to be the smoothest ride yet."

"I'm just saying. I expected a little more skepticism."

"I'm not walking into it blind, and I'll admit that the whole thing has made me a little crazy."

Rose snorted.

I perked up, not letting her get to me. "But today's a new day, and I have a feeling it's going to be a good one. I even got a Brazilian yesterday, just in case."

It was her turn to raise an eyebrow. "Hot wax to the

lady bits for Blane Baker? He'd better appreciate that."

"That's what I'm talking about. Full and complete lady cave commemoration."

She laughed and opened the door. "I'll see you tonight."

"Bye, then," I said, only slightly wounded when she shut the door without responding or asking me to join her, but my smile crept back again. Rose would rather wax her *own* cooch than get up at eight in the morning.

Wuss.

West

I shredded the paper napkin, dropping the strips in a pile on the diner table as Patrick and I waited for Rose in silence. Genie's was our favorite diner, a chain of only three that started in Hell's Kitchen, and they made the best malts I'd ever had. This one was on Broadway, just down the block from our apartment, and we were there nearly as much as Habits.

Patrick and I had spent the night drinking until we passed out. Lily's name was on my lips when I drifted away, and her face filled my thoughts the second I woke. I checked my phone that morning to find texts to Rose, all vague, in part for all the typos. It was a pretty weak cloak and dagger operation. I only asked her to meet us at the diner at eight and to not tell Lily I would be there. She told me to kindly go to hell. So I told her, very simply, that it was important and that I needed her help. She couldn't say no to that.

My coffee sat in front of me untouched. I'd realized as soon as I'd ordered it that the last thing my nerves needed was caffeine.

Patrick sat across from me, back against the window ledge, watching me with concern. "It's going to work out."

I sighed. "I'm sure, one way or another."

The bell on the door rang, and we turned toward the sound to find Rose walking in. She looked tired and definitely annoyed, though somehow still together. A little scary, but together. I couldn't help but smile. Patrick looked like he'd been slapped.

Her eyes were narrowed as she slid into the booth next to Patrick. The waitress appeared out of nowhere and opened her mouth to speak.

Rose didn't even acknowledge her, just grumbled, "Coffee."

The waitress rolled her eyes and walked away.

"This better be good, you shits. This is the face of four hours of sleep. Take a good look, because if you see this again, it might mean you're at the threshold of hell."

Patrick turned in the booth and leaned on the table, gesturing to me. "Go ahead, Romeo."

Somehow, Rose's eyes narrowed even more as she stared me down.

I leaned on the table and took a deep breath, knowing there was only one way to say it. I met her gaze. "I think I'm in love with Lily."

Her eyes flew open. "You what?"

I nodded. "I realized it last night at the opera."

She dragged a hand through her dark hair and pulled in a breath, blowing it out through her nose. "What happened?"

"Nothing. Everything. It hit me when I came to pick her up, but I think it had been coming for days. Maybe longer."

Rose gaped at me. "I can't believe you realized this right now. Bad timing, West."

"I know. Trust me, I know."

She leaned back and folded her arms. "What are you going to do?"

"I don't know how to handle this, Rose. I need your help."

Something in my voice must have reached her because her face softened. "If you had asked me yesterday, I would have told you to go over there right now to talk to her about it. But I just left her singing her high hopes about Blane and tonight."

My eyes were on my coffee as I struggled with what to say.

The waitress brought Rose her coffee. "Thank you," she said, relieved and smiling, and the waitress seemed placated, smiling back with a nod. "If you tell her right now, she's going to flip out, and she's got rehearsal all day and a show tonight. Can you wait to talk to her about all of this until tomorrow night? Noir will be behind us, and she'll have all day off work on Monday to process."

"It's going to be hard to get through tonight with the two of them, but if it's what I have to do, then I'll do it."

Rose reached for the sugar and poured it in with a brief hiss. She picked up her spoon. "Honestly, I'm kind of hoping Blane just lets his bro show so Lily will finally write him off for good. Here's the thing — she *thinks* she cares about him, and I think he's throwing off her radar by pretending to give a shit. He's trying to hang on to her for some reason, but I don't know what his angle is. Maybe he doesn't have one." Rose sighed and picked up her cup. "The whole thing is fucked up. What I do know is that if you talk to her right now, she's not going to know what to say. If you wait until Blane blows over, your chances will be better." She took a sip of her coffee.

"So you think I should tell her?"

Rose nodded. "I definitely think you should tell her."

"That's what Patrick said too."

Patrick looked pleased with himself.

"Well, he's right. You may only have one decent shot at this, but you shouldn't take it until she's ready."

"I'm putting all my hope in Blane making a fool out of himself. What if he's *not* a douchelord tonight? What if she really ends up falling for him? What if I miss the chance all together?"

She reached for my hand. "Listen, you're not going to miss anything. There's too much going on right now to drop this on her too. Things will slow down, and even if she's still seeing Blane, that doesn't mean you can't tell her how you feel. For now, I just think you need to wait and see."

My voice was thick. "How can I pretend?"

"You don't have to put yourself through tonight. Just stay home. You can talk to her tomorrow night."

I shook my head. "I have to go. I need to go."

She nodded. "Then you need to pretend, just for a night."

My only other question burned in my throat — the same one that had plagued me since I'd realized how I felt. "Do you think I have a chance?"

Rose smiled. "Oh, I definitely think you have a chance."

The relief was palpable, hope that I needed to fortify my willpower. "Thank you, Rose."

"You're welcome. Now feed me bacon, Weston, before shit gets real."

Lily

The crowd roared as I bowed again, barely able to see the faces beyond the stage lights. It was a feeling that we all lived for — standing on the stage, listening to the thunderous applause for all of your hard work. That high was the cherry on the sundae, the reward for the pain, the grueling rehearsals, the stress and sacrifice. None of it mattered in that moment.

We made our way off stage, and I hurried to my bag, stuffing everything in unceremoniously. The crew bustled behind me, but I barely noticed, just grabbed my flats and tossed them on the ground with a smack, reaching for my ankle to untie my shoes, then the other. I was an absolute whirl — in a hurry to get to my changing room so I could get home.

Jenni walked up, stopping next to me at her own bag, grinning. "God, I love *Serenade*. I think it might be my favorite."

I laughed and stuffed my shoes in the bag. "You say that about every show."

"Ugh, I know. Congrats, by the way — your Waltz Girl was perfect tonight. Just perfect."

"Thank you," I beamed as I stood and picked up

my bag.

Her smiled faded, brow dropping as she leaned toward me. "Listen, I wanted to talk to you, Lil—"

Anxiety blew through me at the thought of being delayed even for a second. Everyone was waiting on me to get home, and I still had a million things to do. "Can we talk tomorrow? I'm so sorry, it's just that I have plans tonight, and everyone's waiting on me."

She smiled, but she was definitely disappointed, and there was something else there … guilt? I was curious, but I couldn't linger.

"Of course. We'll talk tomorrow for sure."

"You're the best. I'm sorry to run." I leaned over and kissed her cheek before slipping out between the chairs. "Love your face, Jen."

"You too." She still had the smile on, but it was tight. I wondered what she needed, figuring it couldn't have been *too* terribly important, or she'd insist that we talk.

I still had to get dressed, turn my costume in, get home, shower, fix my hair, do my makeup, get dressed — my head spun around, and I started trucking toward the stairs. Dancers and crew were everywhere, and Bastian caught my eye from across the room. He flagged his hand, looking more serious than usual, but I just waved and took off, wondering what in the world everyone needed to talk to me about tonight, of all nights.

CAVEMAN SAYS "UG"

Lily

MY DRESS WAS TOO SHORT and my heels were too high, but I couldn't even find it in my heart to care what anybody thought about it.

It was ten-thirty, and Maggie, Rose, and I had spent the last hour drinking gin — okay, I'd had one, which was my finite limit for the night — and doing our hair and makeup. Rose lined her lips with a deep red in the mirror, with the big, shaggy hair and smokey cat-eye going on while somehow looking like she didn't put in any effort. Maggie sipped her drink and messed with her necklaces, looking sweet in a loose sleeveless dress that was nearly as short as mine, with nude heels and natural makeup.

I felt tricked out by comparison — hair curled, lips hot pink, kohl liner, and a cobalt blue dress that made my boobs look amazing. Not like I had a ton to work with, but man. That dress. I gave my goodies a squeeze as I looked in the mirror, and Rose laughed.

"Don't laugh. These are my magical tickets to the land of O."

Maggie burst out laughing.

I giggled, still checking them out, wiggling my hips to the disco house bumping from Rose's portable speaker. "I'm serious. Blane cannot refuse me in this dress."

Rose picked up her lipstick and popped off the cap. "No man in their right mind would. Or woman, either."

"Aww, well, if you'd do me, then I've already won, Rosie."

I was feeling heady from the gin and the long day of dancing, still zinging from the adrenaline from the performance. I was shiny and fresh and ready. Tomorrow was going to suck, but I swore to myself that after tonight, it was on. I had two weeks to get my body ready for *Swan Lake*. But tonight, it was all or nothing.

Something was going to change. I could feel it.

I checked my phone for the fifth time. "Blane should be here any minute." I stepped out of the tiny bathroom and stood in the hallway with my hands on my hips. "How do I look?"

Maggie leaned to peer around Rose. "Bangable."

"Your legs are ridiculous," Rose sighed.

"Nailed it." I smiled and headed into the living

room, humming along to Rose's music as I gathered my things and put them in my clutch. ID, lipstick, tiny mirror, credit card, cash, phone, and condoms. What? No way was I leaving the apartment unprepared for The Blane. I was so prepared for The Blane, it was almost creepy. Almost.

Someone knocked on the door, and my heart skipped. I took a deep breath, smoothing my skirt as I walked over and pulled it open.

Blane stood in the hallway looking dead fucking sexy. My eyes roamed up his body — tailored shirt and gray coat, pants that hugged that luscious ass of his. A chill ran down my back when my gaze came to rest on his smile as he looked down at me with bright eyes.

"Hey, Lil," he said as he gave me a sweet kiss on the lips, and my knees almost gave out.

"Hey." I laid a hand on his rock-solid chest and grinned up at him.

"You look amazing." He leaned back to get a good look, smiling crooked.

"So do you. Come on in." I turned, swinging my hips as I made my way into the kitchen, congratulating myself on the decision to keep it going with Blane.

He followed me into the apartment, closing the door behind him.

I looked back over my shoulder and caught him looking at my ass. Let me just say that in that moment, I was sure my hips could bring world peace. "Can I get you a drink?"

His lips tilted in a smile. "Sure. Whatever you've got is fine."

I poured him a whiskey on the rocks as Rose and Maggie walked in, whispering. He turned his killer smile on them.

I strutted back into the entryway with his drink in hand. "Blane, I didn't get a chance to introduce you to my roommates last time you were here. I'd like you to meet Rose and Maggie." I gestured to them. "Girls, this is Blane."

Rose's smile was fake — I could tell from across the room — not that he would know the difference. I wondered what her problem was.

She gave a half-hearted wave. "Nice to meet you, officially at least."

Maggie was more genuine. Must have been her dutiful Southern manners. "It's so nice to meet you! Come here, I'm a hugger." She stepped up to give him a hug, and he leaned back a little, surprised. Definitely not something New Yorkers were ever prepared for. "We've heard so many good things about you, Blane. Glad you could make it tonight."

I handed him the whiskey, and he eyed it for a long second before taking a sip. He tried not to cough and failed.

Rose didn't miss it and rolled her eyes when he wasn't paying attention. I gave her a look.

Another knock sounded, and Rose answered it to Astrid who looked stupid awesome in nearly no makeup and with her hair virtually untouched — a shaggy, blond, fabulously unfussy mess. Her white dress was patterned with large jewels, loose enough that it looked vintage and bohemian, short enough that it somehow covered her ass without looking whorey.

"Hey," she said to the room and made her way around, pressing her cheeks to ours and making kiss noises. She raised a blond eyebrow when she reached Blane. "Blane Baker?"

He looked a little flustered, though he shot her the smile and somehow still looked adorable. "Wow, Astrid Thomas. Good to meet you."

"Likewise," she said, bored by his enthusiasm. She hated when anyone openly acknowledged who she was. She found it tacky, much preferring when people just treated her like she was a normal old nobody. She turned to me. "Is there time to drink?"

I glanced at the clock. "We're supposed to leave in a second."

Rose handed her drink over. "Here, finish mine."

She shrugged as Rose handed it over, knocking it back without so much as flinching. Blane watched, fascinated.

The third knock of the night came, and this time it was Maggie who answered. Patrick stood in the doorway, dressed to the nines in a black-and-white houndstooth tailored shirt and black suit. His jaw and cheekbones were chiseled — seriously, the guy could have actually been a marble statue covered in Sharpie — black hair combed back, eyes on Rose, who stood stock still for a long moment as he walked in. She blinked and took a deep breath, turning to Astrid to hide the fact that she was totally eyeballing her ex.

When I looked back to the door, West stepped from behind Patrick, and every thought left my brain.

His hair was down with those deep ruts in the top from running his fingers through it, somehow keeping it messy and tidy at the same time. He was wearing the suit he'd had on the night before, that glorious suit that made him look like a man who made things happen. My eyes caught on his full lips, framed by his beard, but only for a moment because I could feel his eyes on me like a command. My gaze snapped to his, eyes a shade of electric blue with something burning behind them, something he was trying to hide.

My brow bent in question, asking him what he needed, what he wanted, but he broke the connection, looking across the room at nothing in particular.

I picked up my clutch, shaken, tucking it under my arm as I took Blane's. "Everyone ready?"

A chorus of agreement rolled through the group as we stood packed in our tiny entry, and Patrick opened the door. We filed out, everyone chatting as we walked down the stairs and outside. Patrick and West threw up their hands to hail cabs, and two pulled up, one in front of each of them. Patrick opened the door, and Astrid, Rose, and Maggie ended up in the back seat with Patrick in the front, leaving me, Blane and West to the other cab.

West opened the door for me, and I took a step, but Blane headed me off and climbed in first. West watched him like a starving velociraptor — I could almost feel him seething as I climbed in behind Blane. And six seconds later, I was sitting snugly in the back seat between the two of them.

I crossed my legs toward Blane, and he laid a hand on the outside of my thigh, pulling my legs into his. I wound my arms around his bicep, and he glanced over at me. We smiled at each other. Blane was finally happening.

It was everything I'd hoped for.

West was pushed up against the door, scowling out the window. "So, I'm glad you finally decided to come out with Lily. She's been talking you up an awful lot."

I shot him a look.

Blane looked out the window, sounding bored. "Has she? She's never mentioned you before."

My head swiveled as I pointed the look at Blane instead.

West's voice screwed a little tighter. "Funny, that. Sounds like you guys don't do a lot of talking anyway, so I won't take it personally."

My head spun around again. West had always been a little overprotective of the women in his life, but this was ridiculous. Not that what he'd said was a lie, but still. Inappropriate.

"So," I interjected, desperate to change the subject, "West and I went to the opera last night to see *Madama Butterfly*."

"Oh, was *he* the friend you went with?"

I frowned. "Uh, yes. Do you like the opera?"

Blane made a face. "Not at all."

West laughed, then glanced over at him. "Oh, wait. You're serious."

"The way that they sing is so overdone. Plus, opera is never in English. Why can't they be translated?" He shook his head. "The only time I'm reading subtitles is for Kung Fu."

Satisfaction rolled off of West, and I shifted, taking the opportunity to elbow him. I turned my attention to Blane just as his phone rang in his pocket to the tune of a Nickelback song.

West snorted, trying to cover his laughter with a weak cough as Blane shifted, hurrying to quiet it. He used the arm I was wrapped around to reach into his back pocket, forcing me to lean into West to avoid getting elbowed in the boob. Blane glanced down to see who it was, eyes darting to me as muted it, cutting Chad Kroeger off mid-wail.

"So, Nickelback, huh?" West wasn't even pretending not to be an asshole at that point.

Blane leaned forward to glare at him around me. "What's your problem, man? You've been a dick since you walked through Lilypad's door."

There it is. I braced myself.

West fumed. "Look, I don't have a problem with you, *Blaney.* Not so long as you're good to Lily. You fuck that up, and all bets are off."

"What, are you in love with her or something?"

West's eyes were as hard as diamonds. "Why, are you?"

"Fuck you, bro."

"Don't call me bro, you fuckwit."

"That's enough!" I shouted, head swiveling around so they received equal parts of my rage-stare. "What has gotten into you two? Jesus Christ, I didn't know you were going to bomb the cab with testosterone or I would have gotten my own."

The cab pulled up to the curb, and I glared at West, who didn't move, just stared right back at me. "Let us out, West."

He scowled and opened the door. The interior lights of the cab threw harsh light on us as we scooted out, and West offered me a hand that I batted away, leaving Blane to pay the cabbie. He leaned out, looking sheepish.

"Ah, I don't have any cash."

"Oh," I muttered, caught off guard. I opened my clutch, but West beat me to it.

"You know they take cards, right, asshole?" West shot as he passed the money through the passenger window.

Blane fumed, and West shot me a pointed look. He was close enough that I had a hard time breathing with his eyes boring into mine like they were, but he broke the connection, turning on his heel to walk up to velvet ropes.

Thumping bass marked the silence between West and me as the other cab pulled up in front of the club. I took a moment to look around. A massive line wrapped around the side of the building, jam packed with people who watched us haughtily from behind the velvet rope, like we were just a bunch of schmucks who would end up in line behind them. Normally, they'd be right.

The word NOIR was written in thin gold Art Deco letters above the door, and the architecture was all very 20s — black and gold plated panels, inlaid with swirling patterns that were freeform and geometric all at the same time. The building itself must have been from about the same era — even the stone column façade had a sleek, *moderne* feel.

Everyone climbed out of other the cab as Cooper stepped out of the door and past the bouncer, clapping him on the shoulder as he moved the rope.

Paparazzi came out of nowhere as soon as Cooper appeared, flashes strobing, and bouncers flocked toward us, backing the paparazzi away. I felt like I was caught in a mob as we hurried to the door to the sound of photographers shouting Cooper and Astrid's names.

We didn't stop moving, just made our way inside in a train. I watched West's back as he climbed the stairs ahead of me, the wall he'd thrown up between us feeling like it was a hundred feet tall and bulletproof. But I nearly forgot all about it when Blane touched the small of my back and whispered something dirty in my ear. Something that made me really glad I'd gotten that Brazilian.

The music grew louder with every step until we hit the main floor. The club was beautiful, and I gaped as we walked through. Acrobats spun on hoops suspended from the ceiling above an ocean of sequined bodies, dancing under a cloud of cologne, moving like a wave in time to the music. Everything was black, trimmed with gold in lines, starbursts, and swooping patterns. The bar was sleek, plated in gold with black accents, lit by bright lights that made it shine like gold leaf.

It was like we'd somehow stepped back in time and into the future.

We turned for the stairs up to the VIP floor and past a bouncer who looked like Marcellus Wallace from Pulp Fiction. I'm not gonna lie — I almost tripped looking for a Band Aid on the back of his neck. We kept climbing until we reached the top where the space opened up into a smaller, less crowded version of the club downstairs, with wall-to-wall windows so the elite could watch the peasants from the comfort of bottle service and velvet couches.

Cooper led us to a set of black velvet couches around a low, gold table inset with a chiller, full of ice and bottles of liquor and rocks glasses — real, swanky-ass glass, not plastic — mixers, and garnishes arranged on the surface. Cooper swept a hand over the display, looking pleased with himself, and we all laughed and clapped. He bowed dramatically before making his way through the group passing out kisses to the girls and bro hugs to the guys. He stopped in front of Blane.

"How's it going, man? I'm Cooper Moore. You must be Blane." He extended a hand, and Blane took it, clearly starstruck.

"What's up?"

"Just living the life. You know." He smiled that million dollar smile and gestured to the club behind him. "Come on and have a drink, guys."

Rose hooked an arm in mine and dragged me to the couch with Maggie and Astrid in our wake. We took a seat on the couches, and Rose immediately poured drinks for everyone, passing them to Patrick, who handed them out accordingly.

"What do you think Blane wants to drink?" she said over the music.

I shrugged. "I don't think he likes whiskey."

Astrid snorted. "Maybe you should make him an Appletini, Rose."

I made a face at her before turning back to Rose. "Maybe a vodka tonic would be safe."

She poured his last, but Patrick had already taken the other drinks and walked away. I took it and smiled. "I'll give it to him."

They all nodded at me, not seeming to be as amused as I was. But I didn't care. Nothing was going to get me down tonight.

I stood and tugged my dress down a little before striding over to Blane, who had sort of glommed on to Cooper. Coop just sipped his drink, smiling amiably as Blane went on.

I slipped an arm into Blane's. "Here's your drink."

He smiled down at me and slipped a hand around my waist, fingers grazing my ass. A little shock shot through me. "Thanks, Lily."

"No problem." I looked to Cooper. "Thanks for inviting us. This place is amazing."

"I'm just glad everyone decided to come," he said with a smile, eyes darting over to the couch. I guessed he and Astrid were more into each other than I'd realized, and I smiled back at him.

"Me too. I'm gonna get back to the girls."

"Don't go too far." Blane's voice was silky smooth in my ear.

"You know where to find me." I gave him sexy eyes, I think, and made my way back to the couch with my hips ticking like a metronome to the beat of the music that boomed all around us.

I sat between Astrid and Rose, who handed me a drink. "This is the only one, okay?"

"It's water. I've got your back."

"Thanks, Rosie." I raised my glass, and the girls clinked theirs to mine, but it hadn't yet reached my lips when I caught sight of West leaning against the wall next to Patrick, tall and gorgeous in that suit, arms folded across his chest, eyes like lasers on me, brooding. And I was instantly mad as fuck all over again.

"What the hell is West's problem?" I popped at no one in particular. "He was so rude to Blane in the cab. If I hadn't already been sitting between them, I would have separated them."

Maggie made a weird face. "Ah, uh … I think West

said he and Patrick got drunk last night. Maybe he's just hungover?"

I narrowed my eyes. "He's lucky I'm on a date and don't want to make a scene." I took a sip of my drink.

Maggie smiled, changing the subject while trying to be polite, I suspected. "So, Blane seems nice."

I beamed at everyone. "He's being so sweet, guys. I can actually see how this could work out. Thanks for talking me into this, Astrid. Best idea ever." I raised my glass, and Astrid raised hers in answer with a look on her face.

My eyes narrowed with suspicion before my glass reached my lips. "Why do I feel like you're bullshitting me right now?" I looked at Rose and Maggie too, so they'd know they weren't off the hook either. "What has gotten into everybody? We're at this posh-ass club with sexy dresses and bald vaginas. I can't be the only one excited about this!"

A laugh shot out of Rose. "You're the only one with a squeaky snatch."

"I'm just saying. My dream guy has a chance at redemption, here. Why are we not having fun? Why are we not into this?"

Rose was still smiling, but I didn't buy it. "We're happy for you. I think everyone's just worn out. And the best way to turn that around is *always* whiskey."

We all laughed and raised our glasses, cheering, "*To*

whiskey!" before killing our drinks.

SWAN DIVE

West

AN HOUR LATER, I WAS sitting on the couch alone, watching as Blane leaned into Lily. She was pressed up against the wall looking hotter than I'd ever seen her — legs ten miles long, body wrapped in fabric so blue, it practically gave off its own light. That dress left nothing to the imagination while still possessing class and style, and I hated that she was wearing it for that douchebag.

Lily smiled up at him, and he whispered something in her ear. She laughed — I could almost hear the sound in my burning ears just on memory alone. I squeezed the rocks glass in my hand so tight, I thought it might bust.

But I couldn't tear my eyes away from them, just watched them, torturing myself as I drained my glass, hoping the whiskey would ease my nerves.

It didn't.

Cooper sidled up next to me, and I looked away, feigning indifference.

"You all right?"

"Fine." The word was flat.

He eyed me. "You're really not going to tell me what's going on? You've been watching them all night like … well, like *this*." He gestured to me.

I reached for the bottle of Makers on the table and poured well more than a shot. "What do you want me to say?"

"I just want to know why you look like you're ready to throw that glass."

I stared down at the amber liquid. "Lily and I went to the opera last night." I took a long pull, thankful for the comforting burn of whiskey in my chest.

"Is opera code for something?"

I couldn't look at him. "I'm in love with her, Cooper."

He didn't miss a beat. "What's new?"

I shook my head and killed my drink. "Does everybody know?" My voice was rough.

"Everybody but you and Lily."

"Everybody but Lily, you mean." I poured another drink. "Rose and Patrick said I should wait it out until she got through tonight with Blane, but that's feeling like a fucking terrible idea right about now." My eyes found her again, zeroing in on his hands on her waist. I emptied my glass and set it down, reaching immediately for the bottle.

Cooper watched me. "Yeah, I'm thinking *this* isn't much better."

I scowled at him. "Don't even think about taking my drink. I'll fucking deck you."

He looked genuinely concerned, which was disquieting. "Maybe we should go. Let everyone go to separate corners."

"Yeah, except *they're* going to a corner together." I ran a hand over my beard as sweat beaded on my forehead. My shirt felt like a sauna, and I set my glass down to peel my jacket off. "It's fucking hot in here."

"You're drunk, West."

"I'm fine."

"Your fuck-o-meter is off the charts."

"I *said* I'm fine." I fumed. "I'm not leaving Maggie here, and I'm not leaving Lily alone with that jizzbag."

"Look, I'm not crazy about him either, but he's here with Lily. Don't do anything to embarrass her, or you're fucked."

I eyed Cooper, curious. "What did he say to you when he was talking your face off earlier?"

He shrugged. "The usual. He was trying to impress me, said something nasty about our waitress."

"What did he say about Lily?"

"He didn't mention Lily. But the dude puts out the

scumbag vibe."

I sighed. "Yeah, I know."

I watched Rose walk up to Lily, and the girls leaned together, lips to ears to try to talk under the imposing bass. Blane took the opportunity to check out a girl who walked past our table.

My nostrils flared. "Did you fucking see that?" I was already getting up.

Cooper grabbed me by the arm and pulled me back down. "Whoa, buddy."

I turned to Cooper, throwing a hand in Blane's direction. "Who the fuck is this guy? This is bullshit. She doesn't see what a piece of shit this guy is. Somebody's got to tell her."

"She's not going to listen to us right now."

"Not true. She'll listen to Rose."

His brow was low. "Don't you think Rose sees it too? And she hasn't said anything. There's a reason, West. If you go interrupt her right now to talk shit about Blane, she's going to take his side. You can't tell Lily what to do, man — you've got to let her figure this out."

I shook my head, teeth clenched so tight my jaw hurt. "I don't accept that."

Cooper leaned forward, voice hard. "Listen — tonight you're accepting that, or Tricky and I are going to put you in a cab and fucking send you home. Cool it."

I shook my head, voice rough. "She's driving me crazy, Cooper."

He sighed and nodded. "I get it. I really do, but it's all going to work out. Things like this always do."

I picked up my drink and brought it to my lips. "Tell that to Tricky." I took a heavy swallow.

Cooper huffed and sat back. "That's not the same, and you know it. It's been twenty-four hours since you figured out something we've all known for years. Give yourself a break. It's not like she and Blane are leaving here to go to Vegas."

Rage ripped through me at the thought of the two of them standing in front of an Elvis impersonator at the Chapel of Love.

He shook his head, bewildered. "Damn, dude. Look at you. This is temporary, okay?" He waited for my response.

I sniffed. "Temporary."

"Right. So get your shit together. Now. All right?"

I nodded and took another drink.

"And chill the fuck out on the whiskey, will you?"

"No promises."

"Come on. You need a distraction," he said as he stood. "Let's find Tricky."

I filled my drink again before following Cooper begrudgingly through the club. We found Patrick near the dance floor, leaning against the gigantic speaker boxes between two go-go platforms topped with writhing girls in white wigs and beaded, sheer flapper dresses. They spun around, displaying their lack of undergarments, and Cooper waggled his eyebrows.

I smiled, breathing a little easier, thanks to the distance between me and Lily. Maggie, Rose, and Astrid bounced around on the dance floor with their drinks in the air, occasionally pausing to laugh or yell in each other's ears, taking turns cockblocking any idiot who tried to get between them. One drunk guy got close enough to Maggie to try to dry hump her from behind. I'd already set my drink down and taken three steps onto the dance floor when Maggie turned around and poked him in the shoulder. He made a face and put up his hands, turning to the rest of the crowd to look for another woman to mack on.

After a little bit, I was almost relaxed, laughing with Patrick, watching the girls have a good time. And then Lily walked onto the dance floor.

She ignored me completely, strutting in that dress that hugged her body around every curve. The cut of the neckline was shaped like a heart, and my gaze lingered on her cleavage. She beelined for the girls just as Blane stepped next to Cooper and said something I couldn't hear. Cooper gave him a patronizing nod and glanced at me. I emptied my drink and eyed my glass. But I wasn't about to leave now.

Lily joined the girls in their wiggling, but watching her was different. I noticed everything — her hands, her arms, her long white legs. Her hips as they rolled and she turned. The look on her face, lips parted, eyes down. And then she looked up.

Straight at Blane.

He smiled when she beckoned him, and he stepped onto the dance floor, making his way over to her. Her hands slipped up his chest when she reached him, and his found her waist as their hips pressed together, rolling in time to the music.

I thought I might vomit.

I had to get out of there. I pushed away from the speakers and stormed to the table where I poured myself another stiff drink, trying to get a grip. I had to find a way, or I really would need to leave. Cooper was right — causing a scene couldn't end well for me. I turned to look back to the dance floor and saw Lily with her back to Blane, his hands around her waist as he said something into her ear. She smiled over her shoulder and nodded, and he let her go, heading for the restrooms near the stairs. But when he reached the stairwell, he looked back. He was hidden by a wall of people, and once he saw he was covered, he ducked down the stairs.

I set down my drink, suspicious and determined to figure him out, making to follow him. I watched everyone to see if I could sneak by. The girls were huddled together, laughing, and Patrick and Cooper's backs were to me. I trotted down the stairs after Blane.

I nodded to the bouncer, who I hoped made note of my face, and made my way through the packed club. There were people everywhere, so many I almost felt suffocated after the luxury of VIP. I shuffled my way through the crowd, scanning the faces for Blane, trying to remember what he was wearing. I took a lap around the space, pausing once when a girl touched my arm, sliding her fingers down to my hand where she laced her fingers in mine, tugging me gently toward the dance floor. I shook my head and smiled, looking back in the direction I'd been heading. And that's when I saw him.

Blane was leaned up against the wall, just like he had been earlier with Lily. Except caged in his arms was *not*-Lily. The girl was gorgeous — tall and blond like Lily, but without the grace and polish, wearing a black dress that looked more like a very tight, very low cut shirt. He whispered something in her ear. She nodded, and he took her hand, pulling her toward the bathrooms.

I knew exactly what he was doing, and even then, even knowing, all I could think about was Lily upstairs waiting for him. I could barely see straight as I barreled through the crowd just as they disappeared around the corner.

Within a minute, I was in the big room with hanging chandeliers. There were no gender specific restrooms, just the one room with tall, full-length black doors lining each side. The privacy they allowed was perfect for doing drugs. Or fucking.

I blew to the front of the short line, addressing the girl who was next in line.

"Did you just see a blond guy and a girl in a black dress come through here?"

She was so tan she was nearly orange, with big hair and heavy, fake lashes. She hung a hand on her hip, looking justified. "Yeah, that fucka just cut all-a us. He's lucky I just got my nails done."

Adrenaline pumped through me. "Which stall did they go in?"

"That one." She pointed one long, hot pink fingernail at a door.

My palms were sweaty, hands shaking as I approached the door and reached for the handle, expecting for it to be locked, expecting to beat on it until the piece of shit came out. I only paused for a split second before turning the knob to the unlocked door and pulling it open with a whoosh.

The blond was bent over the toilet, hanging onto a shelf meant for holding drinks with her dress pulled up to her hips and her ass exposed. Blane was behind her with his hands full — let's just say that — as he looked over his shoulder at me with his face twisted up with a variety of emotions … rage, confusion, incredulity.

The girl looked downright mortified. Also high as fuck, with eyes ringed with red and pupils like marbles.

"What the fuck?" Blane shouted.

I barely heard him.

I cocked my fist and released, the crunch of my knuckles against his nose almost as satisfying as the blood that burst out of his nostrils and all over his shirt. The girl screamed as I grabbed a handful of his shirt and dragged him out of the stall, swinging him around before popping him in the eye.

"Fuck!" Blane screamed, hands up and cowering. My chest heaved, fist poised to hit him again. But he looked so pathetic, scared even. He had no fight in him.

I let him go. I don't quite know how, but I let him go.

I shoved a finger in his bloody face. "You fucking leave Lily alone, do you hear me, you piece of shit? You leave her alone, or so help me God, I will fuck you up beyond recognition. You don't deserve her."

"What," he yelled, voice muffled by his swollen nose, "and you think you do? Fuck you, asshole. She's not worth all this shit." He turned and looked into the mirror, eyes flying wide open when he saw his reflection. "My nose. I think you fucking broke my nose."

I shook my head at him, disgusted. "Cry me a river,

you fucking pussy."

I turned and blew out of the restroom with a dozen eyes following me, hands shaking and knuckles raw, not sure what to do with myself. I didn't know how a bouncer hadn't come, and part of me expected one to come at me at any second to kick me out. But when I thought about it, I realized that the whole thing must have only lasted a minute before it was over.

Another part of me was waiting on Blane to stop me and finish the fight. But Blane didn't have the scrote to come after me, or he wouldn't have let me put him down like I did.

The ramifications of what I'd done were lost on me in the moment as I walked through the lights and noise and bodies in a haze. All I knew was that I didn't know what to do, only that I needed to find my friends, so I walked back up the stairs with adrenaline pumping through me so hard, I thought my heart might burst.

When I approached the dance floor in VIP, Cooper and Patrick's eyes met mine, and their smiles slipped off their faces and onto the floor. They hurried over to me, drawing the attention of the girls.

"West?" Patrick asked, uncertain as he looked me over, eyes coming to rest on my hands. "Is that … blood?"

I held them up, inspecting my right hand that was speckled with blood, the skin red and raw, knuckles scraped and swollen.

The girls walked up looking confused, gasping when Blane walked up behind me and blew past, nose a gory mess and eye already swelling closed. He stormed over to the couches where his jacket was, and Lily turned on me, eyes full of hurt and anger. She shoved me with all of her weight.

"What did you do to him, West? What did you do?" she shrieked, not waiting for an answer as she ran after him. He was already stalking back, jacket hanging in his hand as he approached. Lily ran next to him, trying to talk to him. She reached out to touch his arm, but he jerked away.

"Please," she begged. "Just tell me what happened."

He stopped and glared at me. "Your fucking *friend* here just assaulted me."

"But why?" she asked, brows knit together. "Why would he do that?"

He looked right at me. "Because he's a fucking dick." He shook his head, turning to address her, angry and drunk, all pretense of pleasantry gone. His face was hard as stone. "There were two things I wanted. To get into this club, and to get another piece of your ass. The first I got for a bouquet of flowers. The second I don't even want anymore." He took a step closer to where she stood, stunned. "You know, everyone talks about how they've tried to get you into bed, and you shoot them all down like you're better than that. I knew it would be easy for me, and I was right. But let me tell you something, Lily. No ass is worth this bullshit. Not even yours."

I roared, lunging for him, but Cooper and Patrick grabbed me, holding me back as the dickbag shook his head, not even caring that Lily's eyes were full of tears, hands over her mouth and nose as she shook her head right back. I broke away, getting far enough to grab another handful of his shirt before they dragged me back, and Blane shoved me in the shoulder.

"Fuck you."

I strained against Patrick and Cooper. "Real fucking brave, you son of a bitch. Come back here!" I screamed at his back as he marched away. "Let go of me, Patrick. Let me fucking go!"

They didn't relax their grip until Blane was out of sight.

"I can't believe you would do this to me." Lily's voice wavered.

The accusation seared me, and I jerked my arms free. "He's not good enough for you."

Her face bent in anger. "That's not for you to decide. Why would you do this to me?"

"To protect you. He's not a good guy. He—"

"How do you know? I don't tell you not to sleep with Christine or whoever you're hiding from me this week, so you can't tell me who to sleep with, either. It's none of your goddamn business, West."

"I don't want you to get hurt, Lil—"

"You're not my big brother. I'm not going to let you push me around like you do everyone else. You think you know what's best for everyone, but you don't."

"I'm not the bad guy here. For fuck's sake, everyone knew he was wrong for you, *everyone*, but no one would tell you. You know why? Because we respect you. We want you to be happy." Frustration twisted in my chest.

"And you think this makes me happy? You think *this* shows your *respect* for me?" She shook her head, tears rolling down her face. She took a shaky breath. "Why? Why would you do this to me?" she sobbed.

"Because I'm in love with you, Lily." I shot the words at her like arrows, angry and hurt alongside her. I don't know where they came from, but my mouth didn't have permission to use them.

She froze, mouth hanging open, brow bent as a tear rolled down her cheek. "No."

My heart was stone. I couldn't breathe.

Her face wrenched. "You don't get to do that. You wreck everything, ruin everything, and then think you can drop *that* bomb on me in the middle of a fucking nightclub when I'm supposed to be on a date? No. I can't believe you. I can't believe this." She took off past us, and I moved to follow her, but Cooper blocked my path and laid a firm hand on my chest.

"Whoa, buddy. You're not going after her right now."

I watched her disappear down the stairs, taking my heart with her. "I have to talk to her, Coop."

"Nope. No way. You're going to have another drink or ten, and then you're going home with Tricky. Hey, look at me." He patted my cheek to get my attention. "You aren't going anywhere, West. Come on."

He dragged me to the couch as Rose blew past with their bags, and I sat down feeling like a sack of bricks. I told her, and she rejected me. I said it when I knew I shouldn't.

I did exactly what I wanted to do, and it turned out exactly like I hoped it wouldn't.

There was no other solution than to drink whiskey until I couldn't remember my name.

Lily

I wiped my angry tears away as I stormed down the stairs and out the door to the curb, throwing a hand in the air for a cab. One pulled to a stop just as I realized I didn't have my purse.

"Fuck," I squeaked, turning back to look at the entrance like I'd been shot. Rose bounded out of the door with both of our bags. I don't think I'd ever been so glad to see her.

She rushed over to me, searching my face with her hands on my arms. "Hey,"

"God, Rose." My chin quivered as fresh tears rolled down my cheeks.

She pulled me into a hug. "Shh. It's okay."

The cabbie leaned to peer out the open passenger window. "You ladies coming?"

Rose nodded. "Yeah, we're coming. Come on, Lil."

She opened the door, shepherding me into the cab and giving the driver our address. I leaned on the door, staring out the window as Blane's words circled through my brain.

He'd played me so easily.

I was humiliated. Tears burned my eyes as the car took off. "West said you all knew this would happen."

She shook her head. "No one could have known Blane would go so low as to say what he just said to you. This isn't your fault. You didn't do anything wrong."

"Except trust him."

"But you didn't really." She scooted closer and threaded her arm through mine. "Remember how you felt before he brought you vagina lilies? I don't believe that's completely erased by one night of him paying attention to you."

I took a shuddering breath as the tears slipped down my face. "He did everything I wanted. I thought we were … I don't know. I thought we could be together. But I was so stupid. So stupid. It was wrong from the start, and I did it anyway." I couldn't stop crying, and my nose was a mess. I sniffled again, and the cabbie offered a box of tissues through the divider.

"Thank you." I pulled out a tissue, grateful, and he smiled back at me. I blew my nose. "I've never felt like such a fool in my entire life, Rose."

She watched me with sad eyes. "I'm so sorry, Lily."

"I can't believe this. And to top it all off, West …"

She sighed. "I know."

"I can't believe he did this. I can't believe he picked a fight with Blane like that. Do you know what happened?"

Rose shook her head. "I know exactly as much as you do about it. I don't know what made him snap."

I looked out the window and dabbed my nose. "He said he was in love with me. Why would he say that?"

"Probably because he's in love with you."

I shot her a look. "How could I possibly be prepared for him to say that to me after he punched my date in the face? God, I'm so fucking mad at him for this. That was so inappropriate and so upsetting on so many levels." Nausea rolled through me. "We can't go backwards from this. I can't pretend like he didn't say what he said. And now, everything will change." The tears started up fresh. "I don't want it to change. I just want to go back to yesterday when things were normal and fine and not completely fucked up."

She threaded her fingers through mine and squeezed. "It's going to be okay. I promise. Okay?"

I stared out the window through a curtain of tears, not understanding how everything had gone so wrong. Not believing myself when I agreed with Rose.

"Okay."

WRUNG OUT

West

I ROLLED OVER IN BED the next morning feeling like I'd been hit by a truck, body aching from sleeping like I was dead and head pounding from the myriad of bad decisions I'd made the night before. I cracked open my eyes and flinched against the sun, waiting a second before I tried again, blinking against the light. The first thing I did when I finally got them open was drain the glass of water next to my bed. And once I'd set the empty glass down, I lay back, taking a minute after the exertion to stare up at the ceiling.

I'd fucked up. That was all there was to it.

I held up my hand and inspected my swollen, raw knuckles. I felt like I'd done some universal justice, restored balance with something so simple as a broken nose. At least I had that going for me.

Lily was another thing all together. My guts twisted

276

with regret at the thought of her. Or from the whiskey. Maybe both.

I replayed it all again, pictured her face when Blane's words hit her, the look in her eyes when I told her I loved her. I'd just blurted it out like she knew. Maybe part of me thought she did. I knew I felt stupid for not seeing it sooner.

The entire thing was a disaster, and all of it was my doing.

I threw off the covers and got out of bed, pressing the heel of my palm to my eye socket. I vaguely remembered getting shawarma, which was probably the one thing that saved me from expelling the contents of my stomach on my way to the coffee machine.

The argument with Lily rolled through my brain in a loop to the sputtering of the coffee pot. I owed her an apology. I owed her an explanation. But more than that — I just wanted to know that she was all right.

I can't say that a large part of me didn't want to know how she felt about me, about what I'd said after she'd had time to think about it. I needed to know one way or another to put me out of my misery. Even if she shot me down. Even if she didn't want me. I had to know.

Patrick walked out of his room, shirtless and in sleep pants, squinting against the sun, ruffling his hair. "Hey." His voice was thick.

"Didn't mean to wake you."

He waved a hand. "Doesn't take much."

I jerked my chin at him. "Feelin' all right?"

"Decent. You?"

"Depends." I poured us each a cup of coffee, and we made our way into the living room. I dropped into an armchair and propped my feet on the coffee table, and Patrick stretched out longways on the couch.

He shook his head. "Last night was fucked up, man."

"I don't remember much after Lily left. Did it get worse?"

"Past you getting tanked, no."

I sighed. "I'm sorry, man. I knew it was going to be rough, but I never imagined it would be *that* rough."

"I can't even believe Blane. Why would he look for ass when he had Lily right there?"

I bristled at the thought of him and Lily's ass doing anything together. "I don't know. I honestly can't imagine what would have possessed him to do it."

"Not that he seems particularly loyal. Maybe he's just a pussyhound. Maybe Lily isn't the only one." He took a sip of his coffee.

"It would make sense, but that almost makes me feel worse. Did you talk to Rose? Is Lily okay?"

"I texted her last night when you weren't looking, which wasn't easy. I had to take your phone so you wouldn't call her."

I ran a hand across my forehead. "Thank you."

"No problem. Rose said she was okay. Angry and hurt, but okay."

I stared at a spot on the coffee table. "I've got to talk to her today."

Patrick shook his head, voice full of warning. "Bad idea, West."

But I shook my head right back. "I listened to y'all when you said to wait to tell her, and look how that turned out. I'm through taking advice. I'm just gonna do what I think is right."

Patrick snickered. "Like punch Blane in the face?"

That memory was a small comfort. "Man, it felt so good. *So* good." But I sighed. "Still a bad move."

"I would have done the same thing, if it had been me. No way I would have let that fuck get away with what he did."

"Did you tell Rose why I hit him?"

"No. I didn't know what you wanted to do, so I kept it to myself."

"Lily needs to know I didn't pick a fight with him for no reason, and I think it might help her move on to know he's not who she thought he was. I don't want her to get hurt."

"Might be too late for that."

I rubbed my beard. "Maybe. But could I save her

from more pain?"

"I still think you need to give her time to process what happened. What if you tell Rose what happened and let her tell Lily?"

I shook my head. "It needs to come from me. I'm the one who saw it. I'm the one who broke his nose."

Patrick laughed again. "Man, I wish I'd seen that."

I couldn't help but smile. "It was so good, though I think he was more worried about his pretty face than me telling Lily." My smile slipped away. Out of nowhere, I was pissed again, anger charging through me, uninvited. "Fuck that guy. Fuck him for hurting her. Fuck him for using her, that son of a bitch."

I seethed for a minute while Patrick sipped his coffee and let me stew. He eventually broke the silence.

"When are you going over there?"

"I don't know. She'll be gone in a few hours until late tonight, and I don't want her to go all day without at least apologizing. I'm sure she's up already. So, soon, I think. Otherwise, I'll have to wait until who knows when."

"You two are so much alike, even down to your sleep habits. I can't believe you never realized it before."

"She was off the table, Patrick — always. From the minute we met, she told me she wasn't interested in dating anyone but her career. And I was dating Shannon at the time. We started off with the unspoken agreement that we would only ever be friends. So when we would have these … moments, you know? Like I would see her doing something mundane, or she'd say something that made me laugh and feel and … I don't know. *Want* her. But I'd push the idea away like I was crazy because we were never supposed to be anything but friends."

"I get that," he said simply.

"And now I know there's more to it, and you can't *un*-know something like that. I want her, Patrick. I need her. Even if I can't have her the way I want, I'll take what I can get because I can't live my life without her in it."

Patrick was stoic and humble. "You should tell her just like that."

I looked away. "I only hope I have the chance to tell her anything at all."

Lily

My bed was a cocoon of fluffy bedding, illuminated by the morning sun shining through my window.
Everything was bright and fresh, cheery and peaceful.

Clearly, the universe was mocking me.

I felt like a wad of gum on somebody's shoe. Smashed. Sticky. Unwanted. Stretched out, chewed up, and discarded.

It was late when we got home, but the first thing Rose did was pour us each a whiskey, which I accepted. I accepted the second one too. And the third. It was the only way I'd be able to sleep, I knew, and as I stretched in bed, I was grateful to realize I wasn't hungover. My stomach was a little tender, but the rest of me was in working order.

I only wish the whiskey could have erased everything that had happened. In a few hours, I'd have to go to the theater and see Blane — the second biggest offender on my list.

I didn't even want to think about West.

I'd be busy enough at work today that I could avoid him, and I was banking on him being too hungover this morning to catch me before I left. I didn't have any idea what to say to him. I was no closer to understanding how I felt about any of it than I'd been the night before.

The sting from Blane's words were still fresh, and the humiliation of being spoken to that way in front of my friends was the salt in the wound. I knew this was it, the last chance, and part of me figured it might be over after that, even though I was hoping it would work out. But I never, ever expected all that to go down. I never thought Blane could hurt me that badly.

I was glad West got a piece of him, even if it was horribly overbearing.

He was a whole other issue. I stared up at my

ceiling, trying to sort it out. He told me he loved me. Shock ripped through my chest again at the thought. I didn't know how I was supposed to feel, but everything made a lot more sense when I framed it up. It was no wonder West was such a dick to Blane all night.

But when it came to me figuring out how I felt, I was lost. I thought about almost kissing him, thought about my jealously over Christine. And then, there was that dream. My body responded to the memory, and I huffed, hating myself. I didn't know what any of it meant. I was still too pissed to even consider not being pissed.

So for now, I didn't want to see anyone.

I heard the front door open, and my face twisted up. There was only one person who it could be.

I flipped off my covers. *I'm going to lose my fucking shit. How dare West use his key to come into my apartment without even knocking after everything last night, that fucking jerkass,* I ranted in my head as I stormed out of my bedroom.

Maggie froze in the middle of the living room, still in her dress from last night, shoes dangling from her fingers and hair a mess.

"Maggie?" I asked like an idiot. "Wait, did you just get home?"

She blushed, brows raising as she put down her shoes and bag. "Please don't tell West."

"You don't have to worry about me telling West

anything, maybe ever again." She frowned, and I changed the subject. "So who's the guy?"

She blinked at me, looking put on the spot.

"Or girl?"

Her blush deepened. "Guy, and nobody."

"Ooooh, a one night stand? Scandalous. Details." Anything to save me from my own mess. I made my way into the kitchen to brew coffee, and Maggie sat down at the table with bright eyes.

She nudged her wild hair, trying to tame it without seeming to know where to start. "Well, he's *super* hot, funny, smart. But he's kind of a whore."

"I think they prefer the term *experienced.*"

She giggled. "Well, he's *definitely* experienced. I mean, I didn't know a man's mouth could do some of the things his did."

"Like in the downtown, central neighborhood?"

"Mmhmm," she hummed.

"So Jimmy never …"

She rolled her eyes. "Nope. I had no idea what I was missing. Before Jimmy, all the guys I dated were too young to know how to really do *that.* I can only imagine that it takes years of practice, which is why I probably won't see him again."

I chuckled. "Aww. What about just keeping him around to rock your vagina out? I don't know if you should squander such a gift."

Maggie laughed and shook her head. "If my brother knew you were trying to talk me into a bootie call, he'd flip."

"Well, luckily your brother doesn't get to decide what I think of things." I shifted in my seat. "So you're really not going to see him again?"

"Maybe. He wants to, but I don't know. I don't want to get involved. I mean, I just moved here, and after everything that happened with Jimmy … I just kind of want to be *unattached* for a while, you know?"

"Trust me, I know. Well, good for you, Mags. At least somebody got laid last night."

"I'm so sorry about Blane, Lily."

"Don't be. Better to find out now, right?"

Shc gave me a comforting smile. "Right."

Someone knocked on the door, and Maggie and I exchanged confused looks. My brow quirked as I got up and peered through the peephole to find West leaning against the doorframe. I spun around, mostly angry but with a traitorous hint of excitement.

I punted that thought straight to hell.

I mouthed *West* at Maggie, pointing to our room, and she hauled ass out of there fast enough that I think she left some bobby pins behind. I turned back for the door with my jaw square and my heart in my throat.

When I pulled it open, it sucked the scent of him straight into me in a whoosh. "What?" I demanded.

His voice was soft. "Can I come in?"

I clenched my teeth hard and released. "Fine." I moved out of the way, and he walked in, hands in his pockets. God, he looked good. He really did. It pissed me off even more. He had no right to be that hot in jeans and a T-shirt and his hair in that stupid bun. Fucker.

He stopped in the middle of the room with a hangdog look on his face. "I owe you an apology, Lil. Last night was a mistake."

I fumed. "You're damn straight it was, West."

His brow dropped, blue eyes sparking like he knew I was justified, but that didn't stop him from being upset about it. "I stepped over more than one line. But last night, I didn't just go after Blane."

I folded my arms across my chest and raised a brow.

He put a hand up in surrender, nodding. "Okay, I kind of went after him, but I didn't pick a fight with him for no reason."

I eyed him. "Go on."

His face somehow looked even more serious, and he leaned against the back of the couch. "I followed him when he went downstairs, and when I found him, he was with somebody."

That simple sentence sent me reeling as anger and shame washed over me. "Somebody who?"

He shook his head, quiet for a moment as he

grappled with how to say what he came to say. "A girl. And when he took her to the bathrooms, I couldn't let it go. I … well, I had to see for myself. He had her … he was—"

I held up a hand with last night's dinner in my throat. "He was fucking her? Just to be clear here."

He nodded solemnly.

"And that's when you hit him?"

"Yes." The word was a simple confession.

I couldn't move, couldn't think. Questions and visions and a million thoughts flew around my brain, crashing together and smashing like glass.

"I shouldn't have hit him, but I can't say I'm sorry. Not for that. But for everything else, I am."

I added disappointment to my pile of emotions. He was sorry he told me he loved me, and I couldn't understand why that made me feel so lost. "Everything?"

Every curve of his face told me how much he hurt. "I shouldn't have told you like I did, but it's the truth. I won't apologize for loving you."

My food charged up my esophagus, and I ran for it, straight into the bathroom, barely making it in time. I hung over the toilet, holding my hair back, retching until it was over. I sucked in a breath through my nose, and the smell of whiskey roundhoused me in the stomach, sending me on another round.

I didn't realize he'd followed me until his hand shifted on my back as I hung onto the porcelain with my eyes closed and nose running. He handed me a glass of water that I accepted gratefully, using it to rinse out my mouth.

Physically I was as good as new. My emotions were another story completely.

"I'm sorry," I croaked into the toilet.

His voice was soft and deep. "Don't be sorry."

I unfolded myself, and he moved out of the way, helping me up as we stood. His eyes told me so much as he looked down at me, and I wished I had the answers to the questions that lay behind them. But I didn't. Tears pricked the corners of my eyes, burned my nose. "I don't know what you want me to say, West. I don't know what to say."

He flinched, brow low. "I'm sorry, Lily. I didn't say it to hurt you. I just couldn't go on another second without you knowing how I felt. I'd been watching you all night with him, wanting nothing more than to pop him in the face and kiss you until you couldn't remember your name. And when I followed him, when I saw what he did, I couldn't stop myself. He hurt you, and I couldn't stand by and watch. You asked me why I did it, so I told you the truth. I did because I love you."

My heart stopped when he said it again, like it was the simplest, most natural thing in the world.

"Not just like that. You're the most important person in my life. That'll never change, whether you feel the same way or not."

"But I can't pretend that I don't know how you feel about me." I tried to take a breath. "I can't … I don't …" I lost the tenuous hold on my tears, and they rolled down my cheeks, fat and hot.

West shook his head, face full of pain. "Don't cry. Please don't cry." He pulled me into his chest, and I lost any pretense of composure that I had with his arms around me and his cheek pressed against my hair. I cried for my friendship that would never be what it was and for my heart that was scrambled up and bruised. I cried for my humiliation and cried for my lost dreams. I cried until I was dry, standing there in my bathroom that smelled like puke and whiskey in my best friend's arms.

My best friend who loved me.

I couldn't make sense of any of it.

"Just give me some time," I whispered, eyes closed, overwhelmed as I wondered why being in his arms made me feel like everything would be all right.

He rubbed my back, and his voice was rough with emotion when he said, "All right, Lil. I'm here. I'm always here."

IF IT'S NOT ONE THING

Lily

A FEW HOURS LATER, AFTER a long, hot shower and a stout cup of coffee, I pulled open the studio door for barre class with my stomach in knots.

I was nearly the last one there, and all eyes flew to me, my entrance marked by a few snickers and whispers, but mostly just a host of judging eyes, including Nadia's. Okay, Nadia wore something closer to murder eyes, but everyone else was just judging me. They knew. I didn't know exactly *what* they knew, but they knew enough. I wanted to melt into the floor and disappear.

Until I saw Blane.

He scowled at me from across the room, nose fat and red, his eye swollen shut and purple. The satisfaction of seeing West's handiwork overcame my anxiety completely, washing it away in a breath.

A smug smile stretched across my face as I strutted across the room, shaking my head.

"Looking good, Blane." I dropped my bag under the barre next to Jenni and bent over to unzip it.

"Fuck you, Lily."

A few *Ooohs* and whispers broke out, but they couldn't touch me, not anymore. "No, thanks. I've had better orgasms on the snowmobile game at Dave and Buster's."

A gratifying chuckle rolled through the room as I grabbed my pointe shoes and sat, pulling one shoe on.

Nadia made a noise and hung her hands on her hips, eyes narrowed to slits. "What the fuck is that supposed to mean, Blane?"

He glared at me, though his face softened when he looked back to Nadia. "Nothing. Absolutely nothing."

I didn't look up, just smiled at my fingers as they wrapped my ribbon. "You weren't calling it nothing when you nailed me in your studio the other night. Oh, or when you brought me flowers. That was so sweet, by the way. Thoughtful, even."

Nadia sucked in a breath that I'm almost positive also sucked out Blane's soul. "You son of a bitch."

"I knew it," Jenni whispered, and I glanced over at her, confused. She was staring at Blane with her face blank, but when she looked over at me, I knew instantly what she was going to say. "I'm so sorry, Lily. I didn't know he was with you too."

Fury blew through me like hot, angry wind, taking my breath with it. "Oh, my god, Jenni." I stood, one shoe on, one off. "Were you fucking Nadia too?"

The look on Nadia's face said the answer was yes.

My eyes narrowed to slits. "Jesus Christ, Blane. Is there anyone you *weren't* fucking?"

Bastian raised his hand, looking mock hurt.

"You're the lucky one, Bas." I lasered in on Blane. "You're unbelievable. And here I thought you fucking some random skank in a club bathroom was a fluke." Nadia gasped. "Did you really think we weren't going to find out?"

He shrugged, but his eyes were hard on mine. "Did you really think I cared about you?"

I laughed to hide my hurt. "Look at what you got for your trouble. A face that looks like it went through a meat grinder, and the wrath of three piranhas in tutus. You should know better than to fuck with us. You dated the one with the sharpest teeth for years."

Nadia's voice trembled. I don't think she'd looked away from Blane. "Never again."

He touched her arm, his voice desperate. "Nadia, I —"

She jerked away from him. "I said *never.*"

The tension in the studio was marred by Ward's entrance, and we all immediately broke away and turned to prep for class. Cardinal rule for my job: Check your shit at the door. Bringing your personal life into the studio was the best way to lose the respect of the masters, and potentially future roles.

Ward glanced around the room, steely eyes bouncing between Jenni, Nadia, and me before resting on Blane. "What happened to your face, Baker?"

Blane glared at me. "*Lily's* friend hit me last night at a bar."

Ward narrowed his eyes at me. "Is that true?"

I took a deep breath and held up my chin with all eyes on me. I could perform in front of hundreds of pairs of eyes watching me, but somehow enduring the scrutiny in the studio was unbearable. "Yes, sir."

Ward's disapproving gaze nearly killed me. "I saw Baker coming from a mile away, but I didn't expect this kind of behavior from you, Thomas." He turned to address the room. "What you do in your personal time is your own business, but when it interferes with *my* rehearsals and *my* show, we have a problem."

"But, sir—" Blane started.

Ward shot him a look that stopped him dead. "I don't know what happened between you two, and I don't care. It's over." He clapped, snapping us all out of the trance. "Let's go." He motioned to the pianist, who began to play the slow warm-up music.

I hurried to my bag and sat to get my other shoe on

in a rush as Ward gave us the first round of choreography, my heart banging as I stood and jumped in. Plié. *Fuck him.* Effacé. *I'm a fool.* Plié. *Poor Jenni.* Effacé. *I can't believe this.* Rond de jambe. *Poor Nadia.* Plié. *Wait, what?*

My thoughts had quieted by a degree by the end of barre, only because it had taken every bit of concentration I had to get through the series of entrechats — the quick jumps and footwork were too much for my whiskey-worn body. I just had to get through rehearsals today and *Morgen* tonight, and then I was off for a day. And I would spend that day sleeping.

I pulled on my booties over my pointe shoes and grabbed my bag, wanting to get out of that room as soon as possible. The whispers and looks had started up again, and I was sweating, not only from barre, but because I felt exposed, vulnerable. The day was going to suck. Blane and I were dancing together for *Morgen,* and we had stage rehearsal that afternoon. It was the absolute last place I wanted to be. The absolute first place being at the bottom of a bottle of gin.

I hung my bag on my shoulder, eyes on the ground as I blew out of the room with Jenni on my heels.

"Lily, please wait. I'm so sorry. I didn't know."

I shook my head, but I couldn't even look at her. "It's okay, Jenni. Neither did I. You have nothing to be sorry for."

"That doesn't stop me from being sorry all the same."

I reached the elevator well but turned for the stairs, not wanting to stop moving. Bastian caught up with us just as we reached the end of the hall.

"Slow down, sister." Bastian said lightly, trying to defuse me. It didn't. "Are you okay?"

I pushed open the door with a smack. "Of course I'm not okay." The words echoed in the stairwell as I trotted down the stairs.

"I'm so sorry," he said.

I spun around when I hit the landing, and they almost ran into me. "Stop apologizing. It's nobody's fault but Blane's."

Bastian's face was soft. "I tried to tell you last night, but you took off."

Jenni shook her head at him, hurt. "Why didn't you tell me about Lily, Bastian?"

"Because it wasn't my secret to tell."

"But mine was?"

"You said you were going to tell her, Jen. I knew what was going on with her and Blane and thought I could help soften the blow by telling her first."

"I just can't believe this," Jenni said. "I feel so stupid. I knew you liked him, but I didn't know if it was still serious after all these years. The entire time, I felt guilty. I shouldn't have done it in the first place. I'm so

sorry I didn't talk to you about it first, and afterward …
well, I was waiting until we had a minute alone to tell
you."

I was mostly numb, except for my chest, which
bubbled with red hot fucking hate magma. Not at Jenni,
and not even at Nadia anymore. Only at Blane. "When
did it happen?"

Her brows knit together with concern and hurt.
"Before the show, night before last."

I blew out a very controlled breath. "He asked what
I was doing that night, but I had plans, so he mauled
me in the elevator. He was pissed when I shut him
down." I ran a hand over my face. "God, this is such a
mess, and for nothing. He was the worst lay I've ever
had."

Jenni snorted, and I watched her shoulders relax
with relief that I wasn't going to deck her, I'm sure. "I
mean, seriously. I knew Nadia was a frigid bitch, but
can you imagine how awkward their love life is?"

"*Was,*" Bastian interjected.

"Was." I took comfort in the fact that Blane was
currently alone. Not even Nadia had his back anymore,
that's how bad it was.

Bastian shook his head and started walking again,
and Jenni and I picked up our feet and followed. "He's
not worth any more pain or stress."

I sighed. "It's not that easy, Bas. It's like slamming

your hand in a door. It hurts like a motherfucker, partly because you feel so stupid." They chuckled, but I shook my head. "I should have known better."

"To be fair," Bastian interjected, "have you seen his ass?"

"No ass is worth all that." I repeated Blane's words, and the comfort I found in the new meaning did it's part to dampen the pain.

Lily

Rehearsal dragged on through the day, and I didn't see Blane again until our stage rehearsal for *Morgen* that afternoon. I survived by pretending Blane didn't exist, like he was just a prop for me to dance with, a soulless tool. It wasn't too far off, at least.

We stood at opposite ends of the stage afterward, the six of us listening as Ward gave us final instructions and dismissed us. I was anxious to get out of there, but hadn't made it but a handful of steps when Ward called my name.

I turned, trying not to look nervous as he waved me over to where he stood near the edge of the stage, away from the pit where the orchestra packed up, away from the dancers as they dispersed. Blane looked back at us, jaw set before he disappeared backstage.

Ward's lips were thin, brow low. Disappointed.

My chest ached.

"I've watched you since you first came to SAB, Lily. The first time I ever saw you dance, I knew that you had something special, knew you would make it far. I wanted to promote you in your first year with the company, did you know that?"

I looked down, humbled. "No, sir."

"We wanted to watch you grow, and you have. Since we promoted you, you've exceeded every expectation. You've been given an opportunity. Don't throw it away. I expect professionalism from all of you. What I *don't* expect is to hear another word about this. If I walk into rehearsal with my dancers fighting again, there will be consequences for all of you. Am I clear?"

"Yes, sir." The words burned my throat.

His face softened by a degree. "I'm only telling you this because I believe in you. I want you to succeed. But succeeding in this company means keeping your head in the game."

"I understand," I said quietly. "Thank you, sir."

He nodded, and I turned and walked away, trying not to hurry as tears burned my eyes. Everyone was gone, backstage quiet as I pulled on clothes over my leotard and scooped up my bag. I flew out of the building, needing distance and time.

I had five hours before the show, and there was only one place I wanted to go, one person who I wanted to talk to.

I headed for the subway station and popped in my earbuds as I made my way toward Columbia.

West

I leaned back in Blackwell's office chair that afternoon, fingers to my lips as I read through an essay. It was impressive — collected and poignant. I flipped back to the beginning and made a note of the student's name, eager to show Blackwell.

I usually spent Sunday afternoons working at the university, finding it easier to focus in the quiet of the empty campus than in my apartment with the distractions of my friends. Especially today. I didn't want to see anyone. I knew they'd all have questions for me that I wasn't ready to answer. I didn't want to talk about Lily with anyone but Lily.

I'd left her apartment that morning with our future up in the air and the feeling of her in my arms still fresh. I'd admittedly been hanging on to the hope that she would tell me she felt the same way about me. But she was confused and upset, still trying to process it all. I couldn't blame her for that. But I wasn't confident the odds would turn up in my favor.

I had the impending feeling that she was going to let me down, let me go. I just hope she did it gently.

Someone knocked on the door and I looked up, surprised. "Come in."

The door opened, and Christine stood in the doorway looking hopeful.

My face hardened. "Yes?"

She bit her lip and stepped in, leaving the door open. "I was hoping I'd find you here today. I looked for you Friday, but—"

"What do you want, Chris?" I hadn't realized how upset I still was and took a breath, trying to temper my anger.

She walked up to the desk more nervous than I think I'd ever seen her. The confident woman I knew was nowhere to be found. "I'm sorry. I really am."

I softened when I realized how much she meant it.

She searched my face. "I know we talked about not being exclusive, about not being together. It was fine at first, but one day I realized how much I care about you. I want more. I just didn't handle it well. I was afraid of … well, *this*."

"But I didn't want more."

Hurt passed across her face. "You've never thought about me that way? You never considered more?"

I sighed and stood, feeling guilty and responsible as I walked around the desk to sit on the surface in front of her. "Of course I considered it, Chris. But we're not the same, you and I. I don't love you. We barely know each other, when you think about it."

She shook her head and stepped closer. "I don't believe you mean that. I know you can feel it. We're good together, West." She laid a hand on my chest, and I covered it with mine. "This makes sense."

"Only in that it's convenient," I said gently. "I'm in love with someone else. I can't be with you, and I can't pretend that I am. And after what you said at the party …"

"I just thought that if I could show you how it felt to be with me, you'd see. You'd understand. You'd want to try."

"I'm sorry." I moved her hand and held it in my lap.

"So it's over?" There were tears in her eyes.

I nodded. "It's over."

Chris took a deep breath, lips bent in a sad smile. "Then there's nothing I can do but say goodbye." She cupped my jaw and kissed me, a final, reverent act.

Before I could pull away, I heard a gasp and broke away. I looked around Chris to find Lily in the doorway, hand over her mouth and eyes wide. She blinked and spun around, disappearing from my view in a breath.

"Lily," I said softly, hearing the pain in my voice. I shook my head and stood. "I'm sorry, Chris." I took off, bounding out of the door.

I caught sight of her at the end of the hall, hurrying away, and I called her name. She didn't turn, didn't stop, not until I caught up with her.

"Please, stop." I touched her arm, and when she whirled around, she broke my heart. Tears streaked her pink cheeks, eyes sparkling with pain as she looked up at me. "It's not what you think, Lil."

She closed her eyes and shook her head. "It doesn't matter, West. I don't have any rights to you. You can kiss whoever you want."

"No, I can't." *I love you. I need you.* The words piled up in my throat. "Chris came to apologize, and I told her goodbye. I don't want her. You know that." I wanted to touch her so badly in that moment, slip a hand into her hair and kiss her. I clenched my fists.

Lily nodded, but she wouldn't meet my eyes. "I'm sorry I showed up unannounced. I just … it was just a hard day, and I needed … I wanted …" She looked down at her hands, unable to finish, just took a shaky breath.

"Come here." I pulled her into my chest, held her in my arms, and she melted into me. "What happened?" I asked after a moment.

She didn't answer right away, and I felt her chest rise and fall against me as she sighed. "Blane was sleeping with Nadia and my friend Jenni, too. None of us knew."

I drew in a breath as a cold tingle climbed up my neck. "That motherfucker."

"And we all figured it out just before rehearsal. Blane and I got into it, and Ward was pissed. He pulled me aside and talked to me, warned me that my reputation was in danger. He was so disappointed in me." Her voice broke.

I squeezed her tighter with my heart aching under her cheek. "It's all right. It's going to be all right."

Lily sniffled. "I couldn't stay at the theater, and I didn't want to go home. I just wanted to … I don't know. I needed to see you." She pulled away, wiping her cheek with the flat of her hand. She still wouldn't look at me. "I should go."

The hurt was almost unbearable. "I'm sorry. For everything."

"It's not your fault."

"That's not entirely true."

She finally looked at me, eyes full of regret.

"Talk to me, Lily."

But she just shook her head again and backed away. "I really should go. I still have the show tonight to get ready for." With every step she took, my world got a little colder. "I'll see you later, okay?"

I nodded, unable to speak, and she smiled sadly before she turned and walked away from me. And all I could do was watch her until she was out of sight.

BAPTISM BY LIQUOR

Lily

I HURRIED DOWN THE HALL fighting back tears, rode down the elevator trying to hold them back, but I couldn't — they found a way to escape, even with my eyes clenched shut. I barreled out of the building and toward the subway with my mind racing and heart pounding, wishing he'd followed me and glad he didn't.

The image of Christine kissing him was burned into my mind, and I couldn't push it away. I believed him, believed every word. I knew he didn't want her, but that moment when I thought it was all a lie had gutted me, leaving me empty. But then he held me in his arms again, and my heart filled back up, even though it hadn't stopped spinning from the confusion of it all. I needed him for comfort — it was the reason I'd gone there in the first place. And somehow, I felt better and worse.

My heart ached the entire way back to the Lincoln Center, burned as I pulled on my pointe shoes and turned on Tchaikovsky, broke when I danced the last act of *Swan Lake* all alone in the studio. I felt Odette's longing, her loss. Her pain was my own as I moved to the music with tears streaming down my cheeks.

I opened my arms, reaching for the prince who I could never have, moving backwards, saying goodbye, gripped by emotion from the dance and the story. From my naiveté and my confusion.

Nothing would ever be what it was before.

The room was bathed in the pinks and yellows of dusk as I dropped to the ground, arms around my waist, squeezing to hold myself together. I had no answers, only hurt and loss and confusion. But I exorcised the emotions one by one, tear by tear until there were no more left to cry. I wiped my cheeks with the flats of my palms and breathed, finding the peace after the deluge, with more clarity than I'd felt in days.

I peeled myself off the floor, feeling alone as I made my way to my bag, pulling out my phone to text Rose, knowing what would make me feel better.

Go out with me tonight.

My phone buzzed in my hand. *What happened to not drinking ever again?*

I think we both knew that was a lie. It's been a rough day. Please?

Of course I'll go with you. Are you okay?

I'll be okay. See you at home.

K. Xoxo

I wiped my runny nose and packed up my things. It was almost time for the show, so I made my way to the stage, calm and a little numb, like a stone in the bottom of a river. I didn't speak much, only what was necessary to do my job. I put on my makeup on autopilot, donned my Carolina Herrera costume in a daze. I twisted up my hair and sprayed it with an obscene amount of hairspray, sewed up my shoes and put them on. And then, it was time to dance.

We danced *Morgen* accompanied by a soprano opera singer, three couples who switched partners through the course of the piece, each dancer looking for love wherever they could find it. It was sort of like my own life, especially when Blane and I danced, our drama forgotten as we wooed each other for the sake of the story. For a moment, I believed it, poured myself into the movement, into the piece. There was just that small moment of joy, and then I passed him by, moved to another man, and Blane found another girl.

West was in my thoughts, in my heart as I danced through the precious time on stage. And then it was over. The piece. The night. My banged-up heart.

We left the stage to the sounds of applause, and I rode the high once more with my mind a twisted knot, willing everything to work itself out so I could find a way to move on.

Lily

"No, Rosie. There's no amount of lube that could have helped me survive Blane."

She laughed so hard, she snorted. It was the tiniest, cutest thing, and we laughed even harder, that silent laugh where your face is twisted up and you can't breathe. And when you finally *can* breathe, you suck in air like a donkey.

There was a lot of breathless donkey laughing happening that night.

As soon as I caught my breath, I picked up my whiskey from the high-top bar table and took a drink. We were tucked into a corner of Habits, exactly where we'd been for hours as I tried to make sense of my life. I'd passed the heavy, pity party portion of the sob-sesh and was well into the Lily-forgets-to-give-a-fuck portion of the night. I was at least four drinks in. Maybe five. Who knew how many Rose had.

We were mostly tanked.

I giggled, watching Rose crack up. "Seriously, though. He just stuffed it in. So awkward. I don't even know how that felt good for him because I know it didn't feel good for me. Maybe he's just not used to normal vaginas." I perked up. "Maybe Nadia's vag is like a swamp. Like, he just rams it in, and it makes that sound like when your boot gets stuck in the mud." I made a rude noise with my mouth, and Rose laughed so hard she couldn't open her eyes. She made a windshield wiper motion with her hand. I think she wanted me to stop.

"Fuck, I can't, Lily. I seriously—" She made some squeaking sounds.

"How can someone that hot be that bad in bed? How is that possible? It was the worst. Like what I'd imagine it would be like to fuck Pinocchio."

Rose hung her arms in the air, dangling them like a marionette as tears rolled down her face. "I'm a real boy!"

I cackled.

She wiped off her cheeks. "Goddammit, I haven't laughed that hard in forever."

I propped an elbow on the table, holding up my drink. "I'm glad my pathetic sex life amuses you. Am I talking loud? I feel like I'm talking loud."

She waved her hand. "Nah, you're fine."

It made me feel so much better about everything to laugh about it. "I don't know what I ever saw in him." I took a drink.

"Astrid called it Blane's douchesparkle."

A laugh shot out of me. "That's so accurate." I

emptied my glass and shook it to clink the ice around inside.

Rose made a face. "Ew, don't do that to flag Shelby down. Haven't I taught you anything?"

I laughed as Shelby walked up, a tiny thing with freckles and caramel colored hair. "You're so pretty, Shelby. You look like a beautiful little fairy. Did anyone ever tell you that?"

She smiled, amused. "Not recently."

"Well, it's true. I'm glad you're here because I need more whiskey!" I crowed.

Shelby nodded with her eyebrows up. "Uh-huh. You look like you need lots more whiskey. Another for you too, Rose?"

Rose shrugged lazily. "Eh, why the fuck not."

"Okay, girls. Be right back," she said before heading back to the bar.

I leaned toward Rose. "I'm prolly going to regret this in the morning, aren't I?"

"Probably," she answered.

I shook my head at my empty glass. "I can't even believe I'm doing this right now. Tomorrow, I'm getting my shit together."

She snorted. "Starting where?"

I rolled my eyes. "Ha, ha. Starting with not drinking, catching up on my sleep, and eating clean."

"And then what?"

My nose wrinkled. "And then, I don't know."

Rose nodded and twisted up her long black hair, throwing the rope of hair over her shoulder. "What are you going to do about West?" She took a drink.

I took a breath and let it out. "I don't know that either. I went to see him today."

She raised a brow. "At Columbia?"

"Mmhmm."

Shelby brought us fresh drinks, and I grinned at her. "Thanks, Shelb."

"No prob. Now pipe down. You're scaring Bob." She jerked her chin toward Bob, who slumped over the table, snoring.

We laughed as Shelby walked away.

"What were we talking about?" I asked.

"You went to Columbia today?"

I nodded as I picked up the drink. I couldn't feel my lips, but I *could* still feel the residual shock from my surprise visit to see West that afternoon. Thanks to whiskey, my feelings were muffled enough that I could pretend to be blasé. "He was kissing Christine in his office."

Rose's eyes bugged, and she set her drink down, gaping. "He what?"

"She came to talk to him, and he broke it off for good, I guess. That's what he says, at least."

"Do you believe him?"

"I do. After everything with Blane and Nadia and Ward, I just needed to see him. And he made me feel … I don't know, Rosie. Safe. I'd had this horrible day, and then he put his arms around me, and nothing could touch me. Everything made sense. For a minute at least."

"The question is, do you want to be with him?"

I looked down at my drinks. There were two of them, and I closed one eye so there was only one. *That's better.* "I dunno. I feel about West like I feel right now. Like I've got double vision, and I can't tell which West is the real one. Is it my friend I've known all these years? Or is it the mirror of him, like a mirage? A shade of himself, the part of him that I don't know. Am I making sense?"

She nodded. "No."

I laughed and shifted in my seat, leaning forward. "Okay, so there's this West that I know so well. Let's call him Friend West. And then there's this other part of him that I have no idea about. Let's call him Boyfriend West. I know how I feel about Friend West. But Boyfriend West? No idea. It's like having double vision. I can see them both, but I don't know which one to grab, and only one of them is right. And if I try to grab the wrong one, I might spill the drink all over myself."

"That's fucking deep, Lily," Rose said reverently.

I scanned the bar with one eye closed. "I need an

eyepatch."

Her face lit up. "Oh! We should make disposable eye patches for drunk people in foil packets like condoms."

"You're a genius, Rosie." I raised my hand for a high five.

She slapped my palm. "I really am. Flower power, activate. So you need a life eyepatch. Which West should you choose? Let's make a pros and cons list."

"Seriously, how did you get so smart?" I pulled a receipt and a pen out of my purse. "Okay. Cons." I chewed the end of my pen. "I can't think of any. Oh, wait. When we break up, we'll still have to be around each other." I jotted it down.

"I mean, that's workable, but it's super awkward. Trust me."

"Still. Definitely a con. Okay, so what else?" I squinted up at the exposed pipes in the ceiling. "I could lose him forever."

"Isn't that sort of the same as the last one?"

"No, because learning to be around each other and losing a friend are two totally different things."

Rose held up her glass. "Fair enough."

I added the point and wrote down another, one that made me feel a little woozy. "I could hurt him."

"Mmhmm," she added thoughtfully.

"He could hurt me." I frowned as I added it to the

list.

She squinted, concentrating. "But, I mean, isn't that *any* relationship?"

I sat up a little straighter and said, matter-of-factly, "Yes, but the stakes are higher than a normal relationship, Rose. This isn't like deciding to date a guy you met in a bar or something. This is *West.*"

"All right." Rose took a drink. "What else?"

"I don't know. Let's move on to pros." I drew a line and wrote PROS a little too big. "He's hot."

She snickered. "Man-bun hot."

"I feel like man-bun gets its own item in pros." I wrote it down. "He smells good. He's got manners. He's kind and generous, humble. He's my best friend."

Rose made a face. "Hey."

"Besides you."

"Thank you."

"He's smart. He makes me laugh. He knows me." I was running out of room and turned the receipt sideways. "He loves me," I said more quietly. "I love him."

She watched me solemnly. "As more than just a friend? Can you see yourself with him?"

I thought about it, thought about his solid arm under my hand as we walked the steps of the Met. Thought about how it felt when he held me this morning, this afternoon. I wanted more. I wanted all of him. My eyes welled with tears. "Yes."

Rose reached for my hand, and I met her eyes. "Can I tell you something?"

"Anything, Rose."

Her eyes were big and shiny, and she squeezed my fingers. "You've loved him forever. You two fit together without having to work, without having to try. You make sense. Like, I see the two of you talking or touching, and it's just *right*. Do you know what I mean? You make your own magic, like you run on the same frequency. How is it that you haven't been attracted to him the whole time?"

"I don't know. I mean, I always *have* been attracted to him, but I've tried to only think of him as a friend. I thought he didn't want that with me. I thought he was unavailable. But sometimes I'd feel it, the connection to him. I'd push it away like I was being silly or lonely, never letting myself consider doing anything about it. I was afraid of what it would mean if I did. What I would lose."

"But what about what you'll gain?"

I shook my head with my eyes on my list. "I … I don't know. What if something terrible happens? Like, what if watching him floss ruins me for life, or what if he's a horrible, drooly kisser?"

Rose snorted.

"Really, though. What if we end up hating each

other? And what if everything is perfect? What if he's my forever?" I slumped in my seat. "All of those endings are equally terrifying. How can I choose?"

"Because there's a very good chance that he'll make you happy. Risk and reward. Is West worth the risk to your heart?"

But I knew the answer. It floated up to the top of my consciousness like a life jacket. I would do anything for West. I would give anything to be the woman he wanted. "He's worth it."

She smiled. "Then there's your answer."

"I want to be with West." I tried on the words, and they felt good. A relief to say, to recognize. "He wants to be with me, and I want to be with him. All I have to do is tell him, Rosie. I have to tell him." I started to get up.

Rose panicked and grabbed my arm. "Whoa, hold up. Not right now."

"Why not?" I balked.

She laughed. "Because you're drunk, and it's almost two in the morning."

I huffed and sat back down. "Well, what the hell am I supposed to do?"

She rolled her eyes. "God, you two are so much alike."

"How so?" I asked, suspicious.

Her face screwed up. "Nothing."

"Oh, my god. You are such a liar."

"I wasn't supposed to say anything."

"Say anything about what?"

"I have a confession to make."

"Well, fucking confess it already, Rose!"

"Okay! Fine!" She took a drink, apparently to fortify herself, then turned in her seat so she was fully facing me. "So you know how West blurted out that he loved you in the club?"

I gave her a flat look. "Yeah, pretty sure I remember that."

She wrinkled her nose. "Well, he kind of told me that morning."

My mouth popped open. "What?"

"You know that breakfast with Patrick? Well, it was really so West could ask me for advice."

I just sort of sat there, staring at her.

"He figured it out at the opera."

My lips parted and I laid my fingers over them, shocked. "Oh, my god. I almost kissed him that night."

"Yeah, that probably wasn't one sided. They hatched a plan to ambush me at eight in the morning over bacon."

"I feel like if there's one place to get ambushed, it's over bacon." She laughed, but I was chewing on what she'd said, putting the timeline together in my head. "So, wait. You and Patrick knew how he felt about me before we went to Noir?"

She chewed on her lip and nodded. "Maggie and Cooper knew too."

My mouth was open again. "Are you serious?"

"And Astrid."

I threw up my hands. "Jesus, Rose!"

"Well, he couldn't tell you until your date was over," she explained apologetically. "Do you really think if West had come over while you were drinking gin and stuffing your bra with cutlets to tell you he loved you that you would have been happy?"

"Okay, first, I don't use cutlets. And second, you're right." I sighed. "I don't like it, but you're right. You guys all kept it from me and basically made the decision for me."

She gave me puppy dog eyes.

"…But I would have been pissed if he'd told me then, and it would have ruined the night before it even started."

"Exactly. The night had to play out. But none of us suspected Blane would do something so despicable."

"Yeah, well," I mumbled and took another drink. "I love whiskey."

Rose laughed. "Me too." She killed hers and leaned back. "So how are you going to tell him?"

"God, I don't even know." I thought about telling him again and fought the urge to find him tonight. "I found out eighteen hours ago, and almost everything I've touched from that point blew up all over me. You should have seen him today. He was so … I don't know, Rose. I've never seen him like this before. He was hurting, and I just wanted to make it better, make it right. I didn't know how." I slumped in my seat. "Are you sure I shouldn't go over there? I really feel like I should go over there. He's not going to be mad."

"No, he wouldn't be mad. But do you really want to talk to him about all this when you're whiskey drunk?"

I sighed. "No, probably not. But I barely care."

"Well, let me be your conscience. You're not going over there tonight. Here's what you *are* going to do."

"Oh, goodie." I perked up. "It makes me feel better that you have a plan."

"I always have a plan."

I eyed her.

"Okay, sometimes I have a plan. So, first — drink that because wasting alcohol is unacceptable." She pointed to my whiskey.

I giggled and brought it to my lips.

"Second, pizza."

"Ooooh, yes. Pizza."

"Then ibuprofen and bed."

I frowned. "I feel like it's early."

"Your brain is lying to you. You're usually in bed four hours ago."

"I am so boring."

Rose snickered. "Anyway, so tomorrow, we're going to wake up and eat Genie's greasy diner food while we hatch a plan for you to confess your feelings to West."

Nerves flitted through me. "I can't believe I'm going to do this."

"Scared?"

"I'm excited and terrified. It's like bungee jumping at a super sketchy carnival. Like, either it's going to be amazing, or, you know. Death."

She snorted.

"But there's nothing to do except tell him. I can't un-ring the bell. I can't *not* tell him."

"I know. And it's going to be okay."

"God, I hope so. We'll know for sure tomorrow. Now, feed me pizza!" I made a whip crack sound.

She laughed and took my arm, and we waved at Shelby as we left Habits. And for the first time in a long time, I felt like everything might just be all right.

STARS AND SONNETS

Lily

THE SUN HAD BEEN ASSAULTING me for hours before I finally cracked my lids, immediately squeezing them closed again. I pulled the covers over my head.

That's better.

My thoughts wandered back to the night before, the day before, and my heart fluttered in my chest. Today, everything would change, and as scared as I was, I was ready. He loved me, and I loved him. And as soon as I told him, we could step into whatever came next. Together.

I reached out and pawed at my nightstand for my phone, and once my fingers were around it, I dragged the phone under the covers with me. It was ten. My eyes flew open. I had way too much to do to lie around in bed all day.

I flipped back my covers and squinted as I dropped

my feet to the floor and stood. Or tried to. The room spun around, and I grabbed my nightstand.

"Whoa. Mmkay, maybe a little slower."

Maggie shot out of bed with her curly hair sticking up in every direction, sleep mask half on her face. "Whasthe fun … barracuda?"

"Go back to bed," I croaked and waved her off, and she flopped back on her pillow, pulling her covers over her head. I shuffled across the hall to Rose's room and opened the door. Her room was so dark, it was like a metropolitan cave, complete with blackout curtains and a box fan whirring in the corner. I felt my way through, buckling when I kicked the end of her bed frame.

"Fuck," I hissed, grabbing my shin. "Shitfuckingdammit."

Rose stirred in bed.

I hobbled over and climbed in with her. "Rosieeeeeeee," I whispered and moved her hair out of her face.

She didn't move.

"Rose," I said a little louder.

Nothing.

I shook her shoulder. "Rose!"

She smacked her lips and sighed.

I slapped her on the cheek, and her eyes flew open. "Good morning, sunshine," I said sweetly.

"Hmm?" She rolled over and rubbed her face.

"It's ten. You promised me bacon."

Rose cracked an eyelid. "How are you so fucking chipper right now?"

"Pizza? Ibuprofen? The gallon of water I drank before bed? Who knows. Get up! Today's the day. I have until he gets off work tonight to get my shit together, and I have no idea what I'm doing."

She reached for a pillow and tucked it into her chest. "Let's just sleep a little longer."

I grabbed the pillow and ripped it out of her arms. "Ah, ah, ah. Wakey wakey."

"Ugh, oppressor." She pulled her covers over her head.

I yanked them off of her. "You love me."

"I hate you, go away." She curled up in a ball.

"Can't. Need your help. Now get up, and let's get bacon and coffee before I detox for a year."

She snorted, and I smiled as I climbed out of her bed and threw open the curtains, leaving her room to the sound of her hisses.

And so, my day began. I was going to tell West I loved him.

Rose and I had breakfast at Genie's and planned out everything in a nice, tidy checklist. Anxiety rolled through me when I met up with Patrick to enlist his help, which he granted me gladly. I hoped it was enough. West deserved something epic.

Excitement flitted around my chest as I dressed up late that afternoon, and I felt electric as I pulled strings of lights and tiny stars out of the box in the courtyard at Habits. And then, I tried not to pass out as I waited behind the corner for him to walk through that door so I could tell him how much he meant to me.

West

I stepped off the train that evening after what might have been the longest Monday I'd ever had. I hadn't seen Lily, hadn't talked to her since she came to Columbia the day before. But as badly as I wanted to see her, she'd asked for time. So time was what I was giving her.

That didn't stop me from thinking about her.

The night before, I lay in bed, picturing her in bed down the hall, wondering what she was thinking. Wondering if she was all right. I'd woken that morning with her name on my lips. Drudged through my classes and graded papers feeling flat and gray. And now I'd go home and start the cycle all over again.

My phone buzzed in my pocket as I climbed the steps out the subway, and my heart hit my stomach when I saw a text from Lily. I stopped dead in the middle of the stairwell, barely moving when a passer-by hit my shoulder.

Meet me at Habits?

My fingers flew. *Of course. I'm just around the corner. You okay?*

Yeah, just wanted to talk. See you in a minute.

Emotion tumbled through me as I unrooted my feet and took off. She wanted to talk about *us.* I realized in that moment that as much as I'd thought about it, I was unprepared for her answer. Every expectation, every scenario that I imagined dissipated, leaving me blind. I felt like I was staring at the sun.

My heart clanged as I walked up to Habits and pulled open the door, finding Rose behind the bar. The smile she gave me sent a glimmer of hope through me, and she jerked her head toward the back exit where the patio was.

I was a man on fire as I walked through the bar and through that door.

Everything slowed down as the door closed behind me, but I saw every detail. Dusk painted deep shadows against the brick walls and corners of the small courtyard, built around an old crabapple tree that stretched up toward the roofs. It was in full bloom, covered in white blossoms that dropped every few seconds, spinning to the cobblestone ground like snowflakes. The tree was glowing, covered in white lights, and from the branches hung small, silver stars that caught the light as they moved every so often, touched by the petals as they fell.

On the small table in front of me was a sheet of parchment, and I took a step closer to pick up the thick paper.

The edges were painted with ink and watercolor, branches that stretched up, covered in lilies and leaves against a night sky and stars. And in the center were her words.

My friend, my friend you'll always be.
And from the very start
You were as steadfast as the sea
And I gave you my heart.
But only as my friend, my friend,
For we could not be more
And so we vowed until the end
There'd be no more in store.
And all this time I've gladly spent
My days and nights with you,
My friend, my friend, without a hint
Of love, without a clue
That you were meant for me, my love
And I was meant for you.

I laid down the sonnet and looked up to find her standing in front of me. The soft pink lace that made up her dress, her blond hair in waves, her skin, her smile —

everything was illuminated by the lights all around us. The petals fell as we stood under the tree, and I looked into her eyes — eyes full of hope, full of fear. Full of love.

I had no words.

She took a step toward me, then another until she was close enough that I couldn't breathe without breathing her in. Her face turned up to mine, and she reached for my hand, twisting her fingers in mine.

"All this time, you were right here. You were right in front of me, and I missed it." She searched my face, eyes soft with wonder. "How could I not have seen you?"

I slipped a hand into her hair, voice rough, only a whisper. "Lily …"

"I love you, West."

I closed my eyes and took a trembling breath, opening them to find her in my arms still. "Say it again."

She smiled, the tears in her eyes sparkling. "I love you," she whispered.

And then I closed my eyes and kissed her.

That kiss changed my life.

I held on to her like she was keeping me standing, hand in her silky hair, arm around her waist, her lips so soft, so sweet against mine, promising forever. My life clicked into place in that moment, and I knew she was all I wanted.

Her hands slid up my chest and to my jaw, fingers in my beard, in my hair. The kiss deepened, her lips parting in submission, and I breathed her in like a drowning man. She said she loved me. She'd be mine.

I was already hers — I'd lost myself to her long before I even knew.

We finally slowed and broke away, and she leaned back, hanging on my neck with bright eyes. "I can't believe I've been missing *that* all this time."

I laughed and pressed my forehead to hers. "Give me time to make up for it."

"Take all you want. I'm yours."

PHILMORE

Lily

WEST PRESSED HIS LIPS AGAINST mine again, and my eyelids fluttered closed, heart thundering in my chest. I melted against him, not wanting to stop. Ever.

The kiss was tender and easy, and he caught my bottom lip between his, sucking so gently. I was grateful for his arms around me, because I didn't know if I could stand on my own.

He broke away and looked down at me with eyes that told me everything I needed to know. I was meant for him. I cupped his cheek, feeling the softness of his beard between my fingers as I smiled up at him. He leaned into my hand.

"Is this real?"

I nodded, watching as the petals fell, tracing the lines of his face, the shadows cast by the glowing tree behind him, committing every detail to memory. "I'm sorry I couldn't answer you yesterday."

"Don't be. This … this is more than I could have ever imagined, Lily." He smiled. "You wrote me a sonnet."

I smiled back. "I did."

"It's beautiful. Perfect." His lips brushed mine, and he pulled away.

My heart beat his name as I looked into his eyes.

"So what do we do now?" He let me go, and I found his hand, not wanting to separate.

"Can I buy you a drink, Mr. Williams?"

West picked up the sonnet and squeezed my hand, tugging me toward the door, smiling. "Not on your life, Miss Thomas."

The first thing I saw once we were inside was Rose staring at the back door, worrying her lip between her teeth, but her face lit up like a Christmas tree when she saw us beaming and holding hands. She bounced, clapping, before running around the bar and bum rushing us, pulling us both of into a hug.

"Finally!" She pulled away, cheeks pink, eyes bouncing between us. "Come on, you two. What are you drinking?" She grabbed my hand and dragged us to the bar.

I took a seat, and West sat facing me, resting one foot on my stool's middle rung. He hooked his fingers under my seat and pulled me closer to him, putting me nearly in his lap. His thigh was against my stool, hand on my lower back. It might have been the most awesome thing ever. I reached for his knee, grinning.

"What are you drinking?" Rose asked, pulling out rocks glasses.

"Neat scotch for me," West answered, fingers shifting against my back. My eyes followed the line of his nose, the curve of his lips before he turned to me.

"You're making this no drinking thing really hard on me, Rose."

She was giddy, eyes twinkling. "Just one celebratory drink. I'll pour it light for you."

I sighed. "Gin and tonic, please." I turned on my stool to face him and smiled like an idiot. "So, you liked my sonnet? Not gonna lie — I might have gotten the idea from *Ten Things,* but I thought it was fitting. Shakespeare is the way to your heart, andI wanted to tell you in a way that meant something more to you than the words alone."

He held it in front of us, and we looked it over. "The words would have been enough, but I love it."

"I tried iambic pentameter, but it sounded so wrong."

He chuckled. "It's perfect. Did Patrick illustrate this?"

"He did."

"So, did everybody know about this except me?"

I glanced up at the ceiling and bobbled my head coyly. "Mmm, maybe. Paybacks for telling everyone how you felt about me before you actually told *me*."

He laughed, the sound deep and rumbling, and I smiled. "In my defense, they all told me to wait to tell you."

"It's good that you did. Doesn't make it any less awkward."

He chuckled and looked over the parchment again. "It really is beautiful. I'm impressed. You're a poet."

"And I didn't even know it." I made a face and laughed.

Rose rolled her eyes. "I thought we had at least a few weeks before you two went full cheeseball on each other."

West and I took our drinks and faced each other. I raised my glass. "To us."

He raised his, meeting mine. "To things to come."

We touched our glasses and took a drink. I set my glass on the bar top, feeling high, and Rose smiled, making her way around the bar to take care of her tables.

I was all smiles. "I don't know what to do with myself."

He grabbed my hand that lay on his knee. "We're just the same as we were this afternoon or a year ago, except now we're more than we were before."

I thought my heart might explode as I stared at him, smiling at me. "I can't think straight. I have a million things to say, and I can't find words for any of them."

He smiled at me. "I know."

I took a breath in an attempt to calm down, looking down at his hand over mine, his thumb as it moved against my knuckles. "Part of me wondered if you meant it, you know."

His brow dropped. "You didn't think I meant it when I said I loved you?"

I nodded. "I worried it was prompted by Blane, you know? That you were mad about him and it had somehow … don't know. Distorted your feelings. Part of me worried that when I told you I felt the same, you'd admit that it wasn't real."

"I meant it. I don't know that I've ever been so sure of anything. From the second I realized it, it became a simple truth, just a part of who I am. I love you, Lily. Whether you love me back or not, I love you."

Tears filled my eyes, and I smiled, touching his cheek as I leaned into him, bringing my lips to his. When I pulled away, he tugged my arm, forcing our mouths back together for a moment longer.

He pulled away, watching his hand as he touched my hair. "I want to kiss you until I know the feeling by heart."

"We should practice, then."

He smiled. "Oh, we will. But not here. I'd like to take you out, Lily Thomas. I want the world to know you're mine before I take you for my own."

My insides turned into jelly. "Let's go now."

West touched my cheek. "Not yet. I've got to make some plans."

I might have pouted a little. "What should we do tonight, then?"

"Well, you know what show we're behind on?"

"*The Bachelor*," we said at the same time.

"Come on, then. Who knows what shenanigans Celeste is going to get in this week." I picked up my drink and drained it in a gulp.

"I can't believe Eric doesn't see her crazy." He shook his head and knocked his whiskey back before pulling out his wallet. Rose hurried around the bar and slapped his hand when he tried to leave some cash.

"Nope. Get out of here with that."

"Come on," he insisted, pushing the money back at her.

She batted it away. "I said no! Consider it my gift to you on this most joyous occasion."

I laughed. "You better give up, West. She's not above shooting you with the soda gun."

Rose grabbed it and pointed the nozzle at him. "She's right. Now scram."

West smiled. "Thank you, Rose."

"You're welcome. Now don't get into any trouble, and hang a sock on the door if there's nakedness happening because I'm not ready for that. You two kissing in the bar is weird enough."

I leaned over the bar to kiss her cheek. "Thanks, Rosie."

"No prob, Lil."

We waved and smiled our way out of Habits, onto the street in the early night, holding hands as we hurried toward our building and up the stairs. His hand was on my back as I unlocked my door and stepped into the dark apartment.

"Mags?" I called. "You here?"

Silence.

"Huh. Guess she's out." I clicked on the lamp, kicking off my shoes as I tossed my keys in the dish, and West made his way around the couch and took off his bag. I padded into the living room behind him, looking over a sight I'd seen a thousand times. But watching him set down his things and stretch — the long line of his torso, the profile of his face and hair, just the sheer height of him — hit me in a way that made my heart ache. It was possession I felt. He was mine.

He smiled over at me, and when I reached him, we flopped down on the couch shoulder to shoulder, feet propped on the coffee table just like we always did as I navigated the DVR and hit play.

I wound my arm around his, found his hand, and we threaded our fingers together. A few minutes later, that wasn't enough, and he let my hand go to wrap his arm around me. I leaned into him with my hand on his thigh and my thoughts focused on him so intently that even the slightest movement garnered my full attention.

A commercial break came on, and I shifted, brought my knees up so I was almost in his lap. His hand found the outside of my thigh, and I beamed at him.

I'd planned on saying something witty, to start a conversation to dissipate the nervous energy buzzing through me, but then I looked at him — his eyes like the summer sky, dark hair tied back in a knot, his beard framing his lips, lips I now knew to be strong and soft — and I was a goner. I leaned into him, breathing the scent of spiced oranges, and met his lips. They moved against mine, telling me things I knew to be true without the complication of words or thought. Just a simple action that said he needed me just like I needed him.

He sucked on my bottom lip, and I hummed, fingers in his hair. They wandered to the knot and tugged until his hair was loose. My hungry fingers wound through it, and then it was his turn to hum. His hand slipped up my thigh, pulling my legs into his solid chest. I needed to be closer to him.

I climbed into his lap and straddled him, the kiss

holding more determination now that we were face-to-face, with nothing in our way but a little bit of fabric. His hands were against my back, fingers twisted in my hair, and I rolled my hips as our mouths and tongues met in waves. My arms were around his neck, keeping his lips against mine where they belonged, and when his hands found my ass and pulled me into his hips, his length pressed against me, sending a shudder through my thighs.

I broke the kiss with a sigh, hanging my head back.

"Lily," he whispered against my neck.

"Yes." My hips rolled.

He flexed his own hips to meet mine and sucked in a breath with a hiss. "Ah, Lil. Not yet."

"Please?" I covered his mouth with mine, kissing him deep.

He pulled away, eyes hot as he looked up at me. "I can't stop when you beg me like that."

"Then don't."

He trailed kisses down my neck, to my chest as he cupped my breast. "I have to," he said against my skin.

I shifted my hips again, grinding against him. "Says who?"

He growled and flipped me over onto my back. A little squeal burst out of me, and he hovered over me, breath heavy. I cupped his cheeks, shifting my fingers in his beard. "Says me. We'll go on a date before I take you to bed, Lily Thomas." He kissed me hard, a demanding kiss that betrayed his chastity.

I huffed when he broke away. My body was not willing to wait for anything so stupid as a meal. "Damn you and your Southern honor. I've known you for four years. Do you really think dinner matters at this point?"

He smiled and shifted on the couch, putting his torso between my legs, his face near the base of my ribs with his hips much too far away from mine. "Doesn't matter. As much shit as I gave Blaney for not honoring that, I'd be a hypocrite not to follow my own moral code, wouldn't I?"

I scowled. "Screw Blane and screw your moral code and screw me."

"I want you to know I'm serious about you, Lily."

"I believe you're serious. Now kiss me."

He laughed. "Tomorrow. Can you wait until tomorrow?"

"I have Spaghetti-O's in the kitchen." I was almost whining. "Can we make those and call it a dinner?"

"Nope."

"Ugh, West." I groaned.

His hand slipped up my thigh, under my skirt, and I slapped him on the shoulder.

"Don't start something you won't finish, Weston."

"Mmm." He pressed his lips to my stomach. "I should go. I don't think I can keep my hands to myself."

Part of me wanted to cry, and rest of me wanted to laugh at the brilliant insanity of it all. I would have sucker punched an old lady if it would mean I could get West to spend the night.

"Don't go," I pouted.

He climbed up my body and kissed my nose. "Tomorrow." Then he kissed my lips. My entire body responded, particularly my legs, which wrapped themselves around his waist. He pulled away and unhooked them, amused.

I folded my arms across my chest, indignant. "Fine. I guess it's just me and Phil tonight."

His brow dropped. "Oh? Who's Phil?"

"Philmore Dix. My vibrator."

A rumbling laugh burst out of him. "Goddammit, Lil."

"Think of me while you're lying in bed all alone."

But he smiled and brushed my hair away from my face. "One night. And then, you're mine." He kissed me, and I honest to God whimpered.

West climbed off the couch and adjusted his pants, but when he looked back at me, he froze. His gaze drifted up and down my body, pausing where my dress was hitched up. His eyes were on fire when they met mine again.

"Tomorrow." His voice was haggard.

I sighed. "Tomorrow."

He moved around the back of the couch and leaned over it to kiss me again, a gentle kiss. Bastard totally held out on me. On a scale of one to lava, it was an electric blanket. His eyes twinkled at me. "Tell Phil I said hi."

"Oh, I will." I chimed.

He touched my face reverently. "It'll be worth it."

My face softened. "I know it will."

"Sleep tight."

"You too."

And then he disappeared from over me, and I heard the door close.

"This sucks!" I threw a pillow across the room before hauling myself off the couch to look for batteries.

West

I adjusted my pants again as I unlocked my door and made my way into the empty apartment, not any closer to calming down than I had been when I'd walked out of Lily's apartment. When I left, I'd been one more kiss away from taking her right then. A big part of me wanted to march back over there and do it anyway. But like I'd said — it would be worth it. I wanted to honor her. Respect her. Even if it meant I had a hard-on straight from hell.

339

I pulled off my shirt and pants, changing into sweats, no shirt, unable to get her off my mind. It was still early enough that I couldn't go to sleep, not that I thought I'd be able to sleep at all that night. I stretched out on my bed and picked up The Fountainhead, but after I'd read the same paragraph a handful of times, I gave up. I turned on music, but the first song's lyrics made me think of her, and I sighed, glancing at my phone where it sat on my nightstand.

She was right down the hall. So close.

I picked up my phone. Opened my messages and found her name. *I've been reciting running backs since I left, but it hasn't helped me stop thinking about you.*

My phone buzzed within seconds. *Too bad you don't have Phil like I do.*

I snorted. *I doubt he'd do anything for me.*

That's a shame. He does so much for me.

You really want me to come back over there, don't you?

Is it that obvious?

My smile stretched wider. *Just a little.*

What are you doing?

Lying in bed, trying not to think about you and Phil.

What are you wearing?

My heart sped up a little, pumping more blood exactly where I didn't want it. *Grey sweats.*

And what else?

Nothing. That's it.

God, West. It's not fair, you know that?

I laughed. *Honey, believe me when I say neither of us are enjoying this.*

Well, I have Philmore, so maybe one of us is.

I groaned. The next time my phone buzzed, it was with a picture, and I legitimately almost bolted out the door and back to her apartment. It was a snapshot of her body as she lay on her side — thighs pressed together, the planes of her naked stomach, the tiny triangle of pink fabric that barely covered her. My hand slipped into my pants.

Still here? She messaged. *Did you bail on me?*

You can't send me a pic like that and expect me to communicate, Lil.

I could practically hear her giggling from apartments away. *I wish you'd stayed.*

Me too.

Tell me again it'll be worth it.

It'll be worth it. I love you.

I love you too.

Where's Phil?

Oh, he's right here. Just turned him on.

Well, he and I have that in common.

Send me a pic.

I leaned back, catching the line of my stomach, my hand in my pants around the long shadow, clear enough through the fabric to gather what I was doing.

It took a minute before she answered. Didn't matter though — I had her photo still open.

Fuck, West. Seriously.

I know. Tomorrow. I promise.

I want you.

I'm yours.

ALL I WANT

Lily

I HUMMED, FEELING LIGHT AS cotton candy as I grabbed my bag the next morning, heading down the hall to meet West. I knocked on his door, giddy when I heard him walk up, giddier still when I saw him standing in the doorway, looking *fine*. He had on a flannel over a white shirt, gray beanie slouched over his hair that peeked out around his neck, jeans and boots.

His smile was as bright as the sun. "Mornin'."

I stepped into the doorway with him and leaned into his chest, tilting my face as I reached for his lips to give them a simple, yet completely satisfying kiss. "Morning. You ready?"

"Ready." He grabbed his bag, closed his door, and took my hand.

"So, where are we going tonight?" I asked as we trotted down the stairs.

"It's a surprise."

"Oh? I'm intrigued."

"Good." He smirked as he held the door open for me. "What's on deck for you today?"

I walked past him and onto the sidewalk. "Avoid Blane like herpes. Nail my Black Swan once and for all. Costume fitting. Then I'm all yours."

West reached for my hand. "Damn straight, you are."

We walked toward the coffee shop at the end of the block. "How about you? How's your day look?"

"Bleak and cold, until I see you again."

"I know. It's going to be a long day." We walked in silence for a moment. "Can I confess something?"

"Anything."

"I'm nervous."

He smiled over at me. "Me too. But I keep thinking about last night. We're going to be just fine."

"I thought it would be weirder than it is, you know? Like, I thought we'd have to ease into it. But after last night, I definitely do not want to ease into anything."

West laughed as we approached the coffee shop. "Me neither." He pulled open the door, and we stepped in.

We got our morning fix and walked the block down Broadway to the subway, through the turnstile and into the terminal. We stood in the noisy station, pressed chest to chest, taking a long moment to say goodbye. The look on his face as he moved my hair away from my face … well, let's just say my ovaries exploded like popcorn.

He kissed me long enough to steal my breath before breaking away.

"I'll see you tonight."

"Just a few hours. Will you text me if you think of me?"

He chuckled. "I don't think my data plan covers that amount of transfer."

I smiled up at him.

"I'll message you. Have a good day." He kissed me once more as my train pulled up.

"You too." I hurried to catch it before the doors closed, moving to kneel in a seat so I could still see him standing on the platform with his hands in his pockets. I laid my palms on the window, closing my eyes as I made a kiss face, and he smiled like it hit him in the heart.

I made it to Lincoln Center by nine-thirty, early for the day, and changed into my workout shorts and leg warmers. I grabbed a new pair of shoes from the shoe room like I was floating and made my way to barre class to stretch with an unstoppable grin.

Until I walked into the studio.

I froze as the door swung shut behind me. I was the second one there — the first was Blane. A mostly naked

Blane. Duct taped to the barre. With the word *slutbag* written across his chest in hot pink lipstick.

He sighed, relieved. "Thank God you're here. Cut me loose." He tried to extend his wrists but didn't get far.

My mouth hung open in a gaping smile as I walked around him to get a good look. "Well, well, well. Who else did you piss off, Blaney?"

A shadow passed across his face. "I don't want to talk about it. Are you seriously going to fuck with me right now? If Ward sees this—"

My smile fell like a pile of bricks. "He'll think I had something to do with it." I put down my bag and dug around for my sewing kit. "You really don't learn, do you?"

He just scowled. I was sure he had something to say, but his desire to get out of his little bind kept his mouth shut.

My fingers closed around my shears just as the door opened, and a pack of dancers came in. Everyone stopped just inside the door that shut with a thump, marring the silence.

A sharp laugh cut through the room — Jenni's — and the entire group broke out in laughter. I heard the click of a camera as someone took a picture. Nadia stood at the edge of the group with her arms folded across her chest, smirking.

She fucking did it.

A laugh bubbled out of me, and Nadia met my eyes with a nod. Blane was flaming red, and I took pity on the poor, steaming piece of shit, grabbing my shears to cut him loose. I'd only just gotten him free when Ward walked in with the pianist.

The dancers parted, framing Ward as he took in the scene. The room was dead silent.

His eyes met mine, and he stared me down. "What is going on here?"

I nearly withered up on the spot. "I don't know, sir. Blane was like this when I got here."

Blane picked himself up off the ground and glared at Nadia. "Lily had nothing to do with this, sir."

Ward's eyes were so narrowed, you could barely see the whites. "And who did?"

Blane shook his head. "It was my own fault."

His nostrils flared. "You'll meet me in my office after barre, Baker. Put a goddamn shirt on."

Blane nodded, face nearly as pink as the dirty word on his chest. "Yes, sir."

Ward turned to the room, voice hard. "This is over. The next incident will end with all involved dancers without a job. Do I make myself clear?"

Yes, sir, rolled through the dancers, and Ward chugged over to the piano to wait impatiently for everyone to arrive and take their places. I made my way to one of the portable barres in the middle of the room and set my bag down, catching Blane's eye. I mouthed *thank you* at him, and he nodded curtly before pulling on his tank and inspecting his duct tape cuffs. He ripped one off with a yelp just as Nadia set down her bag next to mine.

"Karma's a bitch," she said with her eyes on Blane and a smile on her lips.

"And that bitch bites. Well played, Nadia."

Her face went soft with an expression I'd never seen on her before. Humility. "I owe you an apology, Thomas. I had the enemy framed all wrong."

I was shocked silent for a beat. Maybe I was in the Twilight Zone, or it was a dream, and I was about to find myself buck naked. I looked down. *Nope, still clothed.* I met her eyes. "Thank you."

Nadia smirked. "I'm glad your friend decked him for nailing the slag at the club."

I chuckled. "Me too."

She glanced over at him. "I can't believe I wasted years with that asshole. What was I thinking?"

"Dat ass."

She laughed. "Right. Dat ass."

West

"God, this is so good, West." Lily took another bite of

her dinner, and I smiled. She looked so beautiful — blond hair loose, black dress, eyes bright, heart full. The restaurant was busy but quiet enough, dimly lit. We sat at a table for two near a window that overlooked the street.

"I heard about this place and had to bring you. I figured you'd appreciate some clean, vegan food after the last week."

"Seriously. Thank you for not taking me somewhere that would tempt me to eat like absolute shit." She took another bite and moaned. "This is amazing. Want a bite?"

"I've been waiting for you to offer." I reached across the small table for her plate, and she reached for mine.

The tip of her tongue slipped from between her lips as she dug into my food. "I've got to try this creamed corn."

I scooped up a bite of her spinach and almonds. "Go for it."

We brought our forks to our lips and made appreciative noises. Lily pointed with her fork at my plate. "I don't know what they creamed that with, but I accept it fully and completely. Goddamn, that's good."

"So many dirty jokes."

"There aren't many instances in which 'creamed' is used that don't sound dirty."

"Or moist. Even when it's about cake."

Lily laughed.

I scooped up a bite of sweet potatoes. "How was your day?"

"Forever long, waiting for tonight."

"Same. Did Blane lay off?"

Her face lit up, and she put down her fork, the indication that a story was coming. "Oh, my god, West." She leaned on the table, her face animated. "So I walk into rehearsal this morning and find Blane duct taped to the barre in the empty studio with a horrible word scribbled across his chest in lipstick."

A satisfied laugh shot out of me. "Oh, man. Tell me somebody got a picture of that they'll send to me."

She giggled. "I think Jenni might have gotten one. The best part is that Nadia set him up."

I found myself gaping. "Really?"

Lily nodded. "Leave it to Nadia to make public humiliation a blood sport. Ward was *pissed*. Honestly, I think the whole thing is over. Nadia and I sort of … I don't know. Made up? I think she's done with Blane for good, and Ward threatened our jobs if we didn't keep it out of the studio."

I shook my head as I piled a bite of baked beans and cornbread onto my fork. "He deserved all of that and then some." I took a bite and sighed, taking a sip of my drink once I'd swallowed. I watched her across the table, her wide eyes bright, my gaze following the curve of her lips as she smiled. "I'm sorry that he hurt you. I don't know how he could have done what he did."

"It wasn't only me he hurt. And plus, if it weren't for him, you and I might never have figured *this* out."

I smiled back and reached for her hand, winding my fingers through hers. "You know, when I realized how I felt about you, I imagined this. The little things. Holding your hand." I shifted my thumb on her knuckles. "Kissing you. You looking at me like you are right now. Part of me was afraid that it wouldn't be what I imagined. But instead, I'm … well, this all just feels right. Like a natural progression, the evolution."

"I know what you mean. It's *easier* than I thought it would be. I think I've been suppressing my feelings for you for a long time, and now it's like a deluge."

"I think I've been doing the same. Must be, since everyone else in our lives knew before we did. I just didn't think you could want me. That if you could, you already would."

She shrugged and took a drink. "I think we just kicked it off in one direction and stuck to it. You were with Shannon, and to me, that meant off limits. And I was with the ballet. It's been my lover for years. I didn't have time for a relationship, and I didn't have time to meet people. So I found guys who I could just date without strings and at my convenience and let that be what it was."

"I get it."

"And when it came to my feelings for you, I guess I just figured you weren't interested. You were just my super-hot best friend who lived down the hall and didn't flinch when you saw me without makeup or puking. Or ugly crying to movies I love."

"True. The first time we watched *The Notebook* was a real testament to my commitment."

She made a face. "It's not my fault that Nicholas Sparks is an emotionally manipulative bastard who makes me feel things. And anyway, you handled it like a pro." I chuckled, and she smiled. "Still, you know what I mean. I think I thought you thought of me as a sister. Like, there's no coming back from that level of platonic love."

I sighed, smiling. "I never once thought of you like a sister. I thought you were out of my league."

Her face screwed up. "What?"

"I mean, look at you. You're beautiful and smart, the most driven woman I've ever met. You're a professional dancer in one of the most competitive, talented companies of dancers in the world. I'm an English major."

"At *Columbia*, dear sir. Not something to make light of." She shook her head and squeezed my hand. "This blows my mind because I thought *you* were out of *my* league."

I was stunned. "How can you even say that?"

She looked around, baffled. "I don't get it. Almost everywhere we go, girls practically throw their panties at you. Did you even see our waitress? I'm pretty sure I heard her girl parts squeal when she walked up to the table."

I laughed again. "Didn't notice. I was too busy looking at you, I guess."

Lily let go of my hand to pick up her fork, spearing some spinach. She brought it almost to her lips. "Well, she was." The fork disappeared into her mouth, slipping out from between her lips empty.

"You're one to talk about being hot, Lily. If I hadn't had my hands up your skirt last night, I'd swear your legs never ended."

She laughed, the sound awkward because her mouth was full. She swallowed. "I don't think the length of my legs is equivalent to your pheromones. Pretty sure they have a twelve-foot radius." She pushed her plate away. "I'm super full."

"More spinach for me." My fork wandered over to her plate.

Lily watched me, amused. "Look at you, sacrificing a steak dinner for greens and legumes."

"Baby, I'll eat Brussels sprouts for you."

She chuckled. "That's true love, right there."

Lily

The cab was warm and comfortable, and I sighed against West's chest. He was wearing that gorgeous suit of his, and all night long he'd made me laugh, made me swoon, made me want him. The night had been the magic I'd been looking for with Blane but never found, and I didn't even have to try.

Forget self-made magic. West was fairy dust.

We were quiet, content in the silence, anticipating what would come when we stepped out of the cab and into our building. We knew each other so well that there was no grace period before we'd move forward. The step into being together had been easy, something I hadn't known I'd wanted all along.

Everything was new — every touch, every word and smile. But West was just as familiar to me as he ever was.

The cab pulled to a stop in front of our building, and West paid the driver before climbing out, extending a hand once he was on the curb. I took it, and he hauled me out gently.

We hadn't spoken in some time, both of us nervous and excited, I think. It had been easier to fall into each other the night before when there weren't any expectations, but tonight we'd both been thinking about it through the entire date. Or at least I had been. I'd been thinking about it ever since he'd left me with the ladyboner of my life on my couch. Luckily, Phil and I had a long-standing arrangement.

I wondered what West did with his boner and pictured the photo he sent me. I smiled to myself.

"What's funny?" he asked as we approached his door.

"Oh, nothing." I waited next to him as he unlocked it. "Is Patrick home?"

West smiled over at me and pushed open the door. "Gone for the night."

"That is very convenient." I walked into the dark apartment and kicked off my heels, and he closed the door behind us, cutting off the only sliver of light besides the soft moonlight that streamed in through the windows.

And then West was behind me, hands on my hips, breath in my ear. I leaned back into him, trembling. "I've been thinking about this moment since I left you last night."

I struggled to find my voice and took a breath. "Now you have me. What are you going to do with me?"

"Oh, I can think of a thing or two." He turned me around in the dark and found my lips without missing. I breathed him, tasted him, that soft smell of crisp spice in my nose as I sucked in a breath, lips moving against his.

He broke away, and I almost fell into him. "Come with me."

"Anywhere."

He towed me toward his room, though I couldn't see anything in the dark, not until we reached his door and he pushed it open. I drew in a breath.

The lights I'd used on the tree at Habits were stretched across his ceiling, the tiny stars hanging at varying heights, spinning and waving slowly, twinkling at me. The room was bathed in golden light, and I looked around in wonder until I saw my sonnet hanging in a frame next to his bed.

"Last night, I wanted the moment to stretch on forever. I could have stayed right there with you for all my life."

I turned to face him, overcome. "I love it." I breathed.

His face bent with emotion. "I love you."

I cupped his cheek, smiling as he laid his hand over mine.

"Those words mean so much to me, from our friendship to what we are now and through whatever comes next. I want to share my life with you." He dropped his forehead to mine, wrapped me in his arms with his hands on my back, pulling my body into his. "I know it's crazy to say, but it's how I feel. Like everything in my life has led to this."

"It's not crazy, West. I've always loved you, from the first time I ever laid eyes on you. I wish we hadn't waited so long. I wish I'd always been with you. But now …" My heart ached as I took a breath. "Now I can love you even more. Now I can give my love to you. Now I'm yours, and you're mine, and I feel like I'm whole. I didn't even know I was broken."

"I want you, Lily. Stay with me."

"Nothing could keep me away," I whispered.

A ghost of a smile passed his lips before he pressed them to mine with the relief of decision, the promises in our hearts speaking through fingertips and soft lips. The moment stretched on until I wrapped my arms around his neck, and he stood straight, lifting me off the ground, arms around my waist as he carried me to his bed.

West laid me down, the room soft golds and deep browns, only parts of his face visible as he hovered over me — the bridge of his nose, the line of his cheekbone, the curve of his lip. We lay there for a moment, just watching each other, and I committed every detail to memory. The dark strand of hair on his forehead. The bend of his neck. The one corner of his lips that sat just a little higher than the other, bent in the smallest smile.

I held my breath as his fingers trailed my jaw, traced my lips before he leaned in to take them with his own.

The kiss was slow, lips demanding without any need for force, a kiss that burned hotter with every second as he pressed his body into mine. My blind hands slipped inside his jacket, and he sat up to remove it completely, tossing into his desk chair. I sat with him, reaching for the knot in his tie, tugging at the silk as he unbuttoned his vest. He brought his lips to mine as I slid the tie out of his collar and started on his buttons.

I broke away. "Too many clothes."

He smiled and whispered, "So many," before taking my mouth again, pressing me back into the bed so he could kick off his shoes, still shedding clothes until his chest was bare and heaving.

I laid a palm against his hot skin, and he pulled away, lips parted and lids heavy. He slipped his hands under my back and sat once more, bringing me with him, and I wrapped my body around his, squeezing tight until the skin of my upper thighs was flush against his abs. I needed to get close, wanted his skin against mine. His hand ran up my back to the zipper of my dress that he tugged until it stopped. His eyes followed his fingers as he ran them over my shoulders, my heart pounding as he slid the straps until they hung loose against my arms. The neck of my dress drooped, leaving part of my nipple exposed, and I watched him watch me for a long, reverent moment.

I rose up to my knees, and he slipped his hands up

my thighs and higher, pushing my dress up as he went, sucking in a breath when he reached my bare ass. Higher he went, up my hips and waist, up my ribs where he took a moment to trace the vines of my tattoo, and I raised my arms as he pulled it off completely. Everything about his hands, his eyes, spoke of ownership as he touched me, laid his hand on the flat of my stomach and trailed it down. He was so beautiful in the golden light, and when I moved his hair from his face he looked up at me. The connection was so deep, so real that it was tangible.

He reached for me, slipping a hand in my hair to pull me down to him, kissing me again as I pressed my body against his chest. I wanted skin. I wanted him.

I leaned forward to lay us down, hands trailing down his body to his belt that I tugged open, button that I unfastened, our lips never parting, not until I slipped my hands into his pants and found the length of him, hot and hard. I trailed my fingertips up, circled his crown and trailed them down once more, slipping my fingers lower when I reached his base.

He twisted, rolling us over, kicking off his pants, and I leaned back as our legs wound together so I could look at his long body. I watched him as his soft fingertips roamed my skin — the bend of my waist, the curve of my breast, my nipple that peaked under his touch. He leaned in, and I watched him circle my nipple once more before he closed his mouth over it, his lips against my skin hot and wet.

But his hands didn't stop. They trailed up my thigh until he reached the top and slipped a gentle finger inside, squeezing his palm against the bundle of nerves. My body squeezed him back, and I panted as he rolled his tongue in time with his finger inside of me, grazing me with his teeth before he broke away to lick a trail down my stomach. My hips were still grinding against his hand when he lay between my legs to hook my thighs over his shoulders.

His hands held the curve of my waist, pulling me down to him. I could feel his breath against me, and my body ached, needing him.

I slipped my fingers into his hair as he spread me open with his fingers and ran the flat of his tongue up the length of me, closing his lips over my bud when he reached the top. He sucked hard enough to make my thighs tremble, and he moaned gently, sending a rumble straight to my core. My fingers twisted in his hair. He sucked again. My heels dug into his back. He sucked again.

"Yes," I whispered, tightening my grip as he tightened his, the seam where his lips met my body a hard line. I watched him, too close to close my eyes — if I closed my eyes, it would be over, and I wasn't ready for it to end.

I touched his face, urging him to come to me, and his eyes fluttered open. He knew what I wanted and let me go before climbing up to meet me, lying on his side. Our legs tangled together, hearts banging as I rolled my hips against his thigh between my legs, and I kissed him with all the urgency that he gave to me.

He broke away, rolling me onto my back to reach over me for his nightstand, coming back with a condom.

I covered his hand with mine and shook my head. "It's safe. I trust you."

He smoothed my hair. "You're sure?"

"I'm sure." I leaned into him, lips meeting his again. In that moment, my entire world was built around those lips.

The weight of his body was heavy against mine, my heart pounding as he pulled away and looked into my eyes. When he shifted to press his crown against me, I couldn't breathe. And when he flexed his hips and slipped inside of me, I was his.

Neither of us moved, not until he took a shuddering breath and pulled out, flexing again to fill me to the hilt. His lips brushed against mine.

"This," he whispered. "God, Lily." He brought my thigh up, pressed my calf against his ribs as he pulled out slow and went deeper, rolling his hips when he hit the end. "This."

I couldn't speak as he slammed into me again, then again, lids fluttering closed as our bodies met and parted. Every motion bringing me closer, breath shallow, pulse racing until I gasped, back snapping off the bed. A cry passed my lips as my body clenched around him, squeezed for a long moment and released in a pulse to the beat of my heart.

West was right behind me, and I opened my eyes when he slammed into me once and held me still for a breath, twice and his brow bent, and the third time, he came with a gasp and my name on his lips.

I was surrounded by him as he rocked into me slower and slower, his fingers in my hair, his eyes on my face like he was seeing me for the first time.

I smoothed back his hair, trailed my fingers through his beard, and he laid a kiss on my lips. I couldn't speak. No words could find me, not when he rolled over, taking me with him, and my hair fell all around us like a golden curtain. Not when we parted — the longing for him instant. Not as I stood in front of his bathroom mirror and saw myself, pink cheeks and messy hair, looking alive.

I crawled back in bed with him where he lay under the covers, slipped in close to feel the length of his body against mine as he wrapped me in his arms. Our heads were on the pillow — mine tucked under his chin as his fingers dragged up my back and down again. I listened to the steady rhythm of his breath, chest rising and falling against me, the thump of his heart against my palm, drumming to the beat of my own as we drifted off to sleep.

FAITH

West

THE MORNING SUN HAD BARELY broken the horizon when I woke. The room was still mostly dark, but I could see every detail of Lily's face — the tiny freckles on her nose, her dark lashes against her cheek, hair spilled around her, across her pillow and bare shoulder. The sheets were just low enough that I could see a sliver of the darker skin around her nipple, and my eyes followed the curve of her breast that disappeared into the shadows.

It might have been one of the most beautiful things I'd ever seen.

I lay there for a long time watching her, trying to sort through my feelings. Never in all my life had I felt this before. Not with Chris, not even Shannon, who I had been with for all of those years. What I felt for Lily left them all in the dust.

I'd never believed in soul mates — the idea that there's only one person for you, and if you can find them, the power of that love would be unstoppable. The laws of compatibility would say there are thousands of people you could find happiness with. But now that I had Lily, I realized that there are people who, when they find one another, have no choice in the matter, no say. They need to be together just as much as they need to breathe.

Nothing in life is certain. But as long as my heart was beating, it would beat for her. I didn't exist solely for myself anymore because I was hers, and she was mine.

She breathed deep and shifted, lids fluttering as she scooted close, burrowing into my chest.

"You smell good," she said sleepily.

My arms wound around her, pulling her close. "Morning." I kissed her hair.

She hummed. "Can I stay here all day? I don't want to go to the theater."

I chuckled. "That's a first."

Her arms snaked around my waist, one leg finding its way between mine as we wrapped ourselves around each other. "I'm afraid if I leave, I'll find out that it was all a dream. Like the magic will disappear."

My fingers twisted in her silky hair. "I don't think we could stop this if we wanted to."

She kissed my chest. "I don't want it to stop. I want

to freeze time. Stay right here with you. Only get up to eat. Can we make that happen?"

I laughed again. "How about I take off next Monday and we'll do just that. Sunday night to Tuesday morning. Me. You. Chinese takeout. Clothing banned."

"That's so far away," she whined.

I smiled. "Stay with me again tonight."

"I will." Her fingers trailed lazy circles on my back. "I have a show, but can I see you before?"

"Anything you want." The words were a promise far beyond today.

She sighed. "We're going to have to face our friends at some point."

"Well, we're no secret. They might even have a surprise party planned."

She chuckled and shifted, bringing her hips closer to mine when my hand skimmed down to cup her ass. She sighed again.

"What time is it?" she asked lazily.

I glanced at my clock. "Six-thirty."

"Everybody makes fun of me for getting up early, but it means I have more day to my day. It's my favorite time, when everyone is still asleep and the day is full of potential."

I leaned back to look at her. "You have to be at work at ten-thirty?"

Her lips stretched into a mischievous smile, her blue

eyes on my lips. "Mmhmm." She dragged a hand down my chest, down my stomach, then lower. "I have *hours.*"

Her fingers grazed my length, and I pulled in a breath, gripping her thigh. "God, Lily," I breathed. I'd never wanted anyone so badly, so deeply.

"I know," she whispered against my lips before she locked them to mine. I pulled her closer as the kiss deepened, the want — the need — for him overwhelming.

She laid a hand on my chest and pushed gently, urging me to lean back, and she moved with me, hovering to kiss me once more before pulling away. She made her way down my body, breath hot on the skin low on my stomach. Every few seconds as she moved, something would brush against my shaft — her breast, her hair, her fingers — and every nerve was at attention, anticipating her.

I propped up my head so I could watch her — eyes closed, lips parted, tongue extended as she ran the flat up the length of me, pausing to kiss my crown, a hot, wet kiss that sent a shock through my thighs. My hand was in her hair, eyes on her lips as she closed them around me and dropped down. I disappeared inside her mouth.

My fingers tightened in her hair as she pulled back and dropped down, again, then again. It took every bit of my willpower not to slam into her mouth, and I breathed deep, jaw clenched, eyes squeezed shut as her hand worked what she couldn't take with her mouth.

I found her neck and cupped it, urging her to come to me. She sucked hard enough to make me moan as she let me go, kissing my abs as she climbed up my body too slowly. I couldn't be patient, and I sat to meet her halfway, slipping my hand into her hair again, lips hungry, breath heaving. She straddled me, angled her body against my crown, shifted her hips to ease me in agonizingly slow. She was so wet, so warm, and I flexed my hips, my hands on hers, pulling her down until our bodies were flush.

She gasped.

Her lids were heavy, lips swollen, golden hair hanging down her back as she laid her palms on my chest, rocking her body in a wave. Her eyes were nearly shut, her long lashes covering the irises as she looked down, and I trailed my hand up her body, tracing the curve of her waist, cupping her breast, thumb brushing her nipple. She let out a breath, eyes closed and face soft with satisfaction as her hips rolled faster.

I lowered my lips to her breast, and she propped her arms on my shoulders, cradling my head in her forearms, fingers twisting through my hair when my lips closed over her nipple. She sucked in a breath with a hiss when I rolled my tongue with my hands splayed against her back, and her hips moved with more intention.

I dragged my teeth gently against her, and she gasped, flexing once more with a cry as she pulsed around me.

The feeling of her body moving under my hands, against me, around me was more than I could take, knowing my touch gave her satisfaction. And when her legs wrapped around me and her arms cradled me against her, I buried my face in her neck for a long moment. We were wound together, and I was surrounded by her, inside of her, as close to her as I could ever be.

I laid her down, her long hair hanging off the foot of my bed, her eyes drunk from emotion and exertion. I watched her face, caging her in my arms, hands in her hair as I slipped inside of her. She dropped her head back, lips parted, and I pulled out again, filling her with a thrust of my hips. Then again as my hand pressed her thigh against my body. Again as my fingers gripped her skin.

Her eyes cracked open, hand finding my cheek, tear spilling down her temple. "I love you," she whispered.

My forehead dropped to hers as I let go, legs trembling as I hit the end of her and stayed there. My eyes were closed, one hand under the nape of her neck, one resting on the back of her thigh, my heart beating with hers.

And my breath stirred her hair when I whispered in her ear, "Don't ever stop."

DRINK TO THAT

Lily

THAT NIGHT, I LEANED BACK into West, who sat on a stool at Habits with his arms around my waist. He laughed at something Cooper said, the rumble traveling through my chest, and I smiled. We were all giddy, high, sharing looks that all said the same thing. It was a celebration. A marker in our lives.

"I still can't believe you two finally figured this out," Cooper said, shaking his head. "We had a pool going, you know."

I gaped. "You did not."

"We totally did," Rose added, laughing. "I won."

"You would." I rolled my eyes.

Cooper snorted. "I'd almost lost hope that you'd figure it out. I was the first to lose. The first time I saw you two together, I figured Shannon's days were numbered." He motioned to West with his scotch before taking a sip.

I snickered. "That's horrible, Coop, and completely unsurprising."

Rose shook her head. "It's so weird. And awesome. But really weird to see you guys like this."

Maggie shrugged. "I knew from the first time I ever saw them together that we'd end up here. The two of them together doesn't seem strange to me at all, aside from the fact that West's my brother, and thinking of him doing anything remotely sexual makes me queasy." Everyone laughed. "Sometimes, people just make sense together. Whether or not they see it is irrelevant, if you think about it. Everything ends up working out."

I caught Cooper staring at her with an odd look on his face. West was ordering another drink from Rose, and Patrick's eyes were on Rose, too. I was the only one who saw Maggie blush. I made a mental note to ask her about what was going on there.

Rose poured a round of Makers for the group — water in a rocks glass for me — and passed them out before holding up her glass.

"To Lily and West. May your endings be happy and your habits be bad."

We laughed, chorusing *Hear, hear,* and I shifted in West's arms to look up at him, clinking my glass to his. But his lips brushed mine before my glass could.

EPILOGUE

West

EVERYONE IN THE AUDIENCE WAS still as stone as the music rose higher, our eyes on Lily as she danced, face bent in pain, arms outstretched for Seigfried, who reached for her. She was saying goodbye, taking tiny steps backwards on pointe as the swans closed in around her. The only light in the entire theater was behind her, her face falling into shadows as she reached for him, but the swans enveloped her. The music crescendoed. She disappeared. The lights went black.

I gasped, gripped by the shock of my emotions as my eyes burned. And then, the theater exploded in applause.

We were all on our feet as the lights went back up and the curtains parted once more. The company made their way back onto the stage, bowing gracefully. Lily was in front in that beautiful costume, the gems in the white bodice and her feather headdress twinkling. One leg was extended in front of her, one arm out to the side and other curved around her waist as she bowed low. It was so loud, I couldn't hear Maggie as she turned to me, smiling and yelling something unintelligible with tears on her cheeks. I turned and looked back to the stage. Back to Lily.

I could see her tears from the front row where we sat, the bend in her brow from emotion as she bowed again and swept an arm across the corps dancers behind her, then bowed to Blane, who returned the gesture. They waved to the crowd, and he led her off stage as the curtain closed, starting my heart again.

I looked down the line of seats. Rose was wiping her eyes, and Patrick and Cooper were awestruck, gaping at the stage with admiration and wonder. Maggie shook her head, fingers to her lips as she watched the stage with gigantic eyes. Lily and Blane came out for the curtain call, and the applause that had quieted to a dull roar erupted again. Lily bowed low and turned to Blane again, smiling and crying. Bowing once more and waving before they made their way off stage for the final time.

My heart was so full of pride and reverence in that moment, I didn't know if my ribs could contain it all. The house lights came up, and we made our way to the side entrance to backstage as the rest of the crowd funneled toward the exit.

Lily poked her head out from behind the curtain and waved us up, and I charged up the steps, scooping her into my arms, spinning her around as I pressed my lips to hers. She broke away and laughed, arms around my neck and lips at my ear. The sound was absolute joy.

"I've never seen anything so amazing in all my life, Lil."

She tightened her arms, closing any small gap that existed between us. "I feel like I could fly."

I closed my eyes. "You can. I saw you do it tonight."

I set her on the ground, and she reached up on her tippy toes to kiss me before making her way around the group, laughing and hugging them as I watched on from a few feet away.

I didn't see Blane until he had almost reached Lily.

Everyone froze when he approached, the tension hanging between all of us. My fists clenched by my side, smile fading. If he even thought about ruining this night for Lily, I'd bring him a world of pain.

But he only smiled at Lily, a smile tinged with regret. "Congratulations, Lily. You were perfect. I'm honored." He bowed to her.

Her cheeks flushed, eyes darting to me to share in her surprise. "Thank you, Blane."

"It's the truth."

I took a step forward, eyes narrowed, and Blane

turned to walk away, eyeing me.

"West," he said as he passed.

I folded my arms across my chest. "Blane."

Maggie was the only one unfazed. She grabbed Lily's hand, beaming. "That was the most beautiful thing I've ever seen in my entire life."

Lily grabbed Maggie's free hand with hers. "I'm so glad you were here." She looked around the lot of us. "All of you. Thank you so much. I've waited for this night since I was a little girl, and to have all of you here to share it with me just means everything."

"We'd never miss it," Cooper said and pulled her into a side hug.

Patrick nudged me and handed me the bouquet I'd forgotten I'd brought her.

I made my way to her side and extended the bouquet of pink, white, and peach peonies. She took a step closer as she took them. "I am so proud of you."

She touched my cheek with tears in her eyes. "Thank you."

"Now, let's drink!" Cooper crowed, and everyone laughed.

Lily grinned, leaning into my side as she wiped a tear away. "Not for me. I've got to get some rest. But you guys have fun."

"I'll get you home safe." I squeezed her, and she threaded an arm around my waist, smiling up at me.

"I know you will. Let me run and change, and we can head home."

I kissed her forehead before I let her go. She headed to the dressing room, returning a half an hour later with her face scrubbed clean and her feathered tutu replaced with leggings, flats, and a sweater. We left the theater in a group and headed for the subway to make our way home with Lily under my arm, both of us quiet, content as we watched over our friends. We parted ways with everyone at Habits, saying our goodbyes and thank you's before walking the blocks to our building, up the stairs and to my apartment.

It was quiet inside as she set down her bag and I took off my jacket.

"How are you feeling?" I finally asked.

Her eyes were lively, smile still full of wonder. "Amazing. High. My legs are aching, and my feet are cramping, and I don't care." She slipped her arms around my waist and tipped her face up to mine.

"Foot massage? Hot shower?"

She hummed, still smiling. "Yes, please."

"But first … " I reached into my back pocket and pulled out the letter.

She took it curiously, face stretching in surprise when she saw Columbia's watermark on the envelope. "Oh, my god, West."

I just smiled.

Lily took out the letter in a flurry, wide eyes darting across it before looking up at me with pink cheeks. "You got in," she breathed.

"I got in."

She screamed and jumped into my arms. "I knew you would do it. I just knew it."

I held her against me, picked her up and took a moment to appreciate how she felt in my arms, the joy on her face. "And now I have everything I could possibly want."

The kiss I gave her told her it was true.

Acknowledgements

To my husband, Jeff — I did it again, and I only survived because you always have my back. You always support me, even when you have to sacrifice your time and sanity so that I can do this writing thing, something that is such a huge part of who I am. Without your love, without your constant cheerleading and understanding, I would have had to give up long ago. Thank you, forever.

Becca Mysoor — Your spirit is so present in this book that it's part of what makes it a living thing. You've been a sounding board, a ledge-talker, a jokester, and a shoulder to cry on. How could I have ever done this without you? The joy of sharing this experience with you will be something that I'll always cherish. Always. Now, let's do it again.

Brooke Cumberland — You are one of the most generous souls I've ever met. Without you believing in me, coaching me, reading my scribbles and keeping me laughing, I would never be where I am. This book wouldn't be what it is. Every day, I thank my lucky stars that you are such a huge part of my life. You're my compass. Thank you for always pointing me in the right direction with a smile, cupcakes, and a swift kick in the ass.

To my Beta readers — Lori, Zoe, Melissa, Terry, Jenni, Jen, Parrish, Elyse, and Miranda — Thank you for giving With a Twist a roundhouse to the face, because your comments helped put the final polish on the story that makes it shine. Thank you for your time and for your energy, because without it, I'd be lost.

To Lauren Perry of Perrywinkle Photography, Chad Encore, and Alexis Kener — Thank you for being a part of this project. The three of you made absolute magic, and you brought Lily and West to life in a way that touched my heart.

And to you, Reader — Thank you for taking the time to read my little story, this piece of my heart that I put out into the world.

More Books by Staci Hart

Hearts and Arrows
Deer in Headlights (Hearts and Arrows 1)
Snake in the Grass (Hearts and Arrows 2)
What the Heart Wants (Hearts and Arrows 2.5 Novella)
Doe Eyes (Hearts and Arrows 3)
Fool's Gold (Hearts and Arrows 3.5 Novella)

Hearts and Arrows Box Set

Hardcore (Erotic Suspense Serials)
*Volume 1 - **FREE***
Volume 2
Volume 3

Bad Habits
With a Twist - Summer 2015
Chaser - Fall 2015
Last Call - Winter 2016

Nailed - Erotic Shorts
FREE with newsletter subscription

Once
FREE short story on Amazon

NAILED: Erotic morsels

Everyone wants to get nailed.

Sometimes the first thing you feel for someone is lust. Maybe it's for a stranger. It might be someone you've only just noticed, or someone whom you've known, but aren't allowed to want. Maybe you just don't know if they're affected by you, if the sound of their voice or the way they touch your hand makes them as crazy as it makes you.

Or, perhaps they want you just as badly as you want them. Sometimes, it's all you can do to stop yourself from acting on it.

#getnailed

About the Author

Staci has been a lot of things up to this point in her life: a graphic designer, an entrepreneur, a seamstress, a clothing and handbag designer, a waitress. Can't forget that. She's also been a mom to three little girls who are sure to grow up to break a number of hearts. She's been a wife, even though she's certainly not the cleanest, or the best cook. She's also super, duper fun at a party, especially if she's been drinking whiskey, and her favorite word starts with f, ends with k.

From roots in Houston, to a seven year stint in Southern California, Staci and her family ended up settling somewhere in between and equally north, in Denver. They are new enough that snow is still magical. When she's not writing, she's gaming, cleaning, or designing graphics.

Follow Staci Hart:

Website: Stacihartnovels.com
Facebook: Facebook.com/stacihartnovels
Twitter: Twitter.com/imaquirkybird
Pinterest: pinterest.com/imaquirkybird

43448840R00235

Made in the USA
Lexington, KY
30 July 2015